WIND IN TREES

UPHEAVEL

a novel

Arthur M. Doweyko

Kallisto Gaia Press Inc.
PO Box 220
Davilla TX 76523
info@kallistogaiapress.org
(254) 654-7205

Cover Design: Arthur Doweyko
Author Photo: Laura Alexander
Edited by Tony Burnett

ISBN: 978-1-952224-48-5

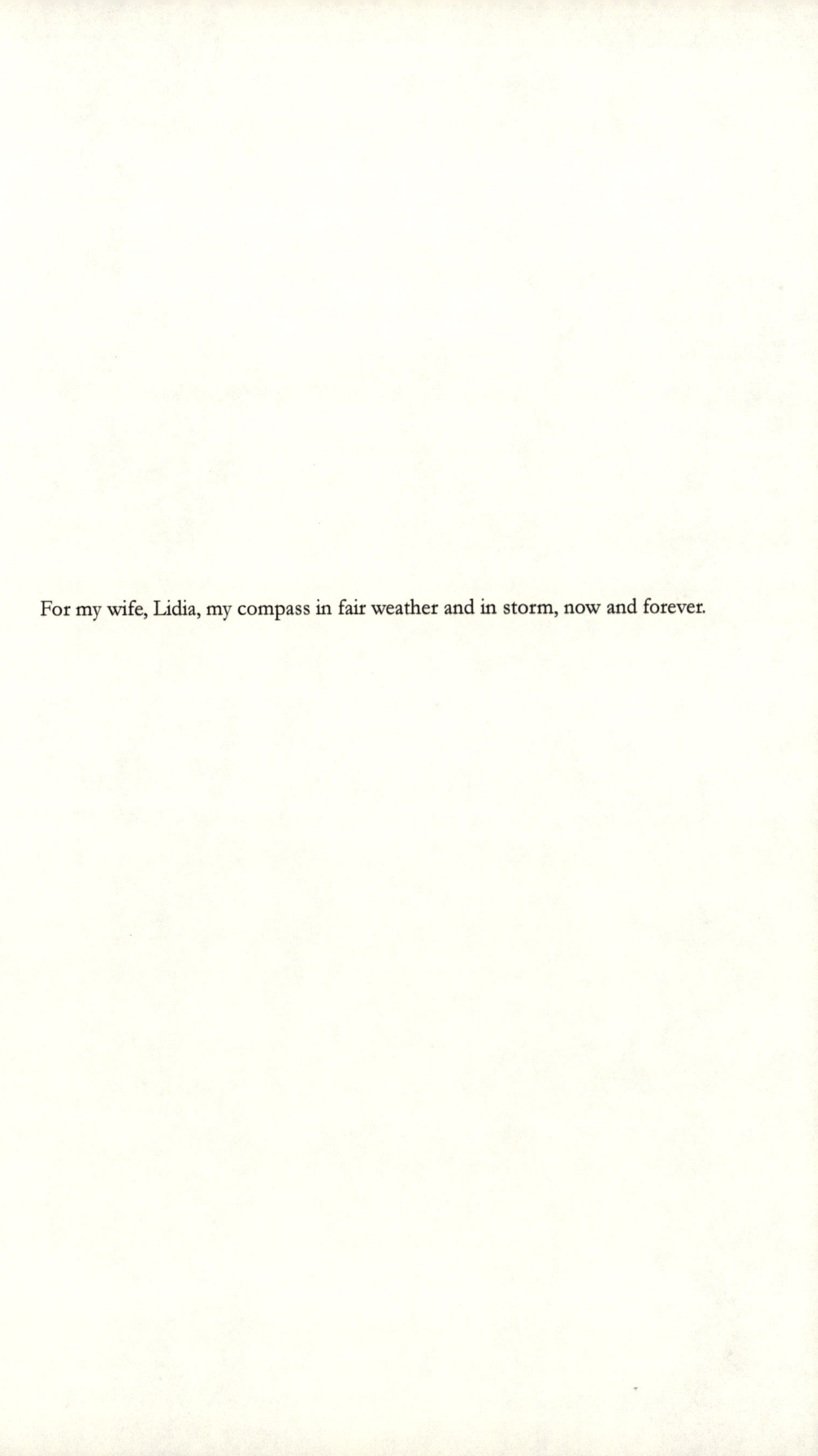

For my wife, Lidia, my compass in fair weather and in storm, now and forever.

WIND IN TREES

UPHEAVEL

a novel

Arthur M. Doweyko

WIND IN TREES

UPHEAVEL

a novel

Arthur M. Doweyko

Attention schools and businesses; for discounted copies on large orders please contact the publisher directly.

Kallisto Gaia Press Inc.
PO Box 220
Davilla TX 76523
info@kallistogaiapress.org
254-654-7205

Cover Design: Arthur Doweyko
Author Photo: Laura Alexander
Edited by Tony Burnett

ISBN: 978-1-952224-48-5

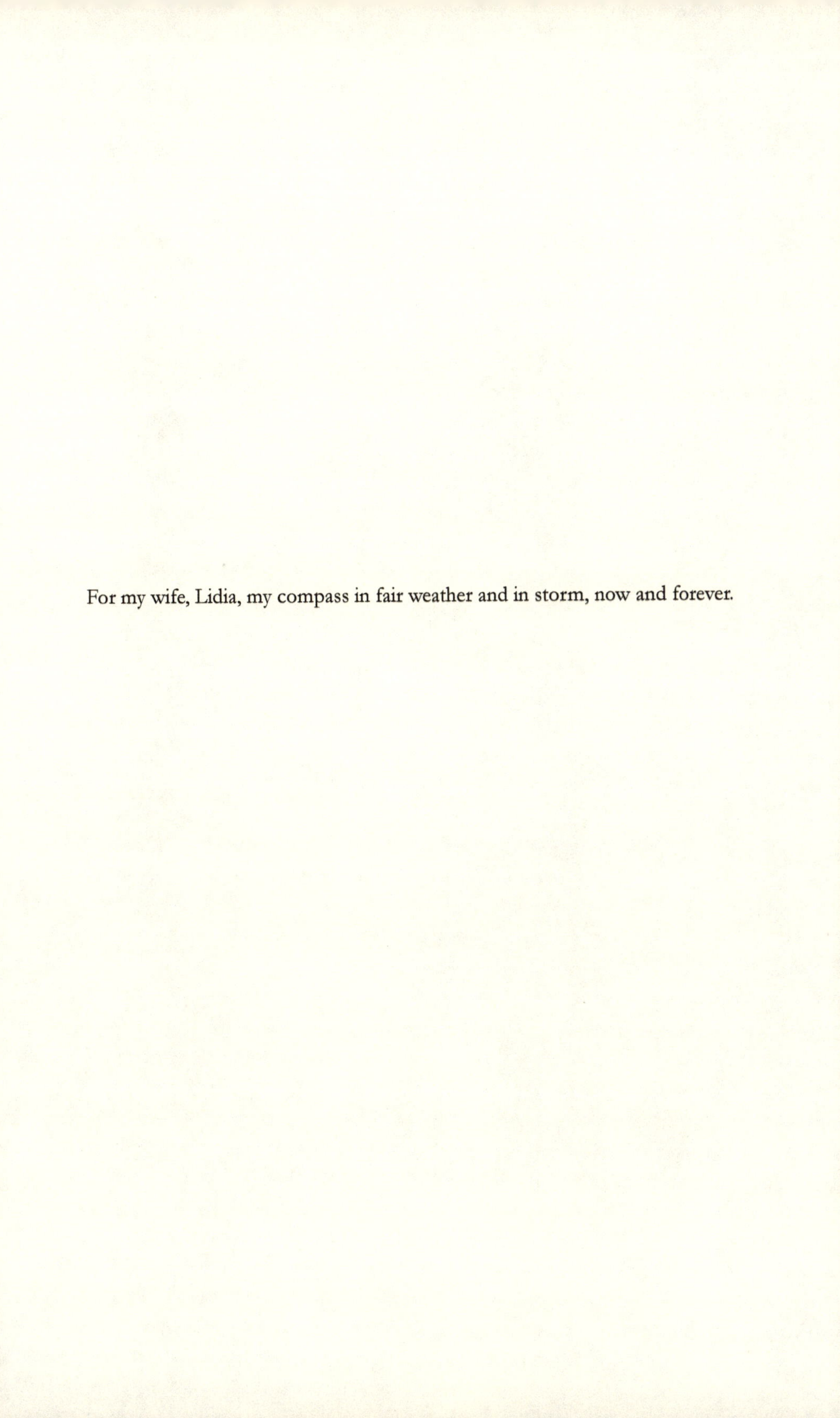

For my wife, Lidia, my compass in fair weather and in storm, now and forever.

WIND IN TREES

UPHEAVEL

a novel

Arthur M. Doweyko

FORWARD

Henry Wind In Trees, a Lakota Sioux Native American, was born in 2081. Twenty years later the Earth suffered an asteroid strike and an ensuing pandemic that left few humans alive. Henry discovered the apocalypse had been orchestrated by an entity known as the Soofysh in preparation for a subsequent colonization by a reptilian species. The Soofysh had chosen him for an experiment—his brain was transferred to a synthetic body made to look like the original. The Soofysh were intrigued by Henry's ability to communicate with his wife through telepathy. Although he had been told his wife was dead, recurring visions convinced him otherwise. With the help of a domestic robot and a few sympathetic reptilians, he rescued her from the Soofysh and the two lived happily for a number of years. Henry's body could not age, and when she died, he decided to end his lonely existence by leaping from a cliff overlooking the Pacific Ocean. And so it was, until the day he awoke.

CHAPTER 1

He heard a faint whisper, a familiar voice, followed by three taps of metal on metal. Recollections drifted by. None made any sense. An image of rising waves in a frigid ocean threatened to inundate what little of his mind was left.

"Seth?" The name spilled out of his mouth. He had a mouth. "Seth?"

He called out to a friend, a close friend. Were his eyes open?

"It is I, sir."

The warm embrace of remembrance.

"Try to open your eyes, sir."

Lifting an eyelid, he saw nothing.

"Shh. Someone is coming."

"Wait. Who am I?"

"Why, sir, you're Henry Wind In Trees. I'll be back in a moment."

◇

What an odd name. A faint glow narrowed to a thin horizontal line. His awakening senses shrieked half in terror and half in pain as the line widened and brightened. He slammed his eye shut. The light had burned, but the movement alone told him he had some control.

He was Henry.

Voices came and went. Were they real? A chest muscle twitched. He ran his tongue along the roof of his mouth, savoring its contours, its texture.

He was Henry.

He dared to open his eye again and the strip of light parsed into blurry forms. The shapes merged into a group of figures—familiar reptilian figures. The odd assortment of creatures stood a few feet away, gawking up at him with their wide, sharp-toothed mouths. He knew what they were. A lifetime of memories jostled for recognition as more of his mind awoke. He lowered his eyelid—an instinct for self-preservation, hoping it wasn't noticed. He yearned to ask what happened or how he got to this point, for all he knew, he could be a prisoner or slated for dinner. The invasion had heralded a new age, a reptilian age. He was surprised to find he understood their lispy exchanges. They spoke of history, colonization, and the last humans.

Why couldn't he move?

◇

Tapping—the metallic sound came from below. Henry looked out into the half-light of a broad room. The reptilians were gone. His fingers and arms tingled. His head swiveled down to see a bronze-colored metallic figure standing knee-high at his side.

"Sir, you are awake."

"Seth. It's you. How?"

"All in due time, sir."

"What happened? Where are we?"

He lifted his head. A pair of humanoid figures came into focus from some twenty feet away. A man and woman stood in front of a cave and appeared to stare back at him. Both were covered in hair, wearing little clothing, and motionless, much like himself.

"Seth, where the hell are we?"

"I'm glad you're regaining your voice, sir."

"Seth?"

"We are in the Museum of Natural History in Atlanta, sir."

Henry fought back the urge to ask a million questions, and instead whispered. "And what's wrong with me? Why can't I move?"

"I'm afraid you are one of the exhibits, sir—quite a popular one I might add."

"Are you kidding?"

"I suggest keeping your voice down, sir. A night guard comes by once in a while."

Henry paused, his mind enthralled by a small parade of events marching past—the search for his wife, Liz, and years later, her death—the view of the ocean from a cliff. The realization that he was still alive angered him. He should be dead. Liz had passed away yesterday and he was alone—the last human in a world populated by reptiles. And now he was a museum exhibit. Things had not improved.

His blue-skinned hand protruded from the sleeve of a stiff deerskin shirt. "I think I can move my fingers. Where did you come from?"

"Like you, I have been on exhibit. A week ago I was revived, and have been working on you, sir."

"We should both be dead."

"We were retrieved, sir."

An image of a swell of water emerged, followed by the crash of a wave against rocks—large boulders at the base of an ocean bluff. He struggled to move, to breathe.

"We were brought here and put on display."

"I remember the water. You were there, too. The cliff—"

"We fell, sir. Do you remember your cabin back on the Marin peninsula?"

"We didn't fall, Seth. You tried to stop me from jumping."

"Perhaps so, sir."

"Damn it all, Seth. You know what happened."

The lights came on. A tall, gangly, green creature wandered in. It paused at each display, bobbing its scaly head up and sideways, reading the placards. After a minute, it left and the room became dark once again.

"Seth, are you still here?"

The small robot stood in front of Henry outlined by indirect floor lighting. "I am glad to see you are returning to the living, sir."

"I'm afraid I don't share your enthusiasm."

Seth paused as if mulling over what to say next.

"It's not your fault, Seth. Last I recall, we were both drowning, isn't that right?"

"That is correct, sir."

"Maybe this is a dream … you know, last thoughts and all that. Maybe we're still under water."

"This is no dream, sir."

Henry ran a hand over his leggings. "I can move my hands and my arms." He gave a tug at his ponytail.

"We were saved by a group of reptilians. By the way, they call themselves Batrans. I believe that may be derived from the name of their planet, Batra."

"I don't care." An image of Anth and Genz flashed by—two reptilians who helped him rescue his wife, Liz. "Are the Soofysh still here?" Henry recalled the strange creature, more mechanical than biological, referring to itself in the plural. Even the reptilians feared it. The Soofysh were responsible for killing off humans to make way for the reptilian colonization, and they were adept at playing with one's perception.

"It does not appear that they are. However, it would also appear that many Batrans have arrived in the years since."

"Wonderful."

"Can you move anything else besides your hands and arms, sir?"

Henry wiggled a foot. "As a robot, I can understand how you survived, Seth. But me ... I have a human brain in this titanium pot. It needs oxygen. How the hell did I survive?"

"I've repaired most of the damage to your legs, sir. Apparently, the Soofysh technology that went into your construction was more robust than we thought. I must surmise that the Soofysh built in some safeguards. Your brain may have entered a kind of stasis, probably triggered when the rest of your body discovered the end was near."

"Damn convenient. So, how long have we been here?"

"You and I were placed in this museum ... part of a tribute to the technology of the human civilization that once existed here on Earth."

Henry shook his head. Although he and Seth were the products of Soofysh technology, the choice of becoming a cyborg was not his own.

Seth said, "According to my internal clock, we've been here for about one hundred years."

Henry swore his legs buckled, but he remained the steadfast statue he had been for a century.

"Are you sure?"

The surrounding shadowy recesses in the hall took on a ghostly veneer—the impression of a mausoleum—Henry's final resting place—a perpetual testament to a morbid choice made several lifetimes ago.

"Quite sure. But do not despair, sir."

"Why the hell not? I'm supposed to be dead. I don't like being here, and I don't want to be here."

"Perhaps you will reconsider, sir."

"Not likely."

"Things have changed considerably since you—"

"Since I committed suicide?"

"Tried to, sir. Although you were a bit damaged from the fall, I'll have you fully operational in a few minutes."

"And that's supposed to make me feel better?"

"I was not able to help you until I was powered up myself."

"Powered up?"

"In a moment, sir."

"Why am I propped up here anyway?"

"The placard announces you as a human-like robot probably because of your blue skin tone. Apparently the Batrans mistook you for an automaton, much like myself."

"Nice." Henry swung his head around. He was surrounded by a variety of mechanical wonders, including several small robots that looked a lot like Seth.

"Anybody in here?" The guard stepped into the hall once again.

Thanks to Liz and her tutoring, Henry understood the hissing tongue. With so many years gone by, her memory lifted his heart. He missed her smile and unflinching optimism. When she died, he had spiraled downward. There wasn't anything left for him.

"What do you mean 'things have changed'?"

The guard came nearer. "Who's there?"

Henry narrowed his eyes and felt Seth snuggle up behind his legs.

The Batran stopped across the way and cast a beam of light over Henry's display. After a few moments it shuffled away, all the while muttering what sounded like incantations to ward off museum spirits.

"He is gone for the moment, sir."

"I can feel my legs, Seth."

"Excellent, sir. Let me close you up, and then we can be on our way."

Henry wiggled a toe for confirmation. "On our way to where?"

"How do you feel, sir?"

"After a hundred years propped up like a manikin, I'm not sure I can walk. And I'm hungry. And thirsty."

"I'll be back shortly, sir." The little robot leaped out of the display and disappeared into the surrounding gloom.

Henry tried to follow, but found himself stuck in place. A tall figure cane into view. "You remember me, Henry?"

He recognized the raspy mechanical voice. A green pinpoint appeared where there should have been an eye. A silver sheen flashed across its human-like form and its bright ceramic teeth.

"You're Mike, aren't you?" A chill ran through Henry's titanium body. He studied the creature—not exactly a cyborg—this one had its human brain replaced with an artificial one. He recalled their last encounter. Mike should be missing most of his brains.

"The one and the same. You don't look happy to see me, Henry."

"It must be resurrection day at the museum. The last time we met you tried to kill me."

Mike pointed to his missing eye. "You tried to do the same to me."

"Yeah. I shot you in that eye. Your brains flew out the back of your head like silver confetti."

"Shooting me in the eye was a stroke of genius. I ended up with some brain damage thanks to you. Now, don't get me wrong, I'm not upset. I'd have done the same if I were in your shoes."

"I don't get it."

"Lucky for me, your shot only took out half my brain. It took a while for the Soofysh technology to knit and repair what was left."

"Damn amazing. You know you should be blind."

"How so?"

"The optic nerves in human brains cross over. Each eye uses the opposite side of the brain."

"Ah … so my left eye gets shot out along with the left side of my brain, leaving a right eye that shouldn't work."

Henry craned his head for a better look. "Got to hand it to those Soofysh."

Mike said, "They knew what they were doing."

Henry looked out beyond Mike's gleaming hulk, anxious for Seth to emerge from the shadows. "They were experimenting, leaving behind lots of dead human beings."

"Look at you, Henry. You're back. You owe your life to the Soofysh."

"You call this a life?"

Mike extended a hand and patted Henry on his shoulder. "We're both here for a reason."

"So, what now? We shake hands and forget about the past?"

"The Soofysh are gone, Henry. I take orders from no one. You might say I'm my own man."

Mike was no more a man than a wind-up doll, despite what the Soofysh promised. An artificial brain would never be human and could never be trusted, except in the case of one small but loyal robot.

Seth peered out from behind Mike and held up a bag. "Unfortunately, the vending machines only carry uncooked meat."

"Did you know about Mike, Seth?"

"He was the one who brought me back, sir."

"I know someone's in here." The silhouette of the guard framed the entrance to the hall.

When the guard approached again, Mike slipped into the shadows of an adjacent display. Henry wondered if he should shout out a warning, but only looked on while the Batran collapsed to the floor.

Mike shoved the body to the side and said, "He's not dead, if that's what you're worried about."

"It's not so much the guard. It's the display you came out of."

"What about it? Some dinos in a kitchen. They kinda look happy."

A family of Batran reptilians sat at a kitchen counter ready to have dinner, while mama filleted a chunk of fresh red meat. A window at the rear of the diorama displayed a pastoral scene of rolling fields of green and a traditional red barn.

"Look at what's in the corral next to the barn."

Mike moved closer. "Those are people … humans. Maybe they came for dinner?"

Henry said, "Yeah. Maybe. Considering this is a museum, that scene is probably old, I wonder if they were the dinner. Seth, you said you were activated by Mike a week ago?"

"True, sir."

"Did you have a chance to look at the other exhibits here? Maybe they tell a story we should know."

"As I mentioned earlier, sir, things have changed. I cannot be sure, but—"

A high-pitched intermittent wailing filled the hall.

Henry lurched away from the troubling display and stumbled. Mike moved in a blur and caught him. "Gotcha, Henry."

Being held up by the very creature he had tried to kill gave Henry the willies.

Mike said, "You're in good hands, Henry."

Seth offered up the bag and said, "Eat up, sir. You'll need your strength."

They entered a hallway which led out of the display area. Henry squirmed out of Mike's embrace, snapped up the bag and staggered ahead.

"Sir, where are we going?"

"I don't know about you two, but I'm going to finish what I started."

CHAPTER 2

Henry pushed through a service door beneath a dull red EXIT sign. He and the two robots spilled into an alley. The early evening twilight outlined several bins overflowing with garbage. The smell put him off for a second, but reminded him of the food he was carrying. He pulled out a strip of meat, closed his eyes and bit in to something that smelled like a decayed piece of roadkill. There was no time to savor the taste. His hunger needed satiating.

"Not much has changed. This meat—what the hell is it? Wait a minute, never mind, don't tell me." Henry's thoughts wandered back to the diorama in the museum.

"It is not human flesh, if that is what you are thinking, sir."

"You're a mind-reader, Seth."

"Sir, your thinking may not be as clear as you wish it to be."

"Seth, you've been a great friend over the years, but the time has come for me to leave. And I don't just mean from this museum."

"What will you do, sir?"

"You know the answer to that. Liz is gone, and you saw what the … Batrans have on display back there. This is not my world anymore. They can have it."

A subtle hum announced Mike's presence. "Henry, you're not alone, buddy. I'm sure we can work out something."

Mike hovered a few inches over the floor.

"I see your magic boots are working well. You and Seth will find a way to survive and maybe even find some meaning … in the new Batra, if that's what they call it now."

Henry walked out of the alley onto the sidewalk and gulped down the rest of the mystery meat. His plastic stomach growled at his first meal in a century. With a mouth that felt like sandpaper, his only thought was to get something to drink.

"Don't follow me."

It wasn't easy for Henry to push aside feelings for Seth. It was better this way. He wanted it all to end, and Seth would only get in the way. What does a robot know anyway?

The alley stench could have knocked over an elephant. The breeze that carried it along with a slight chill hinted at Fall. He sidled along a series of storefronts, struck by the lack of vehicles and that no one was about. Perhaps the Batrans had an evening curfew, or maybe it was too cold to be outside. Corner lamp posts threw a blue glow over the sidewalk. Occasional tufts of grass and trees erupted from cracks in the concrete and larger crevices in the asphalt. Ivy covered many of the buildings lining the street. At least some power coursed through the decaying city, although humankind's footprint was fast fading into oblivion. Each intersection offered up the same ruddy flush with doorways hidden in shadow beneath curtains of green. Henry had stepped out into a landscape that was designed to look like Earth but came up way short.

He continued toward the center of the city. Ragged posters dangling off a line of fencing caught his attention. Although most were faded beyond recognition, one appeared to have retained its color—an announcement of a Chinese festival of some kind. The words were too faded to read, but the illustration looked new—red dragon with a long snake-like body. A deep unease gave Henry pause. The dragon's eyes, yellow-green, stared directly at him, following him as he walked past.

Henry broke into a jog and only eased up when the museum alarm fell away in the distance. He needed a distraction to get his mind off the dragon.

He paused once in a while in storefront alcoves, and turned his attention to the two mechanicals, insuring they were not following and that he had not attracted the attention of anything else.

Taller buildings lay ahead. Black mold had joined the ever present ivy, giving the structures the disquieting look of cowled widows in mourning. The Batrans appeared to have had scant interest in these monoliths. Although crumbling cornices and eaves reflected a century and a half of neglect, all the shops he passed were cleaned out—no merchandise, no furniture, no skeletons. Long dead traffic signals cast their sightless eyes upon what had become an alien landscape.

He was surprised at the absence of desiccated bodies or rusting cars. If nothing else, the Batrans were big on cleanliness. The thought brought up an image of the Soofysh, the entity that destroyed human life more than a century ago. The creature or creatures claimed to have made the planet ready for colonization. No one was certain if the Soofysh were a single entity or some strange amalgamation of many artificial lifeforms. The Batrans had made a deal with the devil—a cleaned up planet in return for resources the Batrans were to provide. And then there were the perplexing images back in the museum—corralled humans. Was that some historical depiction from years ago or was that happening now?

The sound of an eagle's call echoed along the city's stone caverns. Doubtful it was an actual bird, Henry slipped inside a nearby shop and hunkered down in a recess farther within. The ancient display glass shook. A vehicle trundled over the cracked asphalt in the direction of the museum and unleashed another bird-like call. Henry recognized it—a rover similar to the one he rode long ago—a Batran rover, an over-sized VW bus. This one came with tank-like treads.

An image of the two young reptilians who helped him reunite with his wife many years ago loomed up for a moment only to be dispelled by the crunch of those treads biting into the blacktop. It was too dark to see its interior, but Henry knew it could easily accommodate a half dozen eight foot tall Batrans—a daunting force to face, even for a cyborg.

He squatted to avoid a searchlight that panned the street. Once the rover rattled out of sight, he ventured deeper into the vacant store and found a restroom. A quick turn of a faucet yielded an impotent deep-throated, dry groan. His thirst was fast becoming his singular thought.

Once outside, he continued away from the museum. Skyscrapers loomed into view—cold gray edifices streaked with Nature's unrelenting tendrils. The city's eerie silence was beginning to get on his nerves. Had he imagined the museum's visitors? Where were those Batrans now?

An illuminated sign caught his eye—METRO. A waft of warm ozone-saturated air and the muffled squeal of metal wheels drew him closer. A long set of stairs and the remnants of an escalator led down to the sub-terranean complex. The muted yellow lighting from below threw moving shadows across the lower entrance. People, or more probably, Batrans were about.

When a dark shape climbed up, Henry leaped onto the escalator and hid behind its handrails. The high-pitched ragged breathing typical of a human out of breath, got him to chance a quick peek.

A child's voice rang out. "Who you?"

The language was Batran, but the speaker was a human boy, maybe aged ten years or so. His naked body froze, while his eyes darted between the street and Henry.

Henry spoke in the Batran he was taught by Liz many years ago. "Easy, son. I'm human … just different, that's all."

The boy made an effort to lunge past, but Henry scooped him up. "Why are you running?"

"Let go. Let go."

That's when Henry heard footfalls, heavier this time. Several large shad-ows loped up the stairs, moving fast. No time for discussion. Henry bounded out into the street, cradling the boy.

"Can we help, sir?"

Sure enough, Henry's two companions had followed him.

The boy screamed. Mike held Seth in one arm while hovering over the sidewalk. The sight was enough to set anyone into hysterics.

Henry said, "I told you—"

Mike said, "Seth made me do it … to follow you. You know, just in case."

Seth asked, "Who is your new friend, sir?"

The boy continued to scream and squirm. The oblong heads of two spindly Batrans emerged from under the archway of the Metro entrance.

Mike said, "I got this," and swung one arm around Henry and the other around Seth.

A moment later they glided away from the Metro a couple of feet above the ground. Henry craned his head to look back. The Batrans shouted, but their hissing quickly faded away.

Mike turned a corner a few blocks later and alighted on a brownstone stoop. "Henry, you gotta lose some weight."

"Thanks, Mike. I'm not sure what would have happened back there."

Seth said, "It is likely you would have been taken prisoner, sir."

The boy wriggled free of Henry's arm and backed up into the empty street. Sobs punctuated each word. "Who … who you?"

Mike said, "He speaks Batran."

Henry said, "I'm not surprised—few humans, many Batrans. I doubt English or any other Earth tongue has survived. This kid grew up in a world ruled by reptilians."

Seth said, "He looks wild, but well-fed."

Henry used his best Batran. "Son, we mean you no harm. We may look strange to you, but you have nothing to fear from us."

"You be machines."

"It's complicated." Henry pointed. "Mike and Seth. They are machines, but smart ones. Me, I'm mostly machine, but inside here, I am human. For a while, I was sure I was the only human left."

"What be human?"

"That's a good one. Humans are folks like you. Are there others like you?"

"Yes." The boy looked away, toward the Metro station.

Henry coughed

Seth said, "Sir, you need water."

"Tell me something I don't already ..." Henry fell to his knees. "... know."

Mike said, "Stay with him, Seth," and disappeared into the night.

"Batrans come."

Henry slumped forward and held himself up with both hands. "Why are they ... so interested in you?"

Seth said, "Sir, I suggest you refrain from speaking." He turned to the boy and said, "Do you belong to the Batrans?"

"Yes. We do."

"Do they have you working for them … helping clean up and build?"

The boy nodded.

"Do you have a family?"

"Is cold. No allowed here. Too cold."

Henry said, "How many others are there … like you?"

"Not know."

"Show me with your fingers … one for each person."

The boy held up his hands and displayed seven fingers. One finger, extended at first, curled down to leave six up.

Seth reached up and touched that finger. "What happened to this one?"

"He gone." The boy sat on the sidewalk. "Went away."

CHAPTER 3

Mike returned with an oversized black pot resembling something out of a Hamlet play.

Henry said, "What do you … have in there—eye of newt, or wolf's tooth?"

"Better than that."

Mike lowered the cauldron to the ground, splashing water over the sidewalk. Henry plunged his head into the cool liquid, took a pull and bobbed up.

"Sir, take care. Drink slowly."

"Not to worry … damn, it feels good. You guys don't know what it is to be thirsty." He waved at the boy. "Son … a drink?"

The boy scurried over and lapped up the water.

Mike said, "And I brought these." He held out a furry loincloth garment just the right size for the boy.

"That looks familiar. Come to think of it, so does this pot."

"They should. You've been staring at them for a century."

Henry recalled the display back at the museum. "And you weren't seen?"

"Nobody home. I guess they were done with their investigation."

"Probably figured out what went missing."

Seth added, "And perhaps they are now searching for those items."

Henry said, "It's likely. The Batrans at the Metro station will help point out which way we went, and to top things off, I'm sure they'll want this kid back."

When the boy finished drinking, Mike handed him the furry attire. His words hissed out in a Batran whisper, "What this?"

Henry said, "It's clothing," and pointed to his jacket. "I'm wearing clothing … to keep warm. Put it on and you'll feel much better."

The boy's pale skin spoke to a life largely spent out of the sun, perhaps underground where it might have been warmer. The Batrans were cold-blood-ed mammals despite their scaly appearance. Henry wouldn't be surprised if they had adapted to a life in the tunnels, especially in cold weather.

He helped the boy get dressed. "There, now. Doesn't that feel better?"

A nod, the universal human symbol of affirmation, gave Henry hope that at least a trace of humanity had managed to survive through the past century. Humans in captivity and Henry wished his imagination would stop bringing up a number of horrifying reasons.

"Sir, we need to get off the street." Seth had wandered back to the main intersection. "I see several Batrans approaching … they are a few blocks away."

Mike splayed his arms. "Hop on board."

Henry said, "Are you sure we're not too much for you?"

"No way to know unless we try."

Henry took up the boy as Mike wrapped his arms around them both. They rose off the ground and glided over to Seth. Mike's shoes groaned as the four of them lifted a bit more. The boy held onto his arm and whimpered.

Henry said, "Now, now … it's okay."

"Sir, he may be reacting to something else."

Two reptilians rounded the corner. A flash erupted from one of them and the brickwork behind Henry exploded.

"Jeez. These guys are serious."

Mike said, "Here goes nothing," and the odd assembly of humans and mechanicals scooted over the sidewalk away from the charging Batrans.

Henry heard their shrieking but the growing distance garbled their words.

They ascended in an abrupt arc over the featureless and moldy apartment building. The boy's mouth hung open in a half-scream, his eyes wide. Henry felt his stomach turn.

Mike hovered for a moment over a pitted roof which looked like moldy Swiss cheese. "We can't land here." And then his head turned upwards.

Henry's words slipped out in a hoarse whisper. "You're kidding, right?" A monolith of a building towered some thirty or forty floors before them.

Mike said, "To the top?"

Henry gasped, "Why not?"

The feeling was no different than sitting on the outside of a rocket ship. Wind screamed past Henry's ears and the building became a blur. The boy shut his eyes and his grip on Henry's arm tightened.

Seconds later the group alit on the roof, on a cracked concrete surface promising a more secure landing. The boy shifted his arms to Henry's neck. "No let go. No let go."

"It's all right … we're safe for now." Henry set the boy down. "By the way, do you have a name?"

The boy bounded to a parapet and stared out at the darkening sky. Several early evening stars seemed to catch his interest. He shook when he spoke. "No name … name is for Batrans."

Seth said, "Curious, sir. One would assume that the parents or at least the other humans would have names they called themselves."

Henry said, "Yeah, curious. Maybe there are no parents, and the others don't get much of a chance to talk to each other."

Seth said, "A situation which may speak to a dire circumstance, sir."

"I'd say so, but it's not really our business."

Mike said, "What is our business, Henry?"

"All right, not my business. You don't get it. I'm done here. I didn't ask to be resurrected. First chance I get I'll—"

Mike stepped forward. "Go ahead. Jump, Henry. We're at least thirty-some floors up. I'm sure you'll make a fine mess … something that even Soofysh technology wouldn't be able to repair."

"Don't think I'm not thinking about it."

Seth said, "Sir, you have not considered all your choices."

"I'm not happy to leave you, Seth, if that's what you mean."

Seth swiveled and pointed back at the boy. "Not me, sir. There are others that could use your help."

The boy continued to stare up at the sky, caught up in the Milky Way glow. Henry shook his head and edged closer. "Have you seen stars before?"

He laid a hand on the boy's shoulder, who jerked away, as if unused to a fellow human's touch. A moment later, he reached up and curled his arm around Henry's and breathed a deep sigh. However short it had been for the young one, his life had been no picnic.

Henry said, "We can't keep calling you 'boy.' You need a name." The furry loincloth and disheveled ruddy, brown mop of hair reminded Henry of a Kipling story. "I've got it. We'll call you Mowgli. What do you think?"

"Moogly?" The smile on the boy's face said it all.

"Close enough."

"Sir. Does that mean—"

"It means we should avoid large conniving tigers and snakes, and we need to find out what's been happening to Mowgli's people."

Seth said, "We need a Bagheera, sir."

Henry said, "You said it—a friendly panther could come in handy right now."

Mike pointed up. "Whatever we've decided to do, we need to do it right now." A bright spot moved across the jagged city horizon.

Henry said, "Is that an aircar?"

"Indeed it is, sir."

Mike ran over to a ventilator hatch and tore off its cover. "There's a stairway here."

"What's the point? They'll follow us down … and don't forget the other Batrans we left behind down there. They're probably making their way up right now."

Mike said, "It's a big building. You never know what we'll find."

Henry added, "Or what they find."

Mike ground out a chuckle. "Not much of a choice."

The aircar grew larger, morphing into a white oval with a pair of windows at its head. Henry scooped up Mowgli. "If we stay here, we're cooked," and scrambled down the stairs with the other two following. Henry heard Mike replacing the hatch cover. "That won't help much, Mike. I'm sure they've spotted us."

Mike said, "No sense in making it easy for them."

The way down was pitch black, but rendered visible with Seth's help. A twittering beam of yellow light shot out from his eye slit and danced ahead of them, outlining the floor below.

Henry held on to Mowgli. They passed a set of elevator doors and headed to the end of the hallway where a fire door caught Seth's strobe. "Let's get down a few more floors."

As they skittered down the cement steps of an emergency stairway, Henry noted the faded lettering on the outside of each door. At Level 29 he pushed through, allowing Seth to get ahead. A long hallway with a dozen recessed alcoves came into view. Henry said, "Offices. Nothing but offices."

Mike said, "It's going to be easy for the Batrans to check each floor. They're sure to find us."

"Don't be such a Debbie Downer. Besides, I'm the one that's depressed here. Let's check out the intersection up ahead."

A second hallway cut across the main about halfway down. Mowgli squirmed out of Henry's arm and ran. Before he could catch up, the boy rounded the corner.

Mike asked, "Where did Mowgli go?"

Nothing but closed office doors lay ahead, except for one which stood ajar.

Mowgli stared back at them from the office door's single window pane, which sported cracks coated in dust. Once inside, Henry glimpsed the outline of the approaching aircar which drifted over them and landed on the rooftop.

"Stand back." Henry slammed a fist into the window, sending glittering shards flying out into the night.

"Sir, you're not—"

Henry kicked out the remains of the glass and stuck his head out. "Like you said, Seth, things have changed."

"What are you looking for, sir?"

"We're a couple floors below the roof. I'm assuming they'll be taking the stairs down any moment."

"Not an encouraging development, sir."

"Mike, can you use your magic boots and fly up to the roof?"

"I guess so."

"If they all joined in the hunt, maybe the aircar's empty."

Mike said, "I get it. You want me to take the aircar and get back here before they find you."

"If there's still someone in the car, forget it. They do have weapons."

"That's sweet of you, Henry. I'll be careful."

Mike leaped out of the window. A moment later, his green eye rose into view. "I'll be back in a jiffy."

"Sir, I hear something."

Henry stuck his head past the doorway and heard the distinctive clicking of reptilian claws. He eased the door closed.

Mowgli said, "They come. For me."

"Shh. They'll have to get through us first."

The single desk and chair in the office did not offer much in the way of cover. Henry held the boy close. He and Seth leaned up against the wall with the door between them.

"What do you hear, Seth?"

"They are getting closer, sir."

Henry wondered if it would have been better to have Mike give them a ride to the roof, but had nixed that idea for worry that the boy would be exposed to danger. The present situation was not much better, and anyway, what's done is done.

Seth said, "I believe our door is next."

Henry propped up Mowgli in a corner. "Stay here no matter what happens."

The knob turned. The door swing inward. Henry waited for the Batran to step inside. One reptilian might be possible to subdue, especially if surprised.

A tall, thin figure rushed in, followed immediately by another. The Batrans raised their weapons faster than Henry had expected. Spindly hands waved the pistol-like devices, each of which sported a worrisome red glow at its business end.

One of the Batrans ticked its head toward the corner of the room. "We found it."

The other said, "But what of these two?"

One of them stepped toward Mowgli.

Henry blurted out, "Leave him alone."

The Batran's yellow eyes widened. "What's this? It speaks in our tongue."

The other said, "It's the mechanical which was stolen from the museum."

"And the small one—"

Henry said, "His name is Seth. The big one here is Henry. We may be mechanical, but we are also sentient."

Henry wasn't sure the Batrans would understand, but saying something, anything, seemed like a good idea. "We were retrieved many years ago and apparently were considered dead. Seth here is purely mechanical; however, I am human." Henry pointed to his head. "Not exactly human, but there is a human brain in here."

The first Batran said, "Nonsense. Someone has turned you on and is playing with your programming."

The other one reached down to Seth's neck. "There is a switch … somewhere here."

Henry lunged forward but was brushed back. The other reptilian said, "No need to turn them off. Set your weapon to pulse. An electrical reset … they will feel nothing."

A flash filled the room.

Henry blinked, chasing away the purple afterimage. He heard several thumps like sacks of rocks hitting the floor, and thought it strange that he could still hear after being shot with God-knows-what.

"Sir, are you all right?"

The purple faded, replaced by Seth's strobing yellow beam.

"What happened?"

"I happened." Mike leaned in through the outside window. He waved one of the Batran weapons. "It's a damn blaster. Not sure what it's set on."

Henry said, "Bright light would be my guess."

Seth said, "They are still alive."

"Must have been the proverbial stun setting."

Mowgli stepped forward from his corner sanctuary. "We go?"

Picking up one of the weapons, Henry grabbed Mowgli's hand. "We go."

Mike said, "Up the stairs. Our coach awaits."

The group ascended with Mowgli taking the lead and towing Henry.

Once out on the roof, Seth cut off his beam. "The moon, sir."

"Beautiful, isn't it?"

The half-moon cast a silver sheen over the city. Nothing stirred—no cars, no people—an eerie silence blanketed everything, and mirrored the stillness of the prairies and mountains of the west. Henry's synthetic heart paused a moment. He had spent many a night in the western mountains while hunting. There were moments when despite what turmoil man brought upon the world, the stars continued their silent vigil and reminded him of his humble place in an eternal cosmos.

Mike said, "This way," and nodded at the aircar.

A reptilian lay sprawled alongside the vehicle. The car's humming and flickering inner lights suggested it was ready to go.

Henry paused by the prostrate reptilian. "Still breathing."

Mike said, "A gentle smack on the side of its head."

Henry shook his head, "He's naked."

"Not quite, sir." Seth bent down to turn the Batran's wrist.

"Colors and symbols … maybe function and rank?"

"That is likely, sir. It seems they all wear such wristlets."

Mike spoke from the aircar's pilot seat. "Are we going or what?"

Henry guided Mowgli into the front seat next to Mike who reached out and said, "I'll hold that for you." Henry handed the extra weapon over and slipped in behind the two. Seth joined him after inspecting the other row of seats to their rear.

"All set, Seth?"

"Ready."

The aircar's hum turned into a whisper like the wind in a forest and the building's roof dropped away into the night. Henry said, "Now all we have to figure out is where to go."

Mike remained silent. The car gained altitude, then whisked away toward the faint glow of a western sunset.

Henry said, "So, where are we headed, Mike?"

The one-eyed robot ignored the question. Henry's stomach tightened. "Mike, I'm talking to you."

Still no response.

"Mike!"

CHAPTER 4

Mike said, "Sit back and relax."

Henry felt the fool. Mike had both weapons.

Mowgli turned his head and asked, "Is all good?"

Henry said, "Everything will be fine, Mowgli. Isn't that right, Mike?"

"For sure."

Seth whispered, "Sir, I can slip around the side and—"

Mike said, "I can hear you, Seth."

Henry said, "What is going on? We have a right to know."

Mike said, "The less you know, the better."

Henry's mind processed through a variety of scenarios, none of which made any sense. Why was knowing less, better? He leaned back into his chair. "Maybe you can you tell us how long this trip will take?"

"Depends."

"On what?"

"Whether we get blown out of the sky or not."

Mowgli yelped as a sudden turn to the left sent Henry and Seth crashing into the wall of the car.

Henry reached over the seat to the boy's shoulder. "Are you all right, Mowgli?"

The boy sobbed and held his right arm.

"What the —"

A flash of purple reflected off Mike's silvery dome. Wind screamed into the cockpit through a hole in the glass that wasn't there a second ago.

Mike yelled, "Sorry about that, folks. We've got company."

As they dove into a gyrating spiral, Mowgli cried out. Henry twisted round to catch a glimpse of an aircar following their descent. They had travelled beyond the city's limits and the tree tops below grew larger with each dizzying rotation.

Mike leveled them off, skirting above the ground and darting between trees. The forest soon disappeared and gave way to an open field that once might have been a pasture.

Henry said, "I don't see them yet."

The flat field offered little in the way of cover. Henry heard an alarming swish of tall grass running its lithe tendrils along the undercarriage. Mike weaved back and forth, and then whipped the car into a hundred-eighty degree turn while cutting the engines. They slid backwards and settled into a slight depression.

"I guess we'll spot them when they come over the trees." Henry looked around the interior. "Don't we have some weapons?"

Seth angled around Mowgli's passenger seat. "Indeed, this aircar does, sir." He jiggled his diminutive frame next to the boy and pressed a recessed button on the dash. A small screen swiveled into view along with a joystick.

Henry said, "How did you—"

"I just know, sir"

Mike said, "You'll get us all killed."

Henry gripped Seth's arm. "Do you know how to use that thing?"

"In theory, sir."

Mike pointed at the tree line. "Time to put that theory into practice."

The other aircar appeared over the tree tops and slowed to a stop, apparently searching for them.

Henry said, "Maybe they haven't spotted us yet."

Seth said, "Perhaps they are adjusting their aim, sir."

Mike said, "What are you waiting for? Fire the damn thing."

The front of the Batran aircar glowed a dull blue as if in preparation to launch an attack. Seth fired. A second hole exploded inward, leaving a scorch mark where Seth had sat only moments ago. At the same time, a spray of sparks erupted from the underside of the attacking aircar. It wobbled, then spun and descended through the trees at the far side of the field.

Henry said, "Nice shot."

"I aimed at their magneto. That would be the most humane choice, sir."

Henry watched as the Batrans managed a controlled crash a stone's throw away.

Mike said, "Humane? That little robot makes humane choices?"

Henry said, "You might learn a thing or two from him."

Mike said, "I'm way past that human crap. I don't need anyone to tell me how to behave."

"Not saying how you should behave, Mike. Don't be so quick to judge."

Mowgli pointed and said, "They come."

Seth said, "The Batrans are approaching by foot."

Mike said, "They're not coming to thank Seth for his humane shooting," and jolted their aircar up out of the grass. Seth clambered back into the seat next to Henry. As they hovered, three long shadows leaped through the grass. Henry's stomach twisted as Mike drove the aircar straight up into the night sky. A few pinpoints sparked up from the meadow, probably from blasters. They might as well have been lightning bugs for all the effect they had.

After leveling off, Henry shouted over the rush of air coming in through the windshield. "Are you going to tell us where we are going?"

"Relax. Get some sleep if you can. It'll be a few hours, and then all your questions will be answered."

An image of a cliff-side cabin lurched into Henry's mind, and along with it, a tall red-headed girl with a smile that melted his heart. That was yesterday—a yesterday one hundred years ago. Henry looked back at the row of empty seats and sighed—no ephemeral outline of his wife, no whispered encouragement. The deep shadows in the aircar's recesses remained an empty, lonely void.

Seth said, "Sir, try and rest. It must have been quite a shock to come back."

"From the dead? Coming back was the last thing I wanted." Henry turned his face away to look out the window. A gentle touch on his shoulder reminded him that Seth was the closest thing he had to a friend. He forced his eyes closed, and tried not to think of a life he would never have.

◇

Mowgli cried out. "Down. We down." The boy plastered his face against the side window.

Henry pushed himself up from his seat. "Down where?"

Seth said, "By the looks of those mountains and the coloring of the desert, I would say somewhere in the southwest."

Mike said, "Correctamundo. We have landed outside the San Juan Basin."

Henry said, "New Mexico?"

Mike released the door latch, and Mowgli bounded out. The cool air carried with it the unforgettable scents of creosote and sage. The pebbly ground shone dark from an early morning dew. A few hundred years ago this was Indian country. It might as well have been a million years ago.

Henry said, "Beautiful. But why here?"

As they left the aircar, Mike called out to Henry and tossed him one of the Batran blasters. "See. I'm not the enemy."

Henry said, "That remains to be seen."

Mowgli cried out. "Look, look!"

With the rising sun at their backs, the rose-colored mesas could have been islands floating in the desert sea. A glowing dust cloud drifted up in the distance.

Henry said, "Somebody knows we're here."

35

Seth added, "Horses, sir."

Mike said, "We're expected."

"Are you going to tell us what this is all about?"

"It'll all make sense soon enough."

"It better."

The cloud grew larger with each passing second and details emerged. Seth was right about the horses. Henry counted five with a solitary rider leading the pack.

The sudden hum of the aircar turned his head. For a moment, Henry thought Mike had decided to leave, but the one-eyed enigma stood nearby appearing uninterested.

Henry said, "What's going on?"

"Precaution."

The vehicle hovered for a moment and then abruptly scooted off in the direction they had been travelling.

"Worried about what's coming?"

Mike shook his head. "Worried about the Batrans. They can track the car's location, and we don't want them finding us. Sooner or later they'd take over the controls."

Seth said, "True enough, sir."

Henry recalled his first ride on an aircar with Seth at the wheel. "We had to jump out—"

"—while it was moving." Seth added, "It is good to see your memory is intact, sir."

"Yeah. I remember that ride. And how does Mike know what the Batrans can do?"

Mike said, "You two kill me. You know I can still hear you."

Henry said, "Well?"

The answer would have to wait for another day. The sound of horses' hooves pounding the hard desert floor grew louder. The lead rider halted a stone's throw away.

Henry said, "Now there's something I never expected to see."

Seth said, "Do you mean the horses? They are a mixed breed, Andalusian and quarter horses, perhaps. The Andalusian were brought here by the—"

"Not the horses, although they are beautiful."

The setting sun highlighted the woman's hair, giving it a shimmering red sparkle, a painful memory, One hundred years may have passed, but to him Liz had died only a few days ago.

The woman atop the lead horse, a gray mount some fifteen hands high, fixed him with a stare. Her tunic and leggings appeared to be hand-woven cloth mixed with deerskin. A gust of warm air lifted a lock of her long black hair, revealing the deep red-brown of her chiseled features. She dismounted in one smooth motion. A turquoise pendant swung from her neck.

Henry said, "Ya'at'eeh."

The woman's eyes grew large. "It speaks."

"Did I get it wrong?"

"Good day to you, too. What are you?"

"Your English is impressive. I am what I appear to be."

The woman turned to Mike. "Another robot? Is that what we need?"

Henry noted the apparent familiarity between the two.

Mike said, "Henry is no robot. There's a human brain inside that blue head of his. He's what you'd call a cyborg." He pointed at his vacant eye socket. "And don't underestimate him, after all he did this."

She raised her head in appreciation and then reached into a pouch and threw Henry an apple. "Do you eat?"

Henry caught the fruit and handed it to Mowgli. "I do, but this little fellow is probably hungrier than I am."

She said, "And what's this?"

"My name Mowgli."

"A human child. Of no use to us."

Henry said. "Surely, there are other humans that might care for him."

"We are a desperate people. If he wishes to stay with us, he will need to work for his keep." The woman threw a second apple at Henry and then aimed her rigid face at Seth. "And this?"

Henry said, "He is my friend, Seth."

Mike said, "It's of Soofysh design, and very intelligent. Could be quite useful for the task ahead." He swung his arm around to Henry and then to himself. "Actually, we're all Soofysh creations."

Henry said, "And now that we've been introduced, what is your name?"

The woman whispered. "Chooli."

"Ahh, Navajo for strength, like that of a mountain."

She threw Henry a dark look and said, "How do you know our language?"

"My ancestors were of the Lakota. During my early years I was taught some basic language skills."

Her eyes ran over him. "Your skin … a curious choice of color."

"A consequence of my artificial blood. Not my idea."

She drew back. "You are a strange thing."

"Look who's talking. For one thing, you don't look Navajo."

She swiveled and loosened the reins of the other horses. "We need to get moving."

Henry asked, "Maybe you can tell me what's going on?"

Chooli remained silent and quickened her pace.

Seth ambled over to a horse three times his height.

Henry said, "Can you ride?"

"Riding is a matter of keeping one's balance and maintaining authority."

"Right." Henry gave Seth a boost up onto the horse's bare back and handed him the reins. "Good luck with the authority thing."

He turned to fetch Mowgli, but found the child already seated behind Chooli with his arms wrapped around her waist. "Looks like you found a friend, Mowgli."

The remark drew a scowl from Chooli.

Mike leaped up onto his horse, a maneuver which made the animal buck. When the horse settled down, Mike said, "I guess he's not used to someone like me."

Henry said, "Nobody is used to someone like you. Why'd you choose to ride? Why don't you use those jet boots of yours?"

"True enough, but there's nothing like a morning ride through the countryside, right, Henry?"

Henry shook his head. Mike's brain still had some way to go in repairing itself.

Chooli took up the reins of the extra horse and said, "Are you two finished? We have a long way to go."

Henry mounted and asked, "Exactly how far?"

Mike said, "We're on a mission, Henry. It's all top secret."

Clearly, the mission was important, so important that neither Chooli nor Mike would speak of it. And although Mike tried to keep the mood up, the fear he had seen in Chooli's eyes moments ago did little to quell his own growing anxiety. Henry snapped his reins and turned his attention to the glowing eastern sky. The dark blue mesas lining the horizon colored his mood. A foreboding crept up the back of his mind. If he had been reincarnated for a reason, that reason awaited him directly ahead.

CHAPTER 5

The Batran official who stepped inside the office was uncharacteristically nervous.

"I beg your pardon, Councilor Marth, but we have a problem."

"What now?"

The obsequious drudge stepped forward a pace. Marth was quick to notice the pink coloration of his neck and prepared herself for bad news.

"There has been a break-in at the Museum."

She made a show of exhaling a deep sigh. "Which museum and what was taken?"

"Atlanta. Two artifacts were stolen."

Marth raised her voice and hissed, "What two artifacts?"

"A blue robot and a smaller one … a silvery one, one of the old Soofysh drones."

Marth's eyes opened wider to take a closer look at the official. She was vaguely familiar with the two mechanicals. "And what have you done to address this situation?"

"There is more."

"Spit it out."

The official took a step back and continued. "The two stolen robots appear to have been reactivated. Shortly after the theft, a human youngling escaped from our underground operation, apparently aided by the thieves. A pursuit followed, trapping them in a building; however, our forces were overwhelmed and the group flew off in a stolen aircar."

"Overwhelmed? How many thieves were there?"

"Actually, the reports indicate a large robot was behind it all."

"A third robot?" Marth brought a hand to the side of her head. "What kind of robot?"

"A silver one. Apparently it can fly and it has a missing eye."

"Have you been able to track the aircar?"

"Unfortunately, we were only able to ascertain it headed west after which we lost contact."

"After you alert our border stations, give me the names of the incompetents behind this fiasco. Leave me."

When the door eased shut, Marth rotated her chair to face a side alcove occupied by a leather wing-backed chair. The Batran sitting in that chair spoke without turning to look her. "A silver robot, and a blue one stolen from the museum?"

"Robots stealing robots—there must be more to this, but, it's nothing we can't handle."

"I know of only one blue robot that was on display at the Atlanta museum, and it was no robot."

Marth was aware of the inventory, but was short on specifics. "What are you talking about?"

"A Soofysh creation. Human brain in a impervious metal body. His name was Henry, Henry Wind In Trees."

"My brother's name?"

"Your mother and I befriended this creature prior to your birth. We were young and foolish … named your older brother after him. Henry and I defeated the Soofysh, or so we thought at the time." Genz stood from his chair and raised his voice. "Henry led us astray."

"What do you mean?"

"He convinced your mother that we were wrong to colonize this world. She fell for his charm and undermined our work."

"And why didn't my brother ever tell me of this creature he was named after?"

"He didn't know."

"And died without knowing—killed by humans. Why keep such a secret from me?"

"It was no secret, really. Just something that was part of the past … unimportant."

"But my mother—."

"After you were born on the west coast, we returned to our colony in South Dakota. Your mother became incoherent. Every step we took to progress our settlement was undermined by her single-minded desire to abandon all we had accomplished. She had become insane. In the end she was banished."

"Are you telling me she's still alive? When were you going share that detail with me?"

"I'm not sure. In any event, she's dead to me, and should be to you." Genz took the seat opposite Marth's desk. "And that blue robot, that Henry contraption … that cyborg was retrieved from the coastal waters along with its companion some 100 years ago. The damage looked severe. We could not reactivate them. At the time, I was but an aide to Councilor Fernthi, your predecessor. He gave the order to display them, side by side, in the Atlanta museum as a reminder to our people of our early struggles and of Soofysh technology."

"You expect me to forgive you for keeping this from me?"

"Your mother was a traitor to our people. Better you should believe her dead."

"I'm talking about that … that Henry thing."

"Of no consequence at the time."

"Apparently, someone or something considers it of some consequence now."

Genz leaned in over the desk. "Did I hear your aide say that the thief was a robot with one eye?"

CHAPTER 6

The dry heat had climbed to scorching levels by the time they reached the canyons. Sculpted walls of red sandstone several stories high surrounded them at every turn. The floors of many were littered with the dusty and scattered remains of ancient pueblos and other structures flattened by Nature's ceaseless remodeling.

Mowgli's head lolled from side to side against Chooli's back.

Henry called out. "Hey, are we going to take a break soon?"

Chooli said, "We have arrived." Yet another opening loomed into view. "This is part of Chaco Canyon … original home of the Anasazi."

Henry recalled the ancient Native Americans and their penchant for cliff dwellings.

"Who lives here now?"

Mike said, "Someone you know."

The answer gave Henry a chill despite the heat.

Chooli halted at the canyon entrance. Henry brought his horse up next to hers and gave Mowgli a wink. Chaco Canyon formed a nearly perfect circle with dozens of rectangular cave openings decorating its sheer walls. Rope ladders hung from some. Several figures moved atop the surrounding cliffs.

Henry said, "Are you sure they're friendly?"

Chooli heeled her horse forward. "A precaution. Follow me."

They rode in single file. No one stirred at the cave mouths. Chooli led them into a ring of bricks some hundred feet wide at the heart of the canyon floor, the ancient remains of an obscure structure whose meaning was lost to history. At its center she dismounted with Mowgli in tow. Her voice echoed in the enclosed space. "You can get down now."

By the time Henry's feet hit the ground, people filled the recessed wall openings. The dark cave interiors gave them a disembodied floating appearance. Henry wondered if they might be Navajo, but no one uttered a single word.

"So, what's this? How did all these people survive the apocalypse?"

Chooli's brows twisted, giving Henry the distinct impression she didn't understand the question.

He added. "The disease which killed all the humans—you must have some records."

"Ah, the Death. As you can see, the Great Spirit chose to spare some." Chooli took hold of Mowgli's hand and motioned for the rest to follow.

Enigmatic woman. Henry was beginning to think that maybe he was slow, maybe he just didn't get it. He glanced at Mike, hoping for some explanation. Chooli added, "The people you see, including me, are children of children since that time"

Mike said, "You're in for a surprise, Henry."

"Great. Is that supposed to make me feel better?"

Seth said, "Look, sir. Up at the caves."

The hovering faces disappeared. A glance back at the canyon entrance confirmed that at least the guards were still in place.

They entered a narrow opening at the base of the wall sporting most of the caves. The air became cool. Henry sniffed at a trace of cooked meat. "Damn, I'm hungry, and that's not what I should be thinking about."

After a few corners, the group came to a wooden door set flush into the wall. Two guards dressed in thin, hand-woven tunics and leggings stood to either side. An oil lamp set on the wall nearby painted their faces with a ghost-like flickering of shadows.

"Are we going to see the Wizard of Oz?"

"Quite apt, sir. But do recall the Wizard was human."

"You're right about that."

Chooli knocked on the cracked wood.

"Who is it?"

The voice was deep, laced with a commanding tone.

"It is I, Chooli. I have returned with guests."

A few moments passed. Henry heard the rustle of clothing and then a faint metallic clack. The door swung open to another guard.

"Good to see you, Chooli."

"I am glad to see you too, Sequoyah."

Sequoyah's smile and the lingering looks they exchanged suggested they had a deep personal relationship. The guard had the build of a bar room bouncer, tall and wide, muscles on muscles. His smile disappeared as he stared into the eyes of each of the visitors, giving each a disarming inspection.

With his arms outstretched he said, "Weapons."

Chooli said, "No weapons are allowed within this chamber. Fear not, Sequoyah will return them to you when we are finished. I will wait out here with the boy."

Mike and Henry handed over their Batran blasters. An image of an old revolver and a trusted bow came to Henry's mind—reflections of a time long gone. He wondered if those relics still hung on the wall of his cabin.

Sequoyah motioned for them to step inside. "She awaits."

CHAPTER 7

Evan wiped away the cloying sweat from his brow and smirked, realizing there was little of that moisture left. He'd seen many of his fellow workers succumb, falling into a deep sleep, never again to be woken. Then there were those who became sick. The Golden Death is what they called it. Evan recalled seeing bodies glowing, covered in yellow gold, but that was elsewhere, where they mixed rock and acid.

"Back to work."

The gravelly voice jerked him into motion. He lifted his sledgehammer and pounded the rock into smaller pieces. Each swing brought him closer to the end of the day or maybe to the end of all his days. At the risk of getting prodded by a fire stick, he asked Rusty, "Can I have some water?"

The black-streaked silver giant robot drew closer. The ten foot mechanical monster withdrew a leather pouch from its waistband, turned it upside down and shook it to demonstrate it was empty. "Back to work."

Back to work. Evan wondered if it knew any other words in English. Rusty was the name they gave it, and it didn't seem to mind as long as the work was done.

The sun winked out behind the mountains, casting them into purple shadow. Cool dry desert air rolled over Evan's shirtless back, a pleasure so extreme that he trembled. He had survived another day. Soon the wagons would arrive.

No one waited for him at the camp. He often considered making a run for it while his legs had the strength, but there was nowhere to go. Each day they carved out more rocks from ever widening basin. The distant rocky slopes might well have been a prison wall and promised nothing in the way of water or shelter. Besides, big Rusty easily outpaced humans, and the punishment was severe. He swore Rusty enjoyed the torture.

On the day previous, his crew had numbered a few more. Those that embraced the deep sleep were scattered among the rock piles, joining their rotting brethren from countless days and weeks previous. Some of the dead were thrown in the wagons—destined for a fate known only to the reptilian masters back at camp. Vultures circled their digs every day. Rusty wasn't big on tidying up. Evan had seen coyotes spying on them from a distance and was sure that larger animals lurked in the hills waiting for the right moment to descend. Meanwhile, rodents and insects, never bashful, skittered between the rock piles, scouring leftover bones, leaving them to bleach. Each time Evan glimpsed one, he found himself wondering which bone it was, an ulna? A tibia? Maybe a rib? It was a macabre pastime his mind sought out, purposefully denying that the remains had belonged to a man whose dark destiny awaited him and all his fellow workers.

They finished loading the wagon with crushed stone. The shrill burst of a horn ended the workday. The sound of tools dropping to the ground accompanied the squeaking wheels of the rock wagon as it lumbered away on its own, heading to the acid baths. Another set of self-propelled wagons, half the size of the rock coach, arrived to cart them to the campsite. Each steel wagon held ten men and was controlled by some magic commands from Rusty. The trip back to camp took an hour over an uneven dirt trail. Evan used the time to mull things over. What were they doing here?

"You day-dreamin' again?"

Seedy, a giant compared to the rest of the work crew, leaned over the edge of the last wagon and held out a hand. Evan no sooner grabbed it than he found himself seated next to his friend.

Seedy said, "You're awful quiet today."

"No reason to talk."

"Yeah, there ain't any, true enough. But—."

"More quiet than usual?"

Seedy nodded while they watched Rusty hop in. It sat at the back on a special seat designed to allow it to keep an eye on its charges.

As they lurched forward, Seedy said, "This can't be right."

"Meaning?"

"All this … you know … us workin' on those damn rocks. The women back at camp, cookin' shit up to keep us going. What's it all for?"

"I have no woman."

"Sorry, man. Maybe, soon—"

"And don't need one."

"I'm just sayin' that there must be more to life. I heard some of the elders talkin'."

"They've been in the sun too long. And you … ain't you been through school?"

"I know we're supposed to be doin' this for the greater good—survival of the Batran colonies so they can take care of us. I'm beginning to think it's all bullshit." Seedy chanced a look in Rusty's direction. Its black horizontal slits remained enigmatic.

"Yeah. And, so?"

"That's the thing. What of us?"

Evan said, "There is no 'us'."

Seedy dropped his head as if trying to avoid the robot's gaze. "Ain't you ever considered raisin' a family of your own?"

"This is our family. And if you keep talking, the next time the Batrans come for a visit, they might take you back with them." An icy shudder ran up his backside even before he finished,

By the time they arrived in camp, twilight had become pitch. Evan grabbed up his burlap poncho flapping in the stiff wind. He and Seedy trudged to the campfire outside a tent shared with eight others. A short, gray-haired woman wearing a serape over her coarse-knitted dress stood by the fire with a bowl in hand. The flicker of the gas-powered blaze painted her with a bluish glow. She looked like some kind of specter raised from the parched New Mexico desert.

Seedy spilled some of the bowl's soup and embraced her. "I missed you, Bee."

"Careful, that's your supper."

Evan skirted the two and ladled out a few mouthfuls of water from a trough nearby. As he entered the tent, he made a point of waving at Rusty, who had assumed its usual position beyond the campfire. "Goodnight, you rusty bag of shit. See you in the morning, bright and early."

Whether or not Rusty returned the greeting remained the province of the Dark Lord. Evan slipped into the tent, joining several other men and women already laid out on their blankets. He found a bowl waiting for him by his bedding, and whispered through the canvas door flap, "Thanks, Bee."

So it was each day and each night.

Evan bunched up a corner of his blanket to support his head. His eyes refused to close. He considered what Seedy had said. Was this the way life was meant to be? The Batrans didn't care about humans. They used him and the others until exhaustion and death put an end to it. Families were an illusion. The few children that surfaced were taken away once they were independent enough. That was the way of it, and thinking how it might have been different was a waste of time. He forced his eyes shut.

CHAPTER 8

The yellow sheen of a wall lamp draped the back of the figure sitting behind a stone desk, hiding its features. Henry was certain from its size and shape that he was staring at the shadowy silhouette of a Batran. His recent encounters were anything but friendly. He had only met two that were not interested in killing him, and that was more than a century ago. The sound of the door closing brought him back. "Exactly who are you?"

The Batran spoke in perfect English. "Come closer."

All three took a few steps forward.

Seth said, "Sir, do you not recognize the voice?"

Mike clapped Henry's back. "Take a closer look, my friend."

"I'm getting sick of this." Henry took another step to the edge of the desk. "Tell me who you are."

The Batran stood and twisted slightly to allow the light to run across its facial features. It towered over him by at least two feet. "Do we all look alike to you?"

The faded green facial scales, the wide grin, the cat-like eyes—a burst of memories flooded Henry's mind. "It can't be … you're not … you are … Anth?"

"The one and only."

Henry bounded around the desk and the two embraced. To him, Anth and her male companion, Genz, left their west coast home only a few years ago. They had brought their son and daughter by his cabin to say goodbye, having decided to raise their children in the reptilian culture. Liz gushed a fountain of tears. She was alive yesterday.

"My god, you're alive … after all this time."

Anth said, "And you … look at you. You haven't aged a day."

"Sarcasm?"

"I've learned quite a bit since you left us."

Henry paused a moment to reflect. To Anth he must have given the impression of leaving. And now, he was back. "How can this be? You and Genz, and your kids, Henry and Marth. You headed south—"

"Don't remind me. Time has passed. And much has changed."

"You're not surprised to see me."

"An expedition … one of our exploration groups found you and Seth while travelling along the coast. You must have been in the water for a few years when they found you lodged in the rocks."

"I was dead."

"They brought your bodies to our biggest settlement in the city of Atlanta. I was there. I wept when I saw you. You were my dearest friend. I convinced our governing body to put the two of you in a museum, a remembrance of our new beginnings. After some time, I needed to leave Atlanta. There were, and are, terrible reasons why I did so."

"And Mike here?"

Anth paused a moment, perhaps considering what to say next and said, "We came across Mike a year ago."

Mike said, "My brain, that is, the half you didn't blow out of my head, managed to get itself back together. When I woke up outside the Cheyenne Complex, you were gone, and so were the Soofysh. I had no idea what to do. I sat there and waited."

Henry said, "Seriously? For how long?"

"Until these natives came along … I guess it comes out to about a century."

The silence that followed wrapped itself around Henry like a cold, wet blanket.

"You said you left Atlanta. Where's Genz … and your kids?"

"I will discuss that with you in due course."

"Fine, have it your way. Damn, how old are you in reptilian years?"

"Old enough."

Mike said, "So, as I was saying, some Indians showed up. After they tried to kill me, we talked. They turned out to be scouts on a mission to find other survivors. I convinced them that I was friendly and they brought me here."

Anth said, "I remembered a different Mike, Henry. He was Soofysh then, and what he had become … when I saw him again, I was not sure. I was filled with fear and my first reaction was to destroy him. But he was different, not threatening, and at times, helpful. His personality had changed."

Mike said, "Getting one's brains blown out might do that."

Henry said, "Plus the Soofysh were gone, right?"

Mike said, "Could have something to do with it."

Anth said, "When I told Mike about you, he convinced me there was a chance to bring you and Seth back. To prove his point, I sent him to Atlanta."

Mike said, "And here we are."

Seth said, "I sense we are here for a specific reason, sir."

Henry had figured that one out while ago. Anth and company needed him. The big question was for what.

CHAPTER 9

The heat woke him before the morning horn sounded. Evan never slept soundly. Seedy's talk of families had gotten under his skin, crawling about the underside of his mind, pushing out nightmares in a steady stream. Same thing, again and again—Claire, the woman he loved and would never see again, enticing him to join her, begging him to come for her.

He squeezed the sweat from his eyes and sat up. Sunlight filtered through the narrow slit at the tent's entrance, casting a bright line across the floor, which ended at Seedy's blanket. When his eyes adjusted, he realized Seedy was gone. As was Bee.

Evan rose to his knees for a better look, and whispered, "Seedy?"

He scanned the floor of the tent and repeated the question, an action that precipitated less than courteous responses from several of his co-workers that it was too early to get up. Finished with his survey, he stepped outside to greet a sun that had begun its trek over the eastern mountains. The air was cool and no one was about, except for Rusty, who stood at the far end of the campsite.

He approached the robot. "Good morning, Boss." If something had happened last night, Rusty might be willing to share the news.

The tarnished monolith answered without any perceptible movement. "The workday has not yet begun. Return to your tent."

"I know, I know. Just wondering if there's any news."

Rusty took a moment to answer. "Two workers were removed."

"I can see that. Where are they now?"

"They were removed."

The horn sounded.

Several women moved from tent to tent, carrying buckets—food and water. Rusty turned away and silently summoned the wagons. The conversation was over. Seedy and Bee had not escaped. They were removed. If nothing else, Rusty was to the point.

After breakfast, Evan joined the others in their wagon. He could not get the missing pair out of his mind. Seedy had been discontented and perhaps made the mistake of talking too much. Now both he and his girlfriend were gone. This was not the first time people vanished. He suspected Rusty heard a lot better than it made out.

Claire disappeared the same way and probably for the same reasons. She had become too vocal. Unlike the other women, she never accepted her role in camp, being part of the greater family of reptilians. "Better we die trying to free ourselves from this tyranny, than submit as slaves." Those were her last words.

Evan had a vague idea of the term 'slave.' The elders used it, whispering among themselves. They spoke of people who had no hope. He had made a point of never talking that way, at least not out loud.

◇

Several days had gone by since Seedy and Bee went missing. Maybe they had run off; maybe Rusty could lie. But where was there to run to? Why would Rusty lie?

"Back to work."

The robot's grinding tone jerked him back to reality. He focused on the sledgehammer, and with each swing pictured Rusty's oblong metal head dented, flattened and pulverized.

At the end of the day, Evan joined in loading the rock wagon. Rusty inspected its contents, and then sent it rattling its way to a processing site. The routine was the same, day after miserable day.

On the following day Evan feigned exhaustion and dropped to a knee. He expected Rusty would be on him any moment. While the others continued to fill the wagon, he took a good look at the underside of the carriage—three axles, equally spaced maybe six feet apart, stabilized by a central beam that ran the length of its undercarriage. A boxy mount graced the rear axle, likely hiding the motor and a steering mechanism. The clearance between the beam and undercarriage held his interest.

"Back to work."

Rusty loomed over Evan and waved its fire stick.

"No problem, Boss. I slipped is all."

When the wagon was full, Evan took note of Rusty's movement. The robot went through the identical series of steps each day. First, it stood at the rear and scanned the rock cargo. Maybe insuring no one was hiding under the load of stones. Then it walked around to its left side, peered beneath and repeated the process on the right side. Finally, it took two steps back and sent the wagon off with a tilt of its head.

◇

CHAPTER 10

Anth said, "Much has happened after you leaped off that cliff."

Henry winced. "How do you know I jumped?"

"An educated guess, Henry. According to the team that retrieved you, there were two graves at your cabin. One was marked with Elizabeth's name, the other, with your pet's name … Wolfie?"

"He was no pet."

 If anything, he and Liz had been Wolfie's pets.

"And you must have felt alone, isolated from the world you once knew."

"Now you're a psychologist?"

"I know that feeling, Henry. I know it too well."

Henry felt a pang in his chest. Anth had not brought up her significant other, Genz, nor her children.

She added, "I have found a reason to go on."

"I'm not sure that I have."

"Maybe I can convince you otherwise."

"I'm listening."

Anth swept an arm in an arc. "These natives—they are a portion of what is left of the humans in this part of your country. The others, and there are many, are kept by my people." Anth hissed out the word 'people'.

"Kept?"

"You do remember the Soofysh?"

The question needed no answer.

"I have reason to believe they are about to return. We have a contract—a repayment of sorts for the privilege of colonization. The Soofysh expect to be compensated with ore, specifically uranium-enriched ore. We made a promise that we may not be able to keep."

"So what?"

"The Soofysh are not tolerant. We have heard of other colonies vanishing—a result of their failure in fulfilling their contract."

"I'm guessing you're using humans to help do the mining."

"We had limited mechanical resources with which to mine. It was a necessity."

"So, where do I come in?"

"During this past century the Batrans have hunted down the remaining humans. These unfortunates have been manipulated into believing they are an integral part of the Batran way of life, and are taught to be happy to serve their masters."

"As slaves?"

"Precisely. But it does not end there."

"How bad can it get?"

"Those unable or unwilling to work serve a different purpose."

The image of naked humans in a corral in the museum sprang up—an image which included fresh meat in the Batran kitchen.

"Don't say it."

"It is the reason I am here and why we have brought you here. Most Batrans see humans as a breed of clever animals, useful beasts of burden and, I hate to admit it, some see them as a delicacy."

Henry found himself at a loss for words.

She continued. "You know me, Henry, and I know you. Such treatment is unworthy of any specie that considers itself intelligent. We need to do something."

"We? What the hell do you need me for? You've created the demon you wish to destroy. Good luck with it." Henry turned to the door. "I don't need any of this."

Sequoyah blocked the doorway, throwing him an impressive grimace. Henry clenched his fists. "Get out of my way."

Anth said, "Let him go."

In the hallway, Henry leaned against a wall. Misgivings swirled in his mind. This wasn't his fight. For all he cared, the reptilians could all go to hell.

Chooli and Mowgli approached. The boy pulled away and ran up, saying, "Henry, Henry, you help us?" The dirty face, the wide eyes and the expectant grin forced Henry to look away.

With a tug at his leg, Seth said, "Sir, she is gone. She will never return."

"Leave me alone, Seth."

"Look past your own sadness, sir, and you will see the suffering of your people. You are not alone. Mowlgi is one of your people. We are your people. There is no one else we can ask for help."

The air blew out of Henry's chest. It was not the first time Seth included himself as one of Henry's people.

"Damn it all. I'm only one person. What makes me special?"

Seth paused a moment and then said, "You are a legend. You defeated the Soofysh once before. Your people will follow you anywhere, sir."

"You know that's not exactly what happened."

"It's sufficient that these folks believe so, sir. We need a leader, and regardless of what you think, you are it."

Sequoyah and Anth stood at the doorway. Mike peered out from behind them. "You can count on me, too, Henry."

CHAPTER 11

The time had arrived. The windless morning laid a blanket of dry and hot air over wide rocky pit. Evan's nostrils flared with each inhale. He worked to control his breathing, to steady his nerves.

He wasn't hungry, but he left his bowl of gruel cleaner than if it was washed. Neither was he thirsty, but he spent some extra time ladling water down his gullet. And he wasn't cold, but he folded up a small blanket and tucked it inside his trousers. He expected the worst and had the distinct feeling he would not be disappointed.

"Get in."

With luck, Rusty's raspy voice would be a distant memory by the end of the day.

At the dig Evan hid the blanket in a rocky crevice and returned to his job, crushing stone. He paced himself throughout the day, insuring that the workflow remained steady, and took care not to draw attention, although he pushed the boundaries of every break, resting when possible to keep hydrated. His fawning behavior and apparent good mood may have risked Rusty's suspicions, if the robot had any. At the end of the day, the rock wagon arrived.

When the crew finished loading it, Rusty began the usual inspection. When the robot straightened up after checking the undercarriage, Evan rolled beneath with blanket in hand. Had he made a sound? For some reason, instead of returning to the rear of the wagon, Rusty paused at the side. The silence became a vise gripping his heart. He pictured the tin goliath bending down for a second look. The fire stick would swing into view, and then he would scream as the white heat seared through muscle. The robot's eye slits would flare, and a grating laugh would follow, and soon after that, a painful death would end it all.

But Rusty simply stood still.

"Hey, Rusty, you got any brains up there in that tin can? Did you forget something, you bucket of shit?"

Evan recognized the voice. Jacob was the last person he expected to speak up, rarely uttering a word in all the time he knew the man. He must have seen what was happening, and decided on a diversion. Evan was not alone in misery or in rebellion. Rusty's feet marched out of sight, giving him time to wedge himself between the undercarriage and the axle beam. He tucked the blanket between himself and the sharp metal. A moment later Jacob cried out. The whimpering that followed confirmed that the man was still alive. Evan whispered a silent thanks to a hero he probably would never see again, a hero who saved his life this day. He wondered how many others would suffer because of his actions.

The rock wagon shuddered as it began to move. He straddled the covered beam, head forward and stomach down, and came close to falling off at the first turn. The rutted road was a dirt trail laced with stones and potholes. Blinded by dust kicked up by the front wheels Evan curled a corner of the blanket over his face. He needed all his strength to grip the narrow beam. Not knowing how long the trip would be became secondary to his efforts to avoid slipping off and choking on the constant stream of dust and pebbles the wagon kicked up.

The ride seemed like it would never end. Stress and exhaustion took turns torturing his body and mind. More than once, he thought of letting go, leaving his fate to chance. It would be easy to give up, to succumb, to just drift off. He lost track of time, not knowing if a mere hour had passed or many. Each bump, each jarring sway, became his metronome—a kind of knelling of a distant bell. He sang, determined to at least reach the end of each song before giving in to death's siren call.

It was twilight when the wagon jolted to a stop. He coughed up black sputum, and with unfeeling hands rubbed caked dirt from his face. He swung off the beam and passed out.

It was night when he awoke. The ground beneath him felt smooth. His limbs were slow to respond and painful to move, but he forced himself to crawl from beneath the wagon.

He lay on concrete. Tall illuminated outlined several single story buildings in the distance. His nose puckered at an acrid stench and confirmed he had arrived at the notorious processing plant he had heard about. The darkness threatened to give birth to horrors his imagination would not stifle. Any moment could herald dead people covered in yellow dust stumbling out from between buildings.

A metallic whisper announced the arrival of a second rock wagon. It pulled up alongside and ground to a halt, Evan raised himself between the wagons, craning his head to scan the surroundings for any sign of robots or Batrans, or some other nightmare. The darkness yielded only the outlines of a dozen wagons neatly aligned in rows and all loaded with crushed rocks.

He wrapped his blanket over his shoulders to stave off the night's frigid air and stumbled between the silent carts while regaining some feeling in his legs. Hunching down, he shuffled closer to the buildings, pausing at the last line of wagons, reluctant to expose himself.

A tall lamppost illuminated the front door of the middle of three identical and windowless buildings. A breeze whispered beneath the eaves of their corrugated metal roofs as if carrying a ghostly warning. He knew enough of modern equipment to suspect cameras were likely positioned everywhere. Using the line of assembled carts for cover, he emerged at the shadowy far end of the complex and followed an outcrop of rocks to the side of an end building. Several railroad hopper cars stood in the shadows atop a pair of tracks that snaked off toward the east. The acrid odor from the digs was even more pungent. After a few minutes waiting and hoping that no alarms were set off, he approached the railcars.

He scaled the side of one of the hoppers and recoiled when he found it half-filled with yellow dirt. Dirt that was not dirt. Over the years too many stories of the deadly substance had spread though the camp, and each time they came around, the anecdotes became more macabre—walking skeletons, glowing eyes, the dead that did not die. This was the yellow dust they all spoke of—the Golden Death. He leaped off, brushing his hands and slapping at his trousers in an effort to get the clinging powder off.

He followed the tracks to an opening on the side of the nearest building. It was likely that the yellow muck was made inside and loaded onto the waiting rail cars. A small shed stood to the side. Evan checked its doors—unlocked. Digging tools hung within. He grabbed a pickaxe and followed the rails inside.

The apparent lack of security puzzled him. He had expected some activity, if not from humans, then from robots or Batrans. The place gave him the impression of being abandoned, but the half-filled hopper suggested otherwise.

Then the railcars lurched into motion.

◇

CHAPTER 12

Several days of intense discussions included heated arguments on a way forward— what Anth claimed needed to be done. These were tossed up against less aggressive options that Henry preferred.

In the end he found himself part of a team on horseback. Every time he went over it, the plan became less likely to work. But it was too late. He had agreed and would not renege. The group set off at a trotting pace to conserve energy. Anth said the ride would take the better part of a day.

Seth wrapped his short arms about Henry's midsection. "Are we there yet, sir?"

His companion of many years never failed in spirit.

Mike scooted alongside using his Soofysh technology.

Henry said, "You sure you have enough fuel, Mike?"

"No sweat, man. They've never failed me."

"Sounds like a matter of faith."

Chooli and Sequoyah rode side by side, followed by some dozen warriors. His gaze paused at Chooli.

Mike said, "They're a perfect couple, aren't they, Henry?"

Henry slumped his shoulders a bit, "Yeah, seems so."

Mike let out a raspy guffaw. "Hah. Sometimes you really amaze me."

"I don't know what you mean."

"You idiot. She and Sequoyah are sister and brother."

"You don't say."

Henry sat up straighter. "I was just checking on the troops."

"Yeah, troops. They call themselves warriors. I doubt any experienced actual combat. What are they going to do with spears and bows?"

"Some of them have Batran weapons." Henry ran his hand along the string of a borrowed bow. It likely would not amount to much in a fight, but in a world shattered by an invasion no one saw coming, it gave him a sense of place, of meaning, He patted the the Batran blaster tucked in his waistband—insurance of a sort.

Dusk had arrived when Chooli rode past at a gallop and shouted, "Wait here." A trailing dust cloud followed her into a sunset-lit haze. Moments later she disappeared behind a rise.

When Henry brought the column to a halt, Sequoyah came alongside. "We walk." He swung down off his horse and tied the reins to a nearby sagebrush, part of the scrub that littered their rocky path. Henry sucked in the thin air, thankful for the absence of death in its scent. They were at an altitude he had never experienced and was relieved his artificial body remained unaffected.

Minutes later Chooli's silhouette jutted up at the crest of the rise. She was on foot and waved.

Sequoyah said, "We go."

When they reached her, Chooli motioned for everyone to keep a low profile. Waning sunlight cast the valley ahead in deep purple shadows.

Henry said, "So that's the mining operation?"

A large open pit had been dug into the desert floor. At its edge, a huge metallic figure stood to the side, apparently overseeing a loading operation.

Henry turned to Seth. "What do you think they're mining?"

"It would most likely be uranium, sir. The first step is crushing rock."

"And the next?"

"If the objective is to isolate uranium-235, then the rock will be reduced to a yellow cake using acid. Further steps will concentrate the uranium-235, but that requires some sophisticated equipment."

"Why would the Batrans need this stuff? Their technology doesn't require nuclear power, does it?"

"These efforts may be directed at supplying the Soofysh with payment."

"Yeah, payment for services rendered." Henry recalled his previous encounter with the Soofysh. The entity prepared planets for colonization, which included targeted sterilization of the original natives—an extra bonus for arriving colonies. And the Soofysh demanded compensation.

Chooli said, "That is the guard."

Henry said, "A big robot. I've never seen its like. You really think we can take it?"

Chooli threw Henry a frown. "You are the expert. You tell us."

The remark caught Henry off guard, but then he realized why these people sought him out. In their minds he was a legend. He had defeated many robots and vanquished the inscrutable Soofysh. If they only knew how much luck was involved. Anth knew all that, but she still trusted him.

"I guess we need to get closer."

Chooli canted her head as if to say, 'duh'."

Mike said, "Maybe what we need is a distraction. You know … something to draw the guard away while the rest of us get down there and free those people?"

"Great idea, Mike. Why don't you scoot down closer to get that robot's attention? Not too close. We don't know how fast it can move and what weapons it has."

"Me and my mouth."

Chooli offered up her pair of binoculars.

Henry focused them on the guard. "It looks beaten up and worn out—maybe not all that powerful. Assuming it's the only guard, and assuming it follows you, we'll move in from the opposite side, assuming the people down there don't go running off."

"That's a fair amount of assumptions, Henry."

"I have nothing else, Mike. You'll do fine. Besides, you should be faster than that clunker down there."

"You know how to lift a guy's spirits."

Mike took off, gliding above the sloping ground. In the fading light all that Henry saw was a wisp of trailing dust.

Seth said, "He is certainly fast, sir."

"I'm sure he'll do fine." Henry brought the binoculars up. "He's already drawn some attention."

The robot turned away from the pit and turned its head to follow Mike's approach.

Seth said, "He is getting rather close."

Henry said, "He's gotten too close."

Mike stopped some ten paces from the robot. For a moment, neither one moved.

Henry said, "Is it sizing him up? Probably not sure what it has encountered."

Seth said, "The same could be said for Mike."

An explosion of sand erupted between the two. In an instant, Mike rocketed up, stopping to hover high overhead. A bolt of lightning shot out from the robot's arm. It connected with Mike, who twirled in mid-air for a moment and then crashed to the ground. The robot marched toward Mike's motionless body.

Henry said, "We move now."

Chooli said, "To save the people?"

"That and Mike. Sequoyah, get everyone with a Batran weapon and follow me. Mike needs our help. Chooli, in the meantime, get the rest of your warriors to the workers in the pit." Henry leaped up. "Let's move."

Chooli barked out a few orders. Sequoyah waved for the others to follow and ran after Henry.

The robot hadn't yet reacted to them, apparently too curious about Mike. It trundled over the few paces needed to reach Mike's body, while Henry and a group of some half-dozen armed men surged down the slope.

"We're not going to reach him in time. Open fire."

Everyone fell to their knees and fired their blasters. Bolts of blue lit up the darkening sky; however, the distance made accuracy a challenge as most salvos landed wide of the robot, resulting in harmless puffs of exploding rocks. But the robot did take notice.

Henry said, "Keep firing," and ran off at a tangent, hoping to use the barrage for a diversion while getting closer.

The robot took several steps toward the line of shooters and fired off a beam of its own. Henry caught a glimpse of several warriors exploding into human torches. The mechanical juggernaut took a number of direct hits from the Batran blasters, but suffered no perceptible ill effect. In its hand it held some kind of stick-like weapon.

Henry screamed at it, hoping to get its attention. "Shithead. It's me you want."

The robot lurched in Henry's direction, but instead of firing, it lowered the weapon and said, "You are Soofysh."

Stunned by the robot's command of English, Henry sputtered. "That's right … same as Mike, the guy you shot down."

"That was a mechanical and it is only stunned. I will stun you now. My masters will be pleased."

"Not if I can help it." Henry fired his blaster. The burst of energy hit the robot square in its head. It shook it off the burst and raised its weapon. At the same moment it took a second hit from its flank from Sequoyah.

The momentary disruption gave Henry one chance. He aimed for the thing's weapon, firing a continuous stream until his blaster's fiery torrent waned. A blinding red flare erupted from the robot's extended arm. The explosive concussion knocked Henry off his feet and sent him rolling. He yelled through the purple haze, hardly hearing his own voice. "What happened? Sequoyah!"

A hand grasped his arm. "I am here."

His eyes were quick to readjust. The towering giant of a robot lay on the ground, its right arm gone.

Mike stirred. "Nice shot, Henry."

"Are you okay?"

"A little wobbly. And you?"

Sequoyah nudged Henry and pointed.

The robot braced itself on one knee. Henry's weapon was spent. A half-dozen warriors to his rear had closed in and opened fire, as did Mike. The robot stood up on both legs, apparently disinterested in the barrage of weapon fire. At point blank range, the energy bolts barely brushed off patches of rust on its exterior.

The onslaught died down as the weapons expended themselves.

"Soofysh will want to meet you, Henry."

It knew his name. Henry fought back an urge to run. The grinding timber to the metal creature's voice added weight to its grim message. The Soofysh were the real monsters, and his earlier experience with them weighed heavy on his mind. The present monstrosity was nothing in comparison.

Henry took a step closer to the automaton. "What is your purpose?"

Without any discernible movement, the robot replied, "To insure mining operations continue without interruption."

"Where are these rocks going?"

The behemoth remained silent.

Henry caught sight of Chooli and some twenty people carrying sledge-hammers and picks approaching from the basin. Members of Chooli's team, minus several who were vaporized, closed in with spears and rocks in hand. The air pulsated with tension—a portent of an impending cataclysm?

The robot turned to the miners. "I am damaged and unable to continue my function."

One of the miners shouted, "Let's finish it," and raised his pick.

Henry held up his hand, "Hold on." He turned to the robot, "Where are these rocks going?"

Its eye slits glowed, and the air grew warmer.

Seth said, "It would be prudent to move away, sir."

Henry gestured at the workers and his group. "Back! Quick!"

Everyone ran for cover. Henry dove behind a nearby boulder as the sky went from night to day. The detonation shook the ground, sending debris flying overhead, pummeling and ricocheting off the surrounding rock.

When the roaring in his ears died off, Henry threw off the desert dust and peered through the descending cloud of debris. Chooli and Sequoyah emerged from the settling fallout. One by one, the workers strode forward, covered in desert grit.

Henry said, "Damn. I didn't expect that."

"Sir, you have succeeded in destroying yet another Soofysh creation. What now?"

Henry ignored the implied sarcasm. "Good question, Seth. What's important here is what we started."

"And that is, sir?"

"War, Seth. We've started a war."

Chooli strode up. "We will take these workers back with us."

Henry nodded. "I'm staying."

"Our mission is accomplished. We go back now."

"I need to find out what the Batrans are up to." Henry's last contact with the Batrans had left him with the impression that they were reasonable people. Things had changed for the worse, and then there was what the robot had said—the Soofysh wanted to meet him.

The sound of crunching gravel drew Henry's attention to the rock wagon. It trundled away on a rutted dirt trail, no doubt running on automatic, following its routine regardless of circumstances. He imagined the wagon pulled by some desert spirit eager to devour its contents. No sooner than the rock wagon disappeared, three other wagons rattled into view and jerked to a stop nearby.

Henry said, "What are these for? More rocks?"

Seth said, "The workers here have no shelter. It is the end of the working day. Perhaps these are meant to take them back to their encampment."

Henry said, "Where there may be other humans."

Chooli said, "And robots."

Mike said, "Let's take a ride and see."

Henry swung up and into one of the wagons. "Anybody else want a ride?"

Seth and Mike climbed aboard.

Henry said, "Chooli, we'll see where this takes us. With some luck, we'll be back with any others we find in the camp by morning, assuming these wagons are programmed to bring us back."

Chooli yelled to Sequoyah, "Take the workers to the horses and back to our camp, then return here and wait for us." She jumped into the wagon and said, "I am going with you."

Henry said, "Are you sure you want to do this? There's no telling what we'll find."

Chooli said, "I know this land, and … I want to help."

Henry wondered. What was her real reason for tagging along? Maybe she was following Anth's orders, or maybe she was merely curious.

The specter of the Soofysh running the show ran a ripple up his titanium backbone.

CHAPTER 13

"Time to rise, Marth."

The voice echoed between mountains, distant, and easy to ignore. She held her parents' hands as they glided down into a valley. The warm air filled her wings, running its titillating tendrils over her body. It was her first flight, and the feeling of wonder filled her every cell.

"Now."

The valley faded away. Marth opened her eyes, ready to admonish the fool who would awaken her. It was her father.

Genz said, "Come, you have an urgent call."

She shook her head and staggered after Genz into her office. A distraught officer appeared on the wall screen. His voice cracked at times, as if he had trouble believing what he was saying.

"Councilor Marth. I have … some news … excavation 303 in northern New Mexico has gone silent."

"Is that one of our uranium operations?"

Genz nodded while the officer continued. "Our regular contact failed to report."

"By regular contact you mean the overseer?"

The nod sent a twinge of anxiety through her. The mechanicals that were stationed at digs were Soofysh technology—on loan. They were supposed to last indefinitely. And they were supposed to be infallible.

She spoke to Genz. "This is most irritating. The Soofysh will be arriving soon. We cannot have any delays." Turning to the wall display, she said, "Perhaps the problem is technical." She knew what the answer would be.

The officer said, "The overseer has never been late with a report."

Genz said, "The thieves were last seen going in that direction."

"But how would they know of the mining operation? And how were they going to overpower an overseer?"

Genz said, "You should send a military squad to the 303 site immediately. The one-eyed robot is the connection. I have encountered such a one many years ago … and it was also a Soofysh construct. The last I recall was that it had died … destroyed by the cyborg."

"The blue one? The one that was stolen a few days ago?"

"The very same."

Marth spoke to the screen. "Dispatch a squad immediately. I want a full report." She switched off the display. Slumping into her desk chair, she wondered what it all meant. Reactivated mechanicals, a stolen aircar and now, an anomaly at a uranium dig—she sifted through a variety of plausible explanations while somewhere in the back of her mind an unsettling feeling of dread reared up.

She looked up at Genz. "Tell me everything you know of the one-eyed robot and the blue cyborg."

◇

CHAPTER 14

Evan ran outside. The engine at the far end of the track growled into life. Two options surfaced—to stay and discover more about the operations within the buildings, or jump on a railcar and see where it led.

Considering that no one was around and that the operations appeared to be on automatic, the train offered the best chance of survival. He dashed along the rails and managed a hop to grab hold of a ladder on the last car. He hurled the pickaxe in and climbed up.

Fear of the yellow dust kept him perched at the top of the ladder. A foot-hold near the car's coupling offered him a seat.

The three-car train gained speed and at times it was all he could do to avoid being thrown off. The adrenaline rush had eaten away the strength in his muscles, leaving him barely able to hold on. To top things off, he found himself fighting to stay awake.

It was still dark when the train slowed. Evan leaned out to see a station of sorts ahead. He grabbed the pickaxe and jumped down to the gravel bed, tumbling over the rocks and brush to finish in a bruised heap. The engine hissed to a stop a few hundred feet farther along.

A quarter moon cast a glow over the one-story buildings surrounding the rail yard. Two figures climbed out of the engine and entered what he guessed was the station. A minute later they clambered back in the engine and the rail cars reversed direction.

Alarmed that the cars would soon be upon him, he struggled up to a knee, ready to run, but was relieved to see that the train veered to the side. It followed a spur that led to a long building covered by a corrugated roof. Two enormous metal doors slid apart to allow the cars through.

Evan loped to a parallel track and slid to the bottom of its rocky bed for cover. After a few minutes to insure no one had seen him, he crawled over to a window. The moonlight slipping in through the building's entrance revealed few details within.

He heard the two Batrans speaking and understood enough of their language to piece together the disjointed conversation.

"Another load."

"Time to rest."

The crunching sound of footfalls on gravel grew louder. They were getting nearer and there was nowhere to run. He hefted up the pickaxe.

"We rest later."

"Get the other door."

The massive doors pulled shut and the footfalls faded away. The last statement he heard had him concerned.

"The Soofysh will be here—"

The Batran hissing faded away while they walked to a building beyond the station house—perhaps their sleeping quarters. Evan waited for the pounding in his ears to subside. He had heard of the Soofysh—part of the invasion many years ago. When the Batrans spoke of them it was always with a tone of respect, or was it fear?

He sidled to a corner of the building and scanned the yard for other structures. Besides the station, the one at his back, and the one the Batrans were heading out to, there was not much else of note. At least no robots wandered the premises at the moment.

He edged to the double doors and parted them, unleashing a dull metallic squeal. The short train loomed out of the gloom. The pings of cooling metal set his nerves on edge. Farther on, the tracks made their way beneath metal beams holding some heavy machinery whose function was beyond anything Evan had experienced—enormous funnel-shaped contraptions, geared wheels, and pipes made of metal and glass. He turned away, coughing. The air held an acidic stench that made it a struggle to breathe.

With his lungs burning he quick-stepped back to the entryway, happy to suck in the cold, fresh air. As the pain in his chest subsided, he staggered to a corner where a faucet jutted from the gravel floor. After several attempts to turn the valve, it gave way with a spurt of water. He cupped his hands beneath the thin stream and splashed it into his face, rolling his tongue over his lips, savoring the taste of rust. He spent the next few minutes at the faucet sopping up the ruddy elixir, casting aside any reservations regarding its purity. Each swallow brought with it new life and new hope. He couldn't imagine anyone, Batran or human, working under the conditions in the building. The entire setup had to be automated, much like most things Batran seemed to be.

Evan's mind reset itself to his immediate goal—escape. The present structure offered nothing tangible, as did the Batran sleeping quarters. Who knew how many might be in there. He slinked his way to the station, the only two-story building. It was built in the style of the Old West. Evan recalled the images of a children's picture book that his parents had kept—a treasure of the past. No such books existed anymore. He spat into the night air, allowing his disgust and longing to share a ride on the phlegm.

Although the station's broad windows were coated in dust, several were broken and allowed a view within. After checking for movement, Evan gave the glass door a push. It opened without a sound and with surprising ease, revealing a large room littered with several wooden benches. A ticketing window adorned one of the interior walls. A stairway ran up alongside.

Evan walked to the opposite side of the room and peered out a shattered window at the back—no vehicles. He sat on a bench and leaned on the pickaxe, continuing his vigil over the tracks and buildings beyond, wondering how the hell he was going to get away from the damn Batrans. That's when he heard a creak from above.

CHAPTER 15

Henry awoke to the sounds of bird song. No, not song, but cackling, as if a wake of vultures scuttled about, no doubt with expectations. His eyes focused on Chooli sitting nearby, chewing. The heat of a campfire pushed away the icy night air.

They sat in front of a tent identical to several others in the area. On the previous night the few women they found in the camp cried, desperate for their loved ones. Mike's appearance threatened to set them into hysterics. Three robots trying to calm everyone was an image Henry would not soon forget. Eventually, broken English and sign language got the message across that the pit workers were safe and that everyone would be reunited soon. Sleep came much later for Henry. He kept seeing huge robot guards with their eyes sparkling in the dark.

Chooli said, "Want some?" She held out a scrap of jerky. "I was not sure you needed to eat."

Henry said, "Oh, I eat. And drink."

She produced a leather pouch. "Water?"

Henry accepted her offer and rebuked himself for not packing food and water when they first set out. "Thanks. I thought I heard—."

Chooli mumbled a chant between chews. "Me? It's a song we use to thank Mother for her gifts and ask for strength."

"Yeah, that must be it."

Seth spoke up. "Speaking of hearing, sir, I hear an aircar."

A quick look up revealed nothing, but Henry trusted Seth. "We need to find cover and fast."

Chooli said, "What can I do?"

"Get the women inside the tents and tell them to wait."

It took but a minute to usher the women out of sight. The four slipped into an empty tent, leaving a slit open in the tarp covering the entryway.

The unmistakable hum of an aircar became louder.

"What is the plan, sir?"

"Seth, you know the answer."

"Indeed I do, sir."

Mike and Chooli leaned in.

Henry said, "Any of your blasters still working?"

Mike said, "Tapped out, Henry."

Shaking heads confirmed their situation, which portended a grim outcome.

Chooli said, "I have an idea." She grabbed a tattered shawl from the bedding in the tent. "I will come out with the other women and tell the Batrans that the men have not returned. They will likely think I belong here."

Henry said, "Not if they see your face. You did notice how old those women are?"

Ignoring Henry's admonition, Chooli ran to the other tents to convince the women to join her. From what Henry overheard, she told them to complain to the Batrans about their missing men. That's when the aircar arrived.

Mike said, "What is she doing?"

Henry said, "I don't know, but she's doing it."

The aircar landed in a clearing between tents. Chooli led a group of four women out to meet it. Three Batrans, armed with blasters, stepped out.

Chooli used her best Batran. "The men have not arrived. What has happened?" The other women joined in, shouting and weeping.

The nearest Batran, maybe the one in charge, approached her with weapon raised. "Who are you?"

Chooli lowered her head. "We are the servants of Batrans."

The Batran used his free arm to grab her neck. He waved the weapon ahead and spoke to the other two. "Search the tents."

◇

CHAPTER 16

He wasn't alone.

Evan fought down an impulse to run, to get out of the station and head out into the surrounding desert. It took a second to realize that would mean certain death because nothing out there offered respite from the heat and lack of water.

Perhaps the sound came from old timbers in the building as it cooled off from the day's insufferable heat, ancient logs snuggling up to each other in the cold air. He waited, frozen to his bench. A drop of sweat rolled down his nose and perched at the tip. A minute went by, then another. The drop plummeted to the floor, leaving a mini-dust crater. He let out a slow exhale. Then he heard another creak. This time it bore a kind of drag, a foot scrubbing across several floorboards.

He stood without thinking, as if his body had decided to move on its own to gain a better vantage point. After a few minutes of complete silence, Evan shuffled to the base of the stairway. He hefted the pickaxe with his right hand and planted a foot on the first rise, keeping to the side for fear of loose boards eager to announce his presence.

He counted twelve steps. An open doorway led to an open space obscured by shadows. A cage stood at its center. A figure moved within it.

"Who's that?"

The whisper came from the cage and it was in English. He lifted the pickaxe, ready to pummel whoever lurked in the dark, and stepped through the doorway. Evan said, "Who do you think it is?"

"Son-of-a-bitch. I know that voice."

Once he was inside the room, a trace of moon glow danced across a face in the cage. Evan lowered the tool. "I don't believe it. I was sure you were dead."

The chuckle that followed both eased his anxiety and sent a chill through Evan's bones.

"It's me. It's Seedy. Damn, it is you. Evan, how the hell did you find me? How did you get out?"

Evan rushed to the cage and reached through to grasp Seedy's arm. "My God, Seedy. What happened? What's going on?"

"Me and Bee, we snuck out a couple nights ago. Decided to follow the rock wagon's tracks … figuring they might lead to something. No damn luck. We were picked up along the way by some Batran patrol. Just as well … we were near dead from thirst."

"So where's Bee?"

"Don't know. They come yesterday and took her away. My Bee—" Seedy pulled back a sob. "Damn lizards."

Evan gave the cage door a pull.

Seedy said, "But you … how?"

"Took the rock wagon for a ride, then hopped on a train."

"Jeez."

Evan lifted up the pickaxe and said, "Stand back." He aimed at the padlock on the cage door. The first swing sent the lock clattering across the bare wooden floor. Both men remained still for a few seconds, waiting to see if a horde of Batrans were on their way up the stairs.

Evan said, "You okay? Can you walk?"

Seedy stumbled out of the cage and the two embraced. Seedy broke down and bawled.

Of a sudden, Evan broke away and whispered, "Get back in the cage and close the door."

Clippity-clap footfalls, Batran footfalls, on the stairs had Evan gasping. He scurried to the head of the stairway, while Seedy hunkered down.

The Batran who entered had a blaster weapon out and aimed it at Seedy. He hissed in reptilian. "Human. Stand."

Seedy mumbled something and remained prone.

As the Batran approached, Evan walked up behind him, taking care to sync his steps with the Batran's to minimize the possibility of being found out.

When the reptilian reached the cage, he pointed at the broken lock on the floor and said, "What is this?"

As if anticipating danger, the Batran turned with his blaster raised. At the same instant, Evan swung his pickaxe at the weapon and sent it flying. Seedy burst out of the cage and wrapped his arms around the Batran's broad chest. In the next instant, Seedy flew through the air, landing on his back. The Batran swung around, frantically scanning the floor.

Evan mouthed his best Batran. "Looking for this?" He waved the blaster, careful to keep several steps away.

"Who are you?"

Evan said, "Never mind who I am. Where is Bee? This man's companion?"

The Batran's yellow-green eyes went blank. When they refocused, they were trained on the weapon in Evan's hand. "She was taken away."

"Bad answer." Evan aimed the weapon at the reptilian's head.

The Batran said, "To the Albacork Station."

Seedy brushed himself off and approached. "Where is that?"

Evan said, "I bet he means Albuquerque."

The Batran nodded and took a step toward the two. "You cannot escape. Give me the weapon. Get in the cage, and I will not kill you."

Evan said, "Stop right there." He examined the blaster. "I wonder what this switch does."

The Batran said, "No!"

A narrow beam of blinding white shot down into the floor. The blast was noiseless, but a crackling sound followed a distinct odor of burning wood. Evan took a step back, buying a moment for his vision to clear.

Seedy said, "I never saw what one of those do."

Several wisps of black smoke rose from the edges of a jagged fissure in the floor. "Neither have I."

The Batran lunged forward, reaching for the weapon. Before Evan had a chance to react, the flooring gave way under the reptilian's feet. The Batran hissed and flailed as he fell through, splintering wood along the way and crashing onto the floor below.

Seedy peered over the toothy edge. "He's not moving."

The two loped down the stairway. The Batran's body lay draped across several benches. His head assumed a stomach-turning angle.

Seedy said, "Now we're in for it."

Evan said, "It makes no difference. They catch us, we're dead anyway."

Seedy walked over to one of the broken windows. "I hope nobody heard all this."

"The ones asleep don't worry me. Too far away. I wonder where this lizard came from. Maybe there are others around. Here, take this pickaxe. I'm sticking with the blaster."

The two slipped out of the station house. Evan jogged over to what he figured was the processing building where the train cars were parked. When Seedy caught up, he pried the doors open.

Seedy said, "Damn. What's that stink?"

"I think they're treating the yellow dust, probably making it into something really dangerous." Evan held his breath and checked out the dark corners of the facility. He came back with an empty gallon can and said, "Hope it doesn't leak." He turned on the water spigot. "We'll need this."

Seedy said, "So, where to?"

"It's no good going back where we came from." Evan stepped onto the tracks and faced east. "Albuquerque can't be that far."

Seedy said, "I'm guessing 'bout 20-30 miles."

"Like I said."

◇

CHAPTER 17

Henry reached out to a quiver of arrows left behind by Chooli. He nocked one onto his bow and parted the tarp to get a clear view.

Mike said, "Who are you going to shoot?"

"At least they're starting with the other tents." The tip of his arrow protruded an inch beyond the flap. "That one holding Chooli—he's choking her. When I loose this arrow, you take the one on the left. I'll go for the other one."

"Are we killing them, Henry?"

"Do what it takes, and be quick."

"Sir, is there anything you wish me to do?"

"Seth, I don't know how this is going to play out. You do what you think best."

Henry fired off the arrow.

A feathered shaft erupted from the Batran's arm. His body twisted in an arc while his other hand reached for the wooden shaft. Chooli and the reptilian's blaster fell to the ground, followed by the Batran collapsing in a writhing heap. The other two Batrans hadn't yet realized their commander's fix.

Mike flew out of the tent. A split second later he crashed into one of the Batrans from behind, sending him tumbling over the desert sand. Henry's target was quick to react. The reptilian aimed his weapon at Henry. An ensuing bright explosion cloaked the Batran. Henry remained standing, expecting some part of his body to be missing.

"Got him, sir."

Seth held up a blaster. Behind the diminutive hero, Chooli struggled to her feet.

Mike called out. "My guy is unconscious."

Henry said, "Seth, did you —"

"It was on stun, sir."

Unexpected relief flooded Henry's mind. Killing any intelligent creature was wrong, even if it was in self-defense. He thought of the natives who were murdered by the robot, a Soofysh robot. Murder came all to easy for the Soofysh. "Let's gather these guys up. Chooli, Mike, we'll use the tent ropes to bind them."

Chooli lifted a blaster and said, "This pig is bleeding. We should put the animal out of its pain." She pointed the weapon at the Batran's head.

"Hold it, Chooli."

"This filth killed many of our people. Look what they are doing here."

"Killing him would be murder."

Chooli spat on the Batran, lowered her weapon, and kicked his wounded arm. The reptilian's mouth curled but he remained still, throwing Chooli an arrogant stare.

"Wrap some of the rope over the top of the wound and don't pull the arrow out."

Chooli gave the tourniquet an extra tug. The Batran hissed and after a moment to catch his breath, he said, "You cannot escape. We know where you are."

Henry said, "Knowing is one thing. Doing something about it, is another."

The Batran added, "And who are you?"

The last statement caught Henry's attention. Of course, they knew. By now the museum incident had to be common knowledge.

Once they secured the three Batrans inside one of the tents, Henry poked his head in through the flap. "Where did you fly in from?"

The nearest city of any size was Albuquerque. The only sound he heard was moaning from the wounded reptilian. The others turned their heads away, clearly not interested in giving away any information.

Chooli said, "Will those ropes keep them?"

"Doubt it. But we don't need a lot of time."

Mike returned from the aircar. "She's ready to go, boss."

Henry angled into the front, allowing Mike to pilot the vehicle while Seth and Chooli slipped in behind. "What guarantee do we have that the Batrans won't take over the controls?"

Seth held up a handful of wires. "I doubt there will be a problem, sir."

Mike said, "Where to, captain?"

"First, we go back. I want to be sure that Sequoyah and the others are okay."

"And then?

"Then we go sight-seeing. I've never been to Albuquerque."

◇

Henry craned his neck to get a good look at Sequoyah who sat with Chooli in the last seat. The big guy insisted on coming along once they explained what had happened.

Henry asked, "Anybody hungry?"

Sequoyah shook his head and gazed out a window. His drawn face spoke to a deep anger. Henry was sure the dead included some close friends. Chooli, always the most logical, said, "Hunger is our way of life."

"Albuquerque is less than a half-hour away, right, Seth?"

"At this speed, 27 minutes, sir."

"Maybe we don't want to go straight in, and into God-knows-what." He turned back to Mike. "Maybe we can stop somewhere a few miles out, scrounge around, maybe pick up some supplies and food? What do you say?"

Mike said, "There's not much out here. Don't forget, nobody's been around for a long time. A lot of the small towns, made mostly of wood, so they're pretty much gone."

"You're beginning to sound pessimistic."

"Yeah, that's not like me."

"We've been following the railway tracks the Batrans probably used to move their ore. Maybe they'll lead somewhere that's still in one piece."

Mike said, "And maybe they'll lead to a Batran colony."

"That's more optimistic."

Mike said, "I see a collection of buildings up ahead."

Henry said, "Looks to be a small town, or what's left of it."

Mike said, "Even in this dry climate, wood will dry out and rot. I see only one building with a roof."

"That's where we'll land."

◇

Henry wiped the dirt from a car's windshield and lurched backward. A leathery face stared back at him complete with black eye sockets and a toothy smile.

"Are you all right, sir?"

"I guess I'll never get used to it, Seth." A corner street sign read "Main Street." Henry stared down the road that cut through the center of the town. Several cars lay across the broken asphalt with purple sage erupting from the cracks. A variety of cacti had sprouted along the edges of the road and a tree found a home inside one of the roofless buildings.

"There is no reason to get used to it, sir."

Henry shook his head. "What would I do without you, Seth?"

Mike stepped out from the side of a barn-like structure. "The aircar's all squared away inside and out of view."

Chooli said, "Sequoyah and I will scout out the buildings to the left."

Henry said, "Look for water. And, maybe some canned food?"

Mike said, "I'll do the right side."

When the others were out of earshot, Seth said, "Sir, if I may ask, why are you here?"

It wouldn't be the first time Seth displayed an uncanny knack for getting under his skin. Henry sat down on the cement curb. "I don't know."

Seth gave Henry some time. After a minute or two, Henry broke the silence. "I guess it's what's right and what's wrong."

Seth cocked his diminutive head, appearing to nudge Henry further.

"Yeah. Maybe that's not all of it."

"Sir, that's hardly a part of it."

"Damn. What are you anyway?"

"I am your closest friend, sir."

"Yeah, that you are, Seth. There are times I wouldn't know what to do without you. But right now, I want you to leave me alone."

"You do not really want that, sir."

"I know what I'm doing." Henry turned away and stared down Main. Mike slipped in and out of side streets, scooting along on his enchanted Soofysh boots. Although most buildings had collapsed, Chooli and Sequoyah took turns checking out the few storefronts that remained recognizable.

"Those people trust you, sir. They believe you are a leader who has a plan—someone with their interests in mind, not his own."

"So, what is it you believe I'm up to, Seth?"

"If I may be so bold, sir … your interest is personal. You are seeking revenge."

"Revenge? If I had my way, I'd be dead by now. I've said that a hundred times. There's nothing here for me. I don't belong. Liz … she's all I had, and she's gone. She died yesterday and so did I."

Seth leaned in. "There is nothing you can do to get her back, sir."

"You don't think I know that?"

"But you are convinced you can make the Soofysh pay for what they did to you and Elizabeth."

The words hung in the air like a floating billboard, and on it, Liz's face cracked a smile. She never stopped smiling. Behind her hovered a winged banshee—the ephemeral outline of a Soofysh .

Henry pounded the sidewalk with a fist. "Damn right. They'll pay." He cupped his hands over his eyes. He wished that he could shed a tear. "You probably think I'm crazy, insane —."

"It is not insane to seek justice, sir."

"Even against an enemy that might be all-powerful?"

"The Soofysh are not gods. But neither are you. And neither are the people you are leading."

Mike zoomed up. "Hey, man. Found a grocery store." He held out a couple of rusty metal cans with crumbling labels.

"Can you read those labels?"

"Not really." Mike handed a can to Henry. "There's only one way to know what's inside." He poked a finger into the top of the can Henry held and tore it open. The mushy contents had a pale pink sheen and an aroma of burned grease. "Smells and looks okay."

"I didn't know you could smell." Henry gave the spongy mass a quick jab with his tongue.

Mike said, "What do you think?"

"It's awful."

Seth said, "Microscopic visual analysis indicates it should be safe to consume, sir."

Henry said, "What does that mean? No obvious parasites or bacteria?"

Seth nodded. "Nothing you should be concerned about, sir."

Henry downed the contents in one swallow.

Mike said, "You're a braver man than I."

Henry said, "What's the worst that could happen?"

Seth said, "We will see shortly, sir."

Henry said, "Very funny. Save the rest for Chooli and Sequoyah."

At that moment, Chooli loomed up behind Mike. "We found nothing to eat, but we did find a well. The hand pump was stuck until Sequoyah here loosened it up." She gave the big Indian a smirk and held out a dented pail. "The water may be a bit dirty."

Mike held out several cans. "And we have food. Dinner is served."

◇

CHAPTER 18

"How far have we gone?"

Evan stopped, not for the first time, and sat down on a rail. "Maybe ten miles."

Seedy said, "Feels like a hundred. I'm dyin'."

"We need to find some shelter … and soon."

Seedy lifted the water can to his lips. "Here, I think there's enough for one more swig."

Evan hadn't realized how exhausted he was. The heat from the sun ground its flaming fingers into his eyes. Thirst and hunger had become a constant drag, clutching at his throat, whispering in his ears, convincing him to give it up.

Then Seedy said, "There's something ahead." A structure jutted above a low rise a mile off, "Can't tell what it is."

Evan adopted a slow jog. "A water tower." A vision of a vast pool of cool, deliciously pure water painted itself across Evan's eyes. "They used those for the steam locomotives." And when was that? Maybe two hundred years ago.

A few minutes later, the two stood next to a stack of splintered gray wood slats held up by sagging rust-encrusted iron stilts—an ancient paean to a time long gone. The next stiff breeze might collapse it into a pile of twisted firewood.

Seedy said, "Damn. Will you look at all those holes?" He slumped down against one of the water tower's struts. "I'm done, Evan. My legs ain't going no more."

"At least we'll get out of the sun." Evan pointed to a nearby shed. The windowless construction was the size of a small room. Four intact corrugated metal walls held up a partly caved-in metal roof. The corner of a door protruded from the rocky sand.

Evan ran a finger into one of several bullet holes at the side of the open entry. "Someone must have lost their key."

Both men laughed as they entered.

An oil can sat on a metal shelf. An assortment of tools hung on one wall, while a storage cabinet took up the other. Seedy pulled at its handle which broke off. The cabinet's door swung open to the unnerving sound of a rattle. A snake uncoiled and slithered to the ground.

Evan jumped aside. "Must've woken that son-of-a-bitch up. Quick, give me the pickaxe." The reptile slipped outside with Evan close behind. A few minutes later, Evan returned, empty-handed.

"Damn. You should've caught it. I could eat a cockroach ... a whole nest of cockroaches."

"We'll rest here for a while. Later, while we still can see, we'll go into town."

"What town? You gettin' loopy, Evan?"

"Relax. I chased that rattler into an arroyo. The path we took went over a bridge, and I'm sure I saw some buildings beyond that. Probably a town ... even if it's only a couple of buildings, it's our next stop.

◇

CHAPTER 19

"When?" Marth failed to keep the anxiety out of her voice.

"In a few days, Councilor." Tiny tremors ran along her scaled arms. Neither Batran was adept at hiding their emotions.

Marth rose from her desk, in part to conceal her panic and to present the best face she could muster. "Inform all stations at once. Preparations are in order, are they not?"

The aide stammered. "Yes. Almost all."

"Almost?"

"Station 303 may be a little late."

"There is no such thing as a 'little late' to the Soofysh."

"The scouting party has reported that the workers at Station 303 have disappeared, apparently an escape led by several robots."

Marth slammed her desk top. She had a good idea who these so-called robots were. "Where are they now?"

"The scouting party, Councilor?"

"No! The damn robots. The damn workers. Anybody!"

"A search is underway, Councilor. There is something else you should know."

Marth lowered her head and motioned the aide to continue.

"A guard at the 303 processing plant was killed."

"How?"

"He might have fallen to his death when a prisoner escaped."

"Are we completely incompetent?"

The aide drew herself back a step.

"Is this a separate incident?"

"I believe so, Councilor. The two events occurred at nearly the same time."

"Get out. I need time to think."

After the door to her office slid shut, she turned to her father seated in his chair. "Two attacks. Who is doing this? Are they trying to undermine our agreement with the Soofysh?"

Genz stood. "We have generated all the processed uranium and pure gold that the Soofysh required. They should be happy with what we already have produced."

"But they may demand more."

"No more than the contract allows."

"A contract they could alter any time. Who would stop them?" Marth sat back down. The original agreement with the Soofysh had been a bargain with the Demon himself. Any fool would know that such a powerful entity would never be satisfied. "If they asked for more, do you think we can say no?"

"Let's hope for the best."

"We're speaking of the success of our colonization—thousands of people with new arrivals every day, all depending on me to see them through. If the Soofysh get annoyed, there's no telling what they'll do. Hoping for the best is for idiots."

The color of Genz's face shifted from green to deep blue.

"I'm sorry, father. That was a poor choice of words. It's not your fault."

Genz remained standing, as if he expected more.

Marth said, "This blue cyborg … you knew him. What makes him special?"

"Nothing really. He was simply a human being that the Soofysh wished to experiment with."

"Why did they leave him behind?"

Genz limped back to his chair. "I was there. It was I who fired a tank shell at the Soofysh. They left immediately afterward, or at least it seemed that way after the explosion."

Marth's jaw dropped. She sat back and closed her eyes. "You never told me this."

"I was young and naïve, and was convinced I was doing the right thing."

"The Soofysh will arrive any moment to pick up their first payment … with an open-ended agreement to do so every century. In the long view they'll drain our resources. And now you tell me, that they may also be interested in something extra … the cyborg or maybe even you?"

"If we capture the cyborg—"

Marth canted her head. "That seems to be a problem now, doesn't it?"

"Leave it to me."

◇

CHAPTER 20

The subtle scrape of a footfall lured Anth out of her inner quarters. She saw no one, but noted the door moved leaving it slightly ajar. She continued to stare at it and said, "I hate it when you do that."

A second later Genz appeared and laughed. "I can never sneak up on you."

Anth rushed up and embraced him. She whispered, "I miss you. Your Soofysh invisibility gadget is quite effective, but one day my guards will catch on, and then you'll—."

"They can't catch what they can't see."

"Sit down. It's been a while. You look tired."

Anth leaned against her desk, while Genz angled into her chair.

She said, "Your joints?"

"I still get around."

"This isn't a personal visit, is it?"

Genz's demeanor turned sullen. "I'm here to find out what you're up to."

"Only that to which we agreed. The humans need a place to call their own."

"That's not what I'm talking about. We lost a number of workers and a

Soofysh robot. Our production quota for area 303 will be negatively affected. And you're my chief suspect. Any comments?"

"Workers? Don't you mean slaves?"

Genz's voice stepped up a notch. "So it was you. We have reports of a blue robot … you remember him ... Henry. What do you know about that?"

Anth put her best surprised expression forward. "Henry? The cyborg? Didn't he die? Wasn't his body on display in Atlanta?"

"Anth, Anth, after all these years do you think this act of yours will fool me?" Genz rose to face her, his eyes bulging. "You don't know what you're doing. The Soofysh have demands we absolutely must meet."

"What do I care? They're not my problem."

"That may be so. But they are your daughter's problem. Besides, there's no telling what they'll do if we fall short."

"I'm sure she'll have the required shipment ready in time."

"You've been away too long. You don't know her. She's become invested … convinced the Soofysh will have further demands on this trip. And she knows of Henry."

"What about me?

"She believes you are dead."

Anth turned away. "What exactly do you want?"

"I've given you the freedom to help the few humans you find out here. While they stayed away from our operations, I didn't care what they did. But now … now they have decided to interfere. And … Henry … is he really back? You know that Marth will come after that cyborg, and that her efforts will eventually lead to you and your colony here. She's not stupid and she will not be kind."

"Why are you telling me all this?"

"Isn't it obvious?"

"Damn you. There was a time when you fought against the Soofysh. You fought with Henry and me at your side. Don't tell me you forgot all that."

"Time moves on. We do what we have to … to survive."

"And I'm supposed to believe you love me? Too many years have passed, Genz. You've made your choice. Keep in step with the directive and the hell with everything else. Those humans you call workers ... tell me, do you still raise them on farms? Do you eat them alive, or do you kill them first?"

"We are not barbarians." Genz stepped away, lowering his eyes.

"Humans are the creatures that built the cities and roads we enjoy now. They are not slaves, and they are not food. I am ashamed to be a Batran." Anth brought her hands to her face and covered her eyes. "Leave. I cannot help you. You are right. Henry is back, and if there is any justice in this world, he will—"

"Will what? He is one, we are many. There is nothing he can do to change anything. He is an annoyance that we will soon eradicate." Genz straightened himself up. "I pity you, Anth. You have exiled yourself for the good of a species that will soon be extinct, useful only as slaves and as a food source. You remember what they taste like, don't you? Quite a delicacy."

Genz touched a device on his shoulder and disappeared.

◇

CHAPTER 21

Mike said, "And there was something else."

Henry finished a long swallow of the bitter water. "Don't tell me you found a saloon with dancing girls."

Mike said, "Better than that."

"Lead on."

The group followed Mike though a side street that ran between several ramshackle buildings and became a barely visible path heading out into the desert.

Henry asked, "Seriously? You went way out here?"

"When you got skates, you skate."

Several minutes later, a low-lying structure came into view. Henry noted the sagging remains of chain-link fencing. Several placards hanging on the fence were faded beyond recognition, although Henry had the sense that they were warning signs. The building was made of cinder blocks and had no windows. Its entrance, a heavy metal and concrete door adorned with streaks of rust, stood ajar, inviting the curious to enter.

Henry asked, "This place was built to last. What do you think it is?"

Mike said, "You'll soon see."

Henry wondered if Mike's incessant teasing was a programming feature or a personality defect. The humanoid robot was at times a charmer, but if past history was any indication, he was also worrisome. Mike pushed through the door, and the group followed him inside.

At first, the dim interior offered up what any office might after being ignored for a century. Fine sand covered everything—the desk, a monitor, file cabinets. Curled up yellow paper with undecipherable scrawling littered the floor. At least there were no bodies lying about.

Henry gave the wall switch a try.

Mike said, "Yeah, I tried that, too. It's funny, ain't it? It's like you want things to be normal again."

Seth maneuvered to a small square panel door at a corner of the office. "Sir, this may be what Mike wants you to see."

The panel had been slid aside a few inches. A boney finger jutted out at the bottom.

Henry lurched back. "Damn!"

While Mike emitted a low frequency chuckle, Seth leaned over to examine the digit. "It is human, sir."

Mike reached down and pried the panel open. The tattered remains of a uniform spoke to a military function, but Henry could not tell in which service. The body looked mummified with leathery skin stretched taut over its angular remains. A cord wrapped around its neck carried a key.

Seth said, "It appears he was trying to get out, sir." A yellow strobe shot out of the robot's twin slits into the dark opening. "It is a descending shaft."

Chooli, who had been leaning in, said, "Sequoyah and I will wait out-side."

Her tone spoke to her discomfort, perhaps she was spooked by the body. Henry nodded. "Good idea. We don't want anyone to sneak up on us."

When he turned back to the opening, the body had been moved aside and Seth was gone.

Mike said, "That robot of yours has a mind of its own."

"That robot's name is Seth, and he's not mine. He's my friend."

"Touchy, touchy."

Seth called out from inside the shaft. "Sir, you should come down and see this."

Mike said, "After you, Henry."

Henry sized up Mike's width. "I guess you'll have to wait up here."

Mike said, "No problem, amigo, and don't take all day."

The trip down was easier than Henry expected with a ramp equipped with rungs for footholds. Moments later, he emerged into a dark cavern with only Seth's yellow strobe for illumination. They followed a metal staircase that wound down into a black abyss. When they reached the bottom, Henry instinctively fumbled for a light switch. This time the unmistakable buzz of a fluorescent fixture sparked to life. The hallway became illuminated by several sputtering overheads.

Henry said, "What the hell?"

A few steps onward led them to an open doorway and an oblong room equipped with two desks at either end. Computer screens, switches and cables hung from the walls.

"Damn. I know what this is."

"A Minuteman missile control module, sir?"

"There you go again. How is it you are familiar with human technology,

Seth?"

"The Soofysh had done their homework, sir."

"That they did." Henry didn't need reminding of what the Soofysh were capable of. That Seth was one of their creations didn't really bother him; after all, he was one too.

The room ran about thirty feet in length and seven in height. The six foot width provided room for movement along the single countertop festooned with instrumentation. The skeletal remains of a body manned a desk at the far end. Beyond that a large double door entry appeared to be sealed shut. Henry imagined the hysteria that the two occupants must have gone through—monitors showing crazed people in the town with no one to advise them because everyone was either dying or dead, including those in some far off command center. After some time passed, one of the two must have decided to find out what was happening. The move cost both men their lives.

As if reading Henry's mind, Seth said, "They would have died, sir, staying inside or not."

"We don't know how long the Soofysh poison or virus would have remained deadly."

"Then they would have run out of food and water, sir."

"Food and water. Hey, these bunkers should have a good supply."

Henry heard a metallic click. Seth pulled up a hinged wall panel. "This may be it, sir."

A rat jumped out and skittered away into a corner of the bunker. Henry said, "Whew. I guess it was too much to hope for."

Seth said, "Perhaps all is not lost, sir."

Henry joined Seth at the secreted bin and peered inside. "Let's see … forget the MREs. What's this?" He pulled out a large glass jar filled with a white-amber solid.

"Honey, sir. Crystallized, but likely still edible."

Henry put the jar aside and reached in to grab one of two yellowed plastic sacks, one of which had a gaping hole. "Rice. At least the rat left us the other sack."

After additional rummaging, he came up with unspoiled dried beans, bouillon cubes and a tin of sugar that survived the rodent's foray.

Seth pointed to a lower shelf containing several five-gallon cans. "Water, sir."

"Fantastic. We have all the makings of dinner, assuming we can rely on your infrared heat beams for cooking?"

"No problem, sir."

◇

The group opted to remain in the above ground bunker for the night. Dinner that evening was a welcome treat. Seth had located a pot and a few dishes, and served up a savory mix of home-cooked rice and beans in beef broth with honey for dessert.

Later that night, Chooli and Sequoyah dozed at the door while Mike hummed to himself. Henry and Seth sat near the entrance to the bunker module below.

Henry said, "Funny that there's still some power downstairs."

"Likely from underground lines coming from a station nearby, sir."

"Maybe one that the Batrans are using to process the uranium ore." Henry mulled over the implications. "I wonder, Seth."

"If the launch system is still functioning, sir?"

"Even if it was … we don't know where the missile is, or if it's still operable, or if it could be directed to a specific target, or —."

Seth said, "We can find out easily enough, sir."

◇

CHAPTER 22

Evan and Seedy shuffled to the middle of Main Street.

"Somebody's been here."

Seedy's winced at the morning sun. "Why'd you say that?"

Evan kicked a can. "That's been opened and not long ago."

Seedy picked it up and brought it to his nose. "Whew. Smells like shit."

"Exactly. If you smelled it—"

"You dealt it." Seedy chuckled at his joke.

Evan said, "It ain't that funny," and moved to the side of one of the buildings, tugging at Seedy to follow. "See the footprints?"

"Shoes or boots. There's a couple that don't look human."

"Robots?"

Seedy's head spun in every direction. "Damn Batran robots. They come lookin' for us. We can't be standing out here."

"I doubt it." Evan followed the prints farther up the street. "Look here, Seedy."

"Whoa. What happened? One of them robots just plain disappeared."

"I doubt it disappeared. Looks like it flew off."

"Shit. That's worse."

A glint caught Evan's eye. "There's something inside that barn."

The two jogged around several buildings, keeping to the shade, and paused at the opening to a large wooden structure. A mild breeze got the spindly wood structure to creaking.

Seedy said, "This town gives me the shakes."

Evan drew nearer to a wall and peered inside. "Look at that. It's one of them Batran aircars."

"I told you."

A distant humming turned both heads upward.

Evan said, "Quick. Get inside."

"They've come for their stuff. We're done for now."

The two watched the skies through one of many narrow slits in the walls. Moments later a silvery object passed overhead, hovered for a second and then continued off to the east.

Evan said, "They're searching for something."

"Yeah, us."

"Maybe … and maybe there's something else around here besides us that they want."

Seedy scratched his head. "Them that left those footprints?"

"Maybe they're like us. On the run."

Seedy said, "Or maybe they be looking for us, too."

"Doubt it." Evan wished his voice carried more certainty.

Seedy said, "Who besides Batrans fly these things?"

◇

CHAPTER 23

Seth spoke from the instrument panel. "We can test a hypothesis, sir."

Henry said, "And what might that be?"

"These three switches need to be toggled on. If I am correct, they should activate the monitors, and with those we can ascertain if the missile is capable of flight, sir."

"You're not going to accidentally launch it, are you?"

Seth craned his head as if admonishing Henry.

"Okay, okay. Try the switches."

The instrument panel flickered with green and yellow squares. The final toggle brought up a whole array of red LEDs beneath a large flat monitor. An unnerving hum rattled the console.

Henry said "At least I don't see any blue smoke."

The monitor remained dark and the smell of something burning did waft up.

Seth said, "Dust. Most likely fan motors heating up."

Henry slapped at the monitor. "Everything here's too old. This stuff may have been solid state, but I guess even that has a limit."

A flash burst across the flat black display. The word "PASSWORD" showed up at its center.

"Well, what do you know?"

Chooli yelled down from the top of the escape tunnel. "Batrans! An aircar is approaching."

"Stay here, Seth. I want to know if this missile still works."

Henry joined Chooli and Sequoyah behind the massive door and peered through the opening.

Mike said, "They're hovering … maybe scanning the area."

Henry said, "They might have detected our use of electrical power."

Mike said, "They're landing."

Henry patted the blaster in his belt. "I hate this."

The aircar settled a couple hundred yards away along the narrow dirt path that led back to the town. Two Batrans with weapons in hand exited and ambled away toward Main Street.

Mike said, "Well, well."

Henry said, "Don't be too happy. They might have spotted our aircar back in the barn."

Mike said, "Clever lizards." He squeezed past the bunker door. Chooli and Sequoyah followed him.

Henry said, "Wait. What are you doing?"

Mike turned his head. "Sneaking up on the sneakers."

Chooli said, "Henry. You stay."

Sequoyah threw Henry a smile that said 'relax, we got this' that had the opposite effect. Something wasn't quite right.

He watched the intrepid two catch up with Mike who had glided to the rear of the aircar while the two Batrans continued away along the trail. Mike sidled up to a side door. Of a sudden, a series of bright flashes left three bodies sprawled on the ground. Shadows emerged from the sides of the bunker—maybe three or four Batrans. Henry scurried back to the escape hatch, slid inside and closed the panel behind him.

"Sir, what has happened?"

"We've been tricked. The Batrans zapped Mike and the other two. I don't know if they're still alive … they may be coming for us next." Henry gripped the blaster and looked back up the ramp.

Scuffling sounds, clawed feet scraping on a tiled floor felt like something crawling up Henry's back. After a few minutes of complete silence, he resumed breathing and said, "Maybe we'll be lucky. I don't think they noticed the access panel."

He sauntered over to the far wall, all the while fighting off the image of Chooli and the others lying motionless on the desert sand. "What's wrong with this door? It must be the main access point. Why wasn't it used?" He tugged at the wheel lock, which turned easily, but the door would not budge.

"The answer may be here, sir." Seth toggled a few switches below the monitor.

"What about the password?"

Seth pulled up a few wires from beneath the desk.

"Damn, Seth."

Scenes of the outside world flitted by on the main monitor. Some screens remained black—cameras long since succumbed to time, but others displayed discernible grey images streaked with electronic snow. Seth stopped the scrolling. "The Batrans, sir."

Several reptilians loaded bodies into their aircar, jumped in and moments later, they were airborne.

"Did you see that, sir?"

"Yeah, yeah. What do they need those bodies for?"

"No, sir. I meant that one of those bodies moved, sir."

"Then they're not dead. That makes sense. They're looking for escapees from the dig … maybe even us."

Seth said, "And they'll want to get information from those they captured, sir."

"Then there's some hope. We can add their rescue to our objectives."

"What are our objectives, sir?"

"Damn if I know, Seth." Henry was keenly aware of what he wanted most—putting a stop to the invasion and ultimately, to destroy the Soofysh. He shook his head, realizing that he was beginning to think like a madman.

"By the way, sir, I've located the missile." Seth tapped the console and an image of a nose cone loomed into view. "According to the gauges that still function, indications are that it may be capable of being launched."

"How can that be?"

"Solid state electronics and solid fuel, sir; however, launching it is another matter."

"How so?"

"Failure might result in a detonation."

"How far away is this thing?"

"About a mile north of here."

"Ouch." Henry stared at the body still seated at the other desk.

"This may explain the door, sir."

Seth scrolled through several views until the rear of a tattered canvas-topped vehicle came into view.

"What is that?"

"Perhaps the remains of a vehicle lodged against the door."

"It's a damn jeep." There was a time when he rode such a truck—open air, open road, the freedom to explore. Liz sat next to him, her short red hair fluttering in the breeze. They had gone camping somewhere in the northwest. It rained and he wanted to pull over, to draw the canvas up. But Liz laughed and said it didn't matter. They ended up soaked for the rest of the day. And Liz was right—it didn't matter, it didn't matter at all.

"Sir?"

"Sorry, Seth. I was just thinking"

"I understand, sir."

"So that's why they didn't open this door. People were trying to get in and ended up blocking the entryway." The shredded canvas fluttered like a forlorn banner, a testament to a time of terror and lost hope.

"Filtered air, sir."

"What? That's right. But these guys couldn't allow anyone in. They were duty-bound to remain at their stations."

"They must have wondered what was going on, sir."

"Yeah, What a nightmare—watching people die on the monitor."

"Helpless outside, and helpless inside, sir."

Henry snapped up a key from the desiccated body at the far desk. "That's two. Maybe we're not helpless anymore, Seth." Henry ran his fingers across a locked box over Seth's desk. "Like in the movies … one key goes here, and the other—."

"What are you thinking, sir?"

◇

CHAPTER 24

Marth spoke in Batran, wondering if the robot would understand and kept her gaze locked onto its single eye. "You are quite the find."

"Most people say so."

"Ah, you can understand us."

The robot gave the cords wrapped about its arms and legs a test.

"Do not bother."

"What do you want with me?"

Marth circled round and ran a finger across the back of the robot's head. The shiny dome sported an odd indentation. "What happened here?"

"A misunderstanding."

She lowered her head to look back into its eye, while sticking her finger into its empty eye socket. "Must have been serious."

"I have nothing to say to you."

"Come now. Surely you have a name?"

"Name's Mike. That's all you need to know."

"We know you stole some items from our repository in Atlanta. We know you reactivated a cyborg … the blue one called Henry. And the little robot. And then there is the human child."

The silvery mechanical man remained motionless and whispered. "I guess you know everything."

"You're Soofysh, aren't you?"

"Not my choice."

"And what of Henry? He is Soofysh too, isn't he? Are you brothers?"

"Henry who?"

Marth reached back to a small table and held up a blaster-like device with a long needle at its tip. She swung it closer to Mike's face. "We normally use this tool for surgery. The tip reaches temperatures sufficient to melt steel."

"Is that supposed to scare me?"

Marth brought the needle level with Mike's remaining eye. "I wonder what it would be like losing your remaining eye. Not the pain, of course, I doubt you feel pain, but what about knowing that you would never see again? Forever blind?"

"You've been watching too many old movies."

Marth raised herself and spoke to the door. A guard entered dragging a female human.

"One of your friends. I believe she is called Chooli."

The woman barely moved, and when she did she groaned. Blood ran along her temples and chin.

Mike said, "Do you think I care what you do to a human?"

"Let's find out, shall we?"

Marth stepped over to Chooli. The guard raised her by her arms. The needle tip glowed. She turned to look at the robot, insuring it had a good view. "Tell us where the Henry cyborg is."

Chooli spat at the needle. Steam erupted from its tip.

Marth said, "This one has spirit. Cooperate and she will be spared."

"Spared for what? Your next meal?"

"When I'm finished, her boyfriend will be next." Marth waved the needle in front of Chooli's face.

"What is going on?"

Marth froze as the door shut behind Genz—his face grim, his color a deep green.

She said, "This is my business, not yours."

Genz took a moment to examine both prisoners. "The one outside is willing to talk. This female is his sister."

Marth walked over to the robot and grazed its shoulder with the sizzling needle, leaving behind a thin scorch line. "Too bad. We were going to have some fun. Let's see what the male human has to say." She gave Mike a pat on its shoulder. "I'll be back."

Marth retracted the needle within the tool's handle and joined Genz at the door. She paused to speak to the guard. "Stay here. If either one tries to escape, kill them both."

The Batran guard lowered Chooli to the floor, drew his weapon and backed up to the sealed doorway.

◇

Mike had made an effort to remain silent and unmoving throughout the entire ordeal. The pain in his shoulder was minimal but would soon end. Chooli, on the other hand, looked dead.

The guard had positioned himself near the door to Mike's rear. Mike nudged his chair, lining it up with where he guessed the guard might be. He leaned back and tilted backwards. At the same moment his boot thrusters fired, slamming him into the hapless Batran, The wooden chair fell to pieces and he wriggled out of his restraints.

"Whoa, sorry about that, chum."

With the guard crumpled against the door, Mike grabbed up his weapon.

Chooli said, "Good work."

"I thought you were a goner."

She shook her head and swayed to her feet.

Mike said, "I get it. Pretty sneaky."

She smiled and shuffled to the door to listen. "Nothing."

"That's a lucky break. They'll be with your brother."

"We must find him."

"Bad idea. This building is full of them lizards. We need to get out while we can."

"You go. I stay."

It was Mike's turn to shake his head. Chooli moved the unconscious Batran out of the way and eased the door open a crack.

And then Chooli collapsed to the floor.

Mike said, "Just a gentle tap. Sorry, darling. We don't know where he is, or if he's still alive."

Mike wrapped his left arm around her waist and prodded the door open with the blaster. No one seemed to be about. The place was clearly built by humans, an office building or maybe a hotel with windows at either end of a carpeted hallway. Mike shuffled over to the nearest window.

When he heard a shout, he crashed through it, turning his body to protect Chooli from the glass shards. His boot thrusters kicked in and sent them hovering some ten stories in the air.

"Where to now?"

A shrill alarm sounded and several Batrans appeared at the shattered window. Judging by their toothy mouths they looked surprised. Mike noted the Marriott monogram on the side of the building. He scooted a half mile away by the time they fired off their weapons, and landed safely next to a single story structure.

"Where the hell are we?"

It was then he saw the blood. Chooli's face and shoulder were streaked in red, and she was beginning to stir. He paused outside a store front with a long-dead neon display spelling out 'Pharmacy,' and pushed through the broken glass door.

After setting Chooli onto a cushioned chair, he shuffled through several aisles and returned with boxes of yellowed gauze and a half-full bottle of rubbing alcohol. It took but a minute to tie off Chooli's most serious wounds.

She awoke. "What did you do?"

"First aid. Sorry if it hurts."

"Where are we? My brother! We cannot leave him." Chooli rose from the chair and blacked out.

Mike caught her before she hit the floor. He held her close to him and said, "I'm sorry about your brother, too."

He lowered her back onto the seat and checked out the street through a grime-streaked window. The last glimmer of sunlight reflected off the cowling of a dead traffic light. Tall grass sprouted through a maze of cracks in the intersection.

"I guess I'm sorry about a lot of things."

◇

CHAPTER 25

"Did you see that?"

Seedy craned his head in every direction.

Evan pointed. "Down there. Out past the end of town … where that aircar was headed."

"Ain't seein' nothin'."

"I saw a light. Come on." Evan nudged Seedy and the two jogged from building to building. When Main Street narrowed to a dirt road, they took cover behind a rocky outcropping.

Evan said, "See anything yet?"

"My eyes ain't so good, Evan. You tell me."

"It's that aircar … the one we saw flying over… there's some Batrans dragging bodies."

"Them must be the ones belong to the footprints."

"Yeah. They're all in … get your head down, it's taking off." Dust kicked up over the two as the aircar soared over them. When it was out of sight, Evan stood up and said, "Wonder what's in that building."

"I ain't going over there. It's probably full of them lizards."

"Look at the solid walls—way different than those in town. That place was built to last. Come on, Seedy."

"Damn no. I'm staying right here."

Evan shook his head and walked away. A couple of signs lay in the dirt, peeled and faded. He stepped over the twisted remains of chain link fencing. It was clear the place wasn't fond of visitors, or for that matter, it might have been designed to keep its occupants inside. The thick door was made of concrete like the rest of the building.

Evan eased himself inside while holding the Batran weapon out ahead of him. The darkness within gradually eased as his eyes adjusted, revealing a small room. Two connected rooms offered up several desks and chairs coated with sand. When he returned to the entryway he caught a glimpse of a desiccated body behind one of the desks—no news there. Bodies had become the norm.

He gave the morbid interior a shrug as he emerged.

Seedy caught up to him. "Find something?"

Evan said, "Nothing. Those people the Batrans caught must have tried to hide in there."

"What do you think this building was for?"

"Don't have any idea. It is weird, though. A few rooms with a few pieces of furniture … seems nobody actually used it for much anything."

"With a fence to guard it?"

"Let's check the other side."

"Hurry up. I don't like it out here."

◇

Henry held the notebook up to the single working console light. The paper sheets enclosed by yellowed plastic crackled as he turned the pages.

"Every city here has a number."

Seth said, "Launch codes, sir."

"A lot of cities … all over the world."

"The missile is theoretically capable of travelling thousands of miles, sir."

"Looks that way." Henry flipped through the folder. "This is interesting." He slapped the notebook down on the console. "Three numbers don't have cities listed alongside. I see zeroes with degree symbols, and what could be feet and inches."

"Perhaps not feet and inches, sir. Might they represent minutes and seconds?"

"You're right. Latitude and longitude … coordinates."

"The three numbers might be codes for the three warheads."

"What? There is only one missile, right?"

"This missile has multiple warheads, sir. Three to be exact."

Seth flipped a toggle and the image of the main entryway flickered on. "We have visitors, sir."

The monitor displayed the wrecked jeep, but this time something moved other than its tattered canvas.

"More Batrans?"

"Unlikely, sir. One has dark human hair."

Henry bolted to the ramp. "You stay here, Seth."

When he reached the corner of the building and eased his head round, an enormous black wolf greeted him. Its yellow eyes narrowed and jaws spread wide.

He raised his blaster. "Easy boy. No need to get ugly."

The wolf canted its head and then gave Henry a dog-like yelp.

"What the hell?"

The wolf wagged its tail.

"Oh my God. Wolfie? But that can't be." Henry recalled the beast he and Liz had befriended a century ago.

"Why not, Henry?"

The female voice was at once familiar and unsettling.

He blinked to get a better look at the woman standing by Wolfie. She had not been there a second ago, but maybe it was a trick of the waning light. She wore a flowery sun dress, a favorite of his wife, his dead wife.

◇

CHAPTER 26

Chooli seemed resigned to allow Mike to be the decision maker. She was strong-willed, and they were, after all, talking about her brother. Regardless, she was also exhausted and could hardly move without Mike's help.

"So first we need to figure out where we are."

Chooli's eyes glazed over while Mike wrapped an arm around her midriff. After checking the street, they stepped out and shambled from alcove to alcove, using the recessed structures for cover. Time and desert grit left store fronts opaque with little left of signage to read. Grass sprouted from sidewalks and streets, gaining a foothold through every fracture. Tumbleweed roamed the streets with piles gathered in corners as if they were lurking, waiting for a chance to pounce on the unwary. Bleached ivy clinged to walls graced with dark patches of moss. Nature spared no time in recovering her domain, more than happy to leave behind crumbling concrete and rusting steel. Mike shook off the feeling of disconnect that threatened to undo what little sanity he had left.

He gave Chooli a stare and wondered why he was bothering with her. He could move freely if he left her behind. She was a burden—one less human. Why not?

"Damn."

Loneliness was like a knife thrust through his heart. Every time he thought back to better days, the knife twisted. He slumped to the sidewalk and watched Chooli sprawled out on the walkway. Her arms spasmed when she looked up at him—eyes fluttered as she fought to stay awake.

She whispered. "Mike."

The barren landscape beyond the town's limits came into focus and the sour feeling that had eaten through him drifted off like a ghostly daydream. The wind danced over his metal skin and reminded him of who and what he once was. That the Soofysh had removed all his humanity, namely his brain, brought back an urge to right that wrong, to find the fiend and balance the scoresheet.

"You'll be okay."

Dust-encrusted cars, trucks and buses were scattered like discarded toys. A few yet contained dried out zombie-like drivers propped up in their seats, maintaining a steady watch, waiting for the traffic to thin out.

"I'll never get used to that."

Mike gathered Chooli up in his arms, and coasted a few blocks along the sidewalk while scanning the sky for Batrans.

"Funny, I was sure they'd be all over us by now. Maybe we're not that important."

A sign leaning alongside an adobe-like structure came into view. Though weather-beaten and faded, its lettering was easily read. "First National Bank of Albuquerque … how about that? More money in there than I can imagine, and all of it worthless."

A distant metal-on-metal screech caught his attention. He laid Chooli down at the entrance to the bank. "I'll be back in a jiffy."

A few blocks later, he caught sight of a train. Only three cars, it ran along tracks headed west. Seconds later he had Chooli back in his arms. "Our ride has arrived."

Mike and Chooli scooted over the tracks and landed inside an empty hopper car. He gave the setting sun a quick nod. "Now, ain't this convenient?"

Perhaps things were too convenient.

◇

CHAPTER 27

Henry looked away and shook his head. What he had seen was impossible. Liz and Wolfie no longer existed. What had he really seen?

"Hey, you all right?"

The question snapped Henry's head up in time to see two men emerging from behind the wreck of the jeep. One was tall with long dark hair, and the other, shorter and broad shouldered, nearly bald. Both wore ragged robes cinched at the waist with rope—the same clothing worn by the workers at the uranium dig.

Henry lowered his blaster and noted that one of the men had a similar weapon in hand. "Just surprised is all."

The tall one raised his weapon. "I'm Evan, and this is Seedy. What are you?"

Seedy said, "It's blue. Ain't seen nothing like it," and angled himself behind Evan. "It's one of them Batran robots, Evan."

Henry said, "My name's Henry and the reason for the blue skin is a long story … I'm part mechanical and part human." He waved his hand over his torso. "And none of this was my idea."

Evan kept his weapon trained on Henry. "Any more of your kind out here?"

"I do have a friend inside. He's an actual robot, a small one. He's my friend, and he's not blue. Put that weapon away and we'll talk."

Evan said, "First you put yours down, nice and slow."

The conversation was going downhill. Henry laid his Batran blaster on the ground. "Now what? I'm telling you we're on the same side. I just came back from the dig … maybe the same one you fellows were in. How did you get way out here?"

"Seedy, pick up his weapon."

Seedy took one step when Evan yelped. His blaster fell to the ground, and as it did, Henry scooped his up.

Evan rubbed his fingers. "What was that? The weapon got hot. It burned me."

Seth emerged from behind the jeep. "I happened."

Henry said, "Meet my friend, Seth."

Seedy said, "We're done in, Evan."

Henry said, "You're fine. Like I said, we're all in this together."

Henry slipped his weapon into his waistband. "He was protecting me. Used your infrared, Seth?"

Seth nodded and picked up Evan's blaster, handing it to him. "Sorry to have caused you pain, sir."

Evan said, "I don't understand. If you're not Batran, who made you?"

Henry said, "We were created by the Soofysh. Seth here … has a mind of his own and has saved my butt plenty of times. I trust him with my life."

Seedy said, "But your color—"

"Blue blood. My body is artificial." Henry touched his head. "At least

I still have my human brain. We can get into my history later. What about you two?"

Seedy said, "We're both from a dig not far from here."

Henry said, "Did it have a big robot overseer?"

Evan said, "Yeah, Rusty. A real son-of-a-bitch."

Henry said, "No worries there. It blew itself up."

Seedy's eyes bulged. "Damn."

Evan eyed Henry from top to bottom. "You must be something special."

"Not special … same as you … scared of the Batrans and their robots."

Evan tilted his head at the building. "Where'd you come from? That place was empty."

"There's a lower level, which reminds me … Seth, can the missile be launched?"

"I believe so, sir, but I am not sure about the integrity of the warheads."

"Integrity?"

"I am unsure that they will go where we tell them to go or that they will explode when they get there, sir."

"Do you have the ability to determine latitude and longitude?"

"To a fraction of a second, sir."

"Good. We may need that ability."

Evan and Seedy stared at each other, clearly at a loss.

Henry said, "This building is hiding a weapon, a big one. Something we might be able to use against the Soofysh."

Evan said, "I've heard the Batrans speak of the Soofysh, and now you bring them up. Who are they?"

"They're the ones who killed us. I mean they were behind the Batran invasion. They cleaned up the Earth to make way. Even the Batrans are terrified of them." Henry turned away and added, "And they may be near."

Henry was sure of it. How else to explain his visions? They were coming back.

◇

CHAPTER 28

Working rail lines were rare, and one that happened to be running on an east-west track kept the level of coincidence up at a worrisome level. Mike raised his head over the hopper car's side and gazed out at the desert landscape.

"Where are we going?" Chooli coughed on the words and slouched back against the wall of the hopper.

"Don't know for sure, Chooli, just hoping."

"My brother —"

"We'll get back to him when we can do something about it."

Her eyes closed.

Mike wished he had it in him to comfort her, to give her hope. But such emotions were distant memories. A frightening, but familiar sensation came over him—one of loyalty, but not to humans. Dark visions muddled his mind. Each tap-tap of the rails was a nudging reminder. Stay on course. Don't dwell on what once was.

He shook off the eerie mood and focused on the present. He considered scooting up to the engine to see who was driving, but one look at Chooli changed his mind. There was no sense in taking any more risks than necessary. They both needed to get to safety, and better yet, back to Henry. The farther from Albuquerque they traveled, the better he felt. The town was rife with Batrans obsessed with the cyborg.

As the train slowed to round a curve, the jagged remnants of a water tower loomed into view. Things just got more optimistic.

"This is our stop, Chooli"

She pulled herself up. Mike wrapped an arm around her waist and she screamed when they flew out of the car.

Mike hovered over the rails. "That's the trail that leads to town. I hope Henry's still there." They zoomed over the dirt path, leaving behind swirling dust devils. Chooli's eyes were shut. He could only guess what the Batrans did to her.

"Hang on, we'll be there in a second."

When a barn came into view, wary of falling into a trap again, Mike landed behind a nearby building. The dark outline of their aircar showed through several missing slats.

"I hope they're still here."

Mike worried that the aircar might be bait, waiting for Henry to take a bite and opted to observe for a while. Besides, Chooli was unconscious and a rest in the shade should do her some good.

Long shadows ran across the main street that led out of town. The missile station sat about a half-mile beyond, and that's where Mike caught sight of movement.

Three figures plus a small one added up to Henry and Seth plus a couple of unknowns. The group marched steadily down the center of the street. Mike made out the two strangers, both humans, dressed in the rags worn by the diggers, and, thankfully, no Batrans were in sight.

When they got closer, Mike stepped out into the street. "Hey, you miss me?"

The strangers backed up, one raising a weapon.

Henry said, "It's okay. He's with us."

The shorter one said, "But he's a damn robot. Look at him. And only one eye."

Mike said, "You can ask Henry about that."

Henry said, "How did you get free? Where are Chooli and Sequoyah?"

Mike shrugged in the direction of a nearby alley. "Chooli's with me. She's not doing too well."

"And her brother?"

Mike paused a moment, then said, "We had to leave him. No time and too many Batrans."

Chooli staggered out of the side alley and said, "We must … go back … my—," and sagged back into Mike's arms.

◇

"Drink slowly."

Chooli straightened herself up at the table. "I know what to do."

Henry winced. The desert was Chooli's home. She didn't need his advice.

They took refuge in what remained of a diner. He had briefed Evan and Seedy on a short history of Mike, the one-eyed robot, while they finished off Seth's leftover rice and beans. Memories of the Soofysh had him spooked and unable to avert his eyes from the diner windows. The street had faded away into a growing twilight, leaving behind the faint outlines of abandoned cars. Cool, dry desert air drifted in through the open door.

Mike said, "There really was no choice. We had only seconds to get out."

Henry said, "That's the third time you explained. I get it."

Chooli said, "It is best to go at night. The Batrans have trouble seeing in the dark."

Henry said, "Hold on. We haven't decided on our next move."

Evan broke in. "Yeah. Nobody's asked us either. This isn't our fight."

Henry said, "You're free to do what you want. We're talking about a friend, Chooli's brother."

Seedy said, "Evan, maybe that's where they're keepin' Bee?"

Evan said, "And maybe they ate her by now."

Seedy dropped his head. "Don't say that."

Evan patted Seedy on the back. "Sorry. It was a bad joke."

Henry turned to Mike. "Tell me again how you escaped."

When Mike finished, Henry said, "So they left you alone with a single guard and bound to a wooden chair."

"That's where they made their mistake."

"Stand up. Let's take a closer look at you."

"What's up?"

"Seth, come over here."

Seth joined Henry behind Mike. Henry pointed at a one-inch square with a metallic sheen on Mike's lower back. "Can you identify that?"

"Some kind of repair, sir. Or—"

Henry ran his metal finger nails across the enigmatic patch. "Or a present from the Batrans." An edge of the patch lifted and Henry pulled the rest off. He held it out to Seth, "Can you tell me what it is now?"

Seth stared at it for a few seconds, and then said, "A sending device, sir. I detect a signal."

Mike said, "Damn. I knew it."

Henry said, "They must have planted it on you when you were unconscious."

"That means—"

"The whole torture bit was a sham. They wanted you to find me."

Seth said, "If I may be so bold, sir, we should leave immediately. Follow the rail tracks with the aircar, keeping low to avoid detection."

Henry said, "For all we know, they're already on their way here."

"Get the aircar ready, Seth." He nudged Chooli. "Are you feeling strong enough?"

She said, "And what about you, Henry? Are you ready to face your destiny?"

Henry conjured up a smile and said, "Mike, mind giving the town a quick check? I hate surprises."

"No problem. Be back in a few."

Henry said, "Evan, Seedy … Are you guys with us?"

Seedy put his arm around Evan's shoulders. Evan said, "Not looking forward to getting captured. And it's not like we have something better to do, right, Seedy?"

A few minutes later, Mike returned to the doorway. "All clear."

They boarded the aircar with Seth at the controls.

Mike said, "Aren't the Batrans going to detect us … they must know we have their aircar?"

Seth said, "We can fly low, below their detectors."

Henry paused at the doorway and looked in. "How do you know flying low is going to do the job?"

"I know, sir."

His diminutive buddy's extensive database always impressed. But then again, the Soofysh likely designed Seth to assist the Batrans, get them ready for colonization.

The sharp electric smell of the vehicle's magneto engines reminded him of his first encounter with the Soofysh. He recalled the creature or creatures—assuming humanoid outlines without any features, without any feeling. They were adept at slipping into human minds. His recent visions could mean they were close, which raised some doubts about everything he saw or touched.

Henry tossed the Batran tracer patch onto the ground and slid the door shut behind him. "Seth, take a path parallel to the rails, about a mile away from here."

"Sure thing, sir."

"We'll stop by the Marriott on the way."

◇

"We'll stop by the Marriott on the way."

CHAPTER 29

Henry said. "I can't see a thing."

Seth said, "The heat signatures of the desert persist, sir, and the starlight provides ample illumination."

"That might be, but I don't have your infrared vision. What do you see down there?"

"Relatively uninteresting—no towns or roads, mostly scrub and rocky ground. The rail line is off to our left on the order of a mile as you requested."

Henry kept expecting a city glow on the horizon despite knowing better. A town the size of Albuquerque should be easy to spot, but that assumed the city had power—and people. He saw nothing ahead.

"My systems suggest we are a few miles from Albuquerque."

Evan said, "What does it mean … systems?"

Henry said, "He has an internal mechanism which senses location."

Evan said, "Why do you keep referring to the robot as a 'he'?"

"Seth is my friend … my best friend. And Seth is a person, not a machine."

Evan shook his head. "If you say so."

Mike said, "I see the Marriott."

The dark outline of a building some ten stories tall dominated the city's landscape. A faint blush ran along its upper edges.

Henry said, "Any lights besides the few on that hotel?"

Seth said, "Some street lamps, nothing more, sir."

"So there's power. Steer a wide arc around it and see if you can pick up the railway again. Try not to hit any of those wrecks down there."

Chooli lunged for the door. "Let me out. I need to find my brother."

Henry grasped her shoulder, fearful she might try to jump out. "Hold on. I didn't say we were going to forget your brother. Seth, find a spot near the tracks but close enough to hike up to the hotel."

Mike said, "You can't be serious. That hotel is lizard town, and we don't even know if her brother is still alive."

"We'll keep an eye on the hotel. I'm hoping for some action … maybe an aircar or two flying off toward the town we left. That'll give us a chance to do some snooping with less of those bastards to worry about."

A minute later, they pulled into a parking deck across the street from the train station. The deck held dozens of abandoned cars and vans. What was once a human being sat in a nearby convertible. Empty sockets stared out at the station, patiently waiting for someone to arrive. Henry tore his eyes away and gave the distant hotel a closer look. The top three floors were visible with the penthouse level completely lit.

Everyone clambered out except Evan and Seedy.

Henry said, "You guys coming?"

Evan said, "Not our fight."

Seedy said, "What about Bee? She might be in there."

"Then you go. I'll stay here."

Seedy paused as if to say something more, and then stepped out of the car. "I'm going, Evan."

Evan looked away and remained silent.

Henry said, "That's fine, Evan. We'll be back in no time. I just want to see what's going on up there."

Henry led the way through a maze of derelict vehicles. Nature's scavengers had removed most of the bodies on the walkways and streets, leaving behind shreds of bleached clothing and shoes—lots of shoes, some with ankle bones protruding.

A lone traffic signal flickered ahead, caught between red and yellow, yet another reminder of a lost civilization. Chooli kept loping ahead, clearly impatient with their slow but steady approach. Henry kept checking on Seedy who had opted to take up the rear.

Seth said, "Sir, I see some movement."

Henry joined Seth at a support column. A thin bluish blur lifted off the hotel's roof.

"What the hell is that?"

Mike said, "It looks like—."

Henry said, "A flying saucer?"

Seth said, "More precisely, a flying disk, and it's headed west, sir."

"Good. Give it a minute to get out of sight. I have to say it looks familiar."

Seth said, "It should, sir. It is Soofysh."

◇

CHAPTER 30

Henry staggered back against the convertible's hood. "Damn. Damn." He reached for the windshield to steady himself, fighting back a sensation of nausea. The feeling was human and for a moment came across as a memory. Liz and Woolfie spun before him. Bitter snow stung his face, a monstrous grizzly bear reared up with blood erupting from its neck, an electric humanoid phantasm crackled, looming nearer. Something had turned on a part of his memory coughing up images, moving into and out of focus.

"Sir. Sir, are you all right?"

Liz appeared once again. She caressed his face and kissed him on the cheek, staring into his eyes. "You must be strong, Henry."

"I, I don't know —"

The visions dissolved into darkness, leaving Seth standing before him. "Sir, it is all right. We are here."

Henry shook his head. "I don't know what happened."

Seth said, "It is the Soofysh, sir. They may not know where you are, but your mind must have developed something of a sensitivity to their presence."

When the parking garage settled back down, Henry said, "Where's Chooli?"

Mike spun about. "Gone, Henry."

Seedy pointed at the far end of the parking deck where a prominent EXIT sign dangled on one rivet. "I saw her go that way."

Henry slid off the convertible's hood. "You all right big guy?"

Mike seemed disoriented, and took a second to respond. "I was dizzy. I'm okay. What do we do now?"

"It must be the Soofysh. They're here. To answer your question, we go after her."

Henry led them out, zigzagging between derelict cars, thankful that their grimy windshields hid what stomach-turning remains might repose within. Nausea remained a possibility, especially having a biological brain; however, a robot complaining of dizziness set off alarms. If Mike had experienced what Henry did, that could be a problem, especially because Mike had been in the service of the Soofysh and those bastards had to be near. Who knew what exactly was going on in that electromechanical half-brain.

The hotel was several blocks away when Henry heard the hum of Mike's boots. "Hey boss, what if I scoot on up there, and what do they call it … reconnoiter?"

"Are you sure you want to do that? You were the one who complained about all those Batrans."

Mike's stony grin set Henry on edge.

"Be back in a jiffy."

Henry turned to Seth. "Well?"

"Mike is not to be trusted, sir."

"I wonder if I'm to be trusted. Where's Seedy?"

Seth said, "He may have returned to the parking garage, sir."

"That's great. This is turning into a fine mess. Chooli takes off, Mike's might be unstable, and Seedy disappears."

"That leaves the two of us, sir."

"Your mathematical prowess never ceases to amaze."

"It is a comfort, sir."

"We better head up to the hotel. Who knows what the hell we'll find."

Three blocks later the two skulked between vehicles and trees that had erupted in the sales lot of a used car dealer. The hotel's glow reflected off a Ford Mustang nearby. "I bet that's a 2049 model. What a beauty. My father had one of these. All electric."

"It is a treasure, sir."

Henry eyed the others. "Antiques. Every single one." He rubbed the sand off the Mustang's windshield, leaving behind the words 'Clean Me.'

Seth said, "A joke, sir?"

"Yeah. A big one."

They scurried across the street to the front of a restaurant, staying hidden from the hotel only a block away. Its wide open doors seemed to invite the pair for dinner.

Henry said, "Shall we?"

"After you, sir."

Once inside, Henry weaved between tables and chairs, through the kitchen doors into darkness. His foot crunched something on the floor. "That's not what I think it is."

"I am afraid it is, sir."

His next steps were taken with care as he approached the back door. He eased it open. The hotel's upper floors illuminated a half-empty lot, and at the far end, a street that ran alongside the rear of the hotel.

"Sir, take care. I hear a motor."

A moment later, a vehicle screeched to a halt directly in front of them.

"That looks gas-powered … a truck?"

"More precisely, a delivery van, sir."

"Figures. That's probably the only vehicle they found that they fit in."

Two Batrans emerged and hefted several large bundles out of the back of the van. They leaped onto the loading platform and disappeared into the hotel.

"Can you tell what they're carrying?"

"My infrared sensors suggest meat, sir. Raw meat."

"Where would they get—." Henry paused. The possibilities registered. Images of cattle flashed by, but that would be food for humans.

"I suspect the meat was cattle, not human, sir."

"As usual, Seth, you're one step ahead of me."

"A small step, sir."

"Wait, did you see that?"

"It was Chooli, sir."

"She's gone in after the Batrans."

Henry stepped out. "We need to go after her."

They raced across the lot to the van. After Henry made sure the vehicle contained no surprises, he checked the front and returned with a bent metal rod in hand. "Can you believe this van uses a crank?

"The van does appear to be modified."

Henry peered within. "You're right. The steering column looks shorter … and the seat, it's pushed way back. You smell that?"

"The scent of gasoline, sir?"

The outline of a metal tank in the van's rear was barely visible. "Makes sense, and a starter motor would need a battery."

"No battery lasts a century."

"Exactly, thus we have a manual crank to turn the engine.

"And a source of fresh fuel."

"Right again, Seth."

Henry scanned the loading dock area. "Do you see any cameras?"

"There are a few, but none are in working condition."

"I bet there are more inside."

"I can see one such camera through the double doors above the dock, sir."

"Which means they might have spotted Chooli."

"What do we do, sir?"

"We go in." Henry pointed at an open window on the first level, "But through there."

◇

CHAPTER 31

"Yes, yes, I can see her." Marth leaned back from the monitor. Her spindly fingers drummed a staccato beat on the desk.

Genz stepped closer, hovering over her. "The Soofysh will be annoyed."

Her father had a talent for understating the obvious, and there were times when she was certain he mocked her.

Genz said, "The Soofysh are here for one reason."

"We can only hope this episode is no more than a curious distraction for them."

"Distraction? Henry was their masterpiece. And now that he is back, I suspect they may consider him with considerable interest."

Marth pointed at the screen. "That cyborg will come for her." She steadied her hand and waved it. An array of camera feeds filled the screen. "Heroes cannot help themselves."

"Neither can villains."

"What do you expect me to do? Ever since that cyborg was revived, it has been nothing but trouble. It destroyed a Soofysh robot at the uranium dig and freed dozens of human workers. Some of our people were killed and it endangered the Soofysh ore shipment."

"Henry is a he. And only one of our people was killed, which by the way, you know was an accident."

"An accident during an escape—I'd call that murder."

"Nonetheless, it was not his fault. Perhaps you should consider having a discussion with him, you know, to see what exactly it is that he wants."

Marth saw where this was going. "Why are you defending that abomination?"

Genz moved away and sat in a chair facing a window. "There was a time when we were friends."

"Yes, yes, and my mother and you named their firstborn after him. I know the story."

"When his companion, Elizabeth, died, he decided to kill himself. We had taken his world and there was nothing left for him here."

"Too bad he failed."

"Cruel words, my child. How would you feel if you were one of the last of our people?"

Outrage clouded her senses. Her father was doing it again. She was the leader of the Batran colony. Hard decisions had to be made for the good of her people.

"It … he threatens our relationship with the Soofysh, and thus our survival. You know what will happen if we fail our side of the bargain. We will capture and deliver him to the Soofysh. That should please them."

Genz remained silent,

She paused at the door, certain that there was no other course to take. As she closed the door behind her she heard Genz speak in low tones.

"There is no pleasing them."

◇

CHAPTER 32

Seedy lowered his head to look into the aircar. "I ain't liking this."

Evan said, "What are you doing here? Aren't you supposed to be with the others, saving the world?"

"It ain't none of my business."

"What if they have Bee up there in that hotel?"

"There's no telling where she is. She probably dead by now." Seedy lowered his head, avoiding Evan's stare. "I'd go if I weren't scared out of my mind. When they had me in that cage, I swear they be planning on having me for dinner. We need to get out of here."

Evan stepped out of the aircar and put an arm around Seedy. "You know how to drive this thing?"

"Nope."

"Neither do I. That doesn't leave us with a whole lot of choices."

Evan slammed the side of the aircar. The train station sign caught his interest.

"A new idea, Evan?"

"Same dumb idea. We keep moving."

They crossed the street to the station.

Evan said, "First, we find something to drink and eat."

The subtle glow of the hotel's top floor illuminated a shop in front of the station, its windows and door still intact. As they neared, a warm breeze caressed Evan's back, feeling like the embrace of an old friend, but he also knew that the night was about to turn that feeling into a bitter struggle for survival against an unceasing frigid wind.

"Maybe we'll stay here tonight."

Seedy motioned at the parking deck. "What about them? They be looking for us for sure."

"Last place you look is under your nose."

"That's a good one, Evan." Seedy tried the door and it swung open.

They sauntered into the dim interior. Peeling wallpaper cascaded over wall shelves. Other shelves filled the middle of the floor, several at precarious angles. Evan said, "This might be what they used to call a grocery store … my mom told me stories. You'd go into one of these stores and pick out what you wanted to eat. Look at this stuff."

Several racks displayed cans with cracked labels. A line of buckled paper boxes lined the higher shelves.

Evan said, "Can't see crap in here."

Seedy pulled a can from one of the shelves.

Evan said, "There's food inside those."

Seedy wandered farther into the darkness. "Evan, what's this?"

Evan caught up with him at a table and ran his hands over the items. "Cans, but these are stacked up with some care."

"Somebody's been busy."

"That'd mean—"

Something cold and hard prodded the back of Evan's neck.

"Who are you and what you want?"

Seedy said, "Who the hell said that?"

"Tell him shut up and stay where he is."

"Do that, Seedy."

The voice had a high pitch—a sound that reminded Evan of children. Young ones were reared by Batrans, a custom decades old.

Evan said, "We're no threat to you. We're humans like you ... least I think so."

"You working with them outside?"

Evan knew of some humans who took on special duties, other work that excused them from the digging. "That ain't us. We're running from them and, I'm guessing, you are too. Put away whatever you got on my neck."

Evan heard a rustle of footsteps, and then the stranger grunted.

"That's done."

Something clattered on the floor. Evan turned to Seedy's voice and saw a pair of hands wrapped around a head covered with curly black hair.

Seedy screamed. "Damn! I'm bit."

Evan pulled up his Batran weapon and said, "Hold it, don't move."

The hair whipped back for a moment to reveal the face of a young girl with dark skin. She was a teenager and not the ruddy-faced digger Evan had expected.

Her eyes narrowed at the sight of the blaster. "I was right. You be with them stinkin' lizards. Go ahead, shoot."

She shook off Seedy's grip and backed up a step. The frayed white tunic and torn pants spoke to a significant time alone.

Evan said, "Like I said, we're like you," and slid the blaster into his waistband. "What are you doing here?"

"I got the same question."

"Fair enough. My name's Evan, and that there is Seedy. We escaped a work camp some twenty miles or so west of here. We think the Batrans are after us and we're hoping they don't have a clue."

Seedy said, "Tell her about the aircar."

"Yeah, we came here using one of their aircars. There are a few others with us, but they went on to the hotel. Seems they're going to try and free a friend of theirs." Evan didn't think the girl needed to know about the robots and Henry.

"You can drive that aircar?"

"No such luck."

"So why you don't go with them?"

"Not our problem."

The girl nodded and said, "No one come back from there."

Evan said, "That may be. What's your story?"

"I'm Mays. My mom had me out of work camp year ago."

Evan noted her eyes averted his. She was lying.

"And your father?"

"Just me and mom."

"Where was this?"

"Atlanta."

"How did you get here?"

"Batran lizards took me, brought me to the digging camps. After a while I ran off."

Another lie.

Evan stooped down and picked up her weapon. "Damn. A shotgun. Two barrels at that."

"Give me that."

"No problem. You sure you know how to use this?"

"I know plenty."

"Just promise not to shoot us."

"Ain't nothing to worry. Ain't loaded."

Evan held back a smile. "You're right next to the train station. Aren't you afraid the Batrans will find you?"

"Been here a while. No trains stop here. No lizards neither."

"Evan, I see lights." Seedy raced to a window. "What the heck is that?"

A moving object flitted in and out of shadows a few blocks away.

Mays said, "They come once a while … go to hotel."

Evan said, "Is that one of them gasoline-powered cars?"

Seedy said, "Gasoline?"

"A fuel."

Mays said, "You moving on or staying?"

Evan said, "We'd like to stay tonight. Don't really know what we'll do tomorrow."

"I got the back room. You sleep out here. Help yourself to what you can eat. There's water in those bottles and don't touch my cans."

A door slammed and she was gone.

◇

CHAPTER 33

Henry lifted Seth to the window.

"Sir, I am not sure this is a wise idea."

"Can you open it or not?"

"It is unfastened."

Henry shook his head. A beat later they were inside an office.

"A century goes by and this place looks like someone just stepped out for a break."

"It seems the cleaning crew forgot to dust, sir."

"Is that a joke, Seth?"

"Perhaps, sir."

Henry noted the loading dock. "This office might have been used to manage shipments." Furniture consisting of a desk, lamp and a file cabinet.

"At least there's no body in here."

"The Batrans are a tidy people.

Henry eased the door open, letting in a muted glow from a nearby stairwell. "Is that the camera you were talking about?"

"Correct, sir."

"Lucky for us it's pointed back at the dock."

The two moved to the base of the stairs. "Seth, go first. Stay close to the wall. Can you spot a live camera before it spots you?"

"I'll try, sir. Would you like me to disable them?"

"Seriously? You can do that?"

"These models operate on a short range signal whose frequency is easily jammed."

"You could have told me that before we climbed through the window."

Seth remained silent.

Nine stairwell landings and three jammed cameras later, the two positioned themselves outside a steel fire door equipped with a square window.

"One more floor, Seth."

"I hear something, sir."

Henry pressed his head against the door, but heard nothing. "What is it?"

"Batrans … speaking to each other … it's the food. One is complaining that the meat is old and that the Councilor would be displeased."

"Must be the two from the van. I wonder who the Councilor is."

"The other mentioned that the Councilor should be happy with any meat."

Henry raised his head to catch a glimpse through the door's glass portal. Two Batrans stood at the end of a well-lit hallway. They began walking.

"They're coming this way. Time to go up to the next floor."

"Sir, what if they are headed up too?"

"Fingers crossed, Seth."

Seth looked down at his four-fingered hand.

"Let's go, and keep the sarcasm to yourself."

When they reached the tenth floor landing, the fire door below squealed. For several seconds Henry heard only his own mechanical heartbeat, and then the fading scrapes of clawed feet descending the stairs.

When he turned to look at Seth, the robot extended his hand with two jointed digits crossed.

"Very funny."

Henry chanced a peek through the glass. "So far, nobody home. Can you put your super hearing to use?"

"I hear nothing."

"Weird." Henry noted the stairs continued upward. "Maybe we should check the roof."

The stairway ended at a windowless door. Henry nudged it open. "Nothing. No Batrans, no aircars, and thankfully, no Soofysh."

"Perhaps they have all gone searching for us."

"They should've been back by now, and probably in a pissed off mood."

That's when Henry heard something on the stairway. "You hear that, Seth?"

"I hear nothing unusual, sir."

"A panting, like that of a dog."

"Or a wolf, sir?"

"Damn it. If you don't hear it, then—.""

"The Soofysh, sir. They must be close, close enough to once again affect your perceptions."

"We need to get to cover."

"May I suggest the floor below, sir?"

"Lead the way." Henry bounded down the steps right behind a surprisingly lithe robot. They paused at the tenth floor fire door.

Seth gave Henry a quizzical tilt of his head.

"We're good. I don't hear any panting. We're going in."

Henry worried about Chooli, and for that matter, Sequoyah. And where the hell was Mike? The corridor was empty. The two reconnoitered along the central hallway, stopping occasionally to listen at closed doors.

"Did everyone board the Soofysh ship?"

A door swung open and a voice echoed along the hall. "I'd say it's unlikely."

"Mike!"

Henry moved toward the robot, but Seth held him back with an extended arm. "Remember what we discussed, sir."

"Where are the Batrans? Didn't you say this hotel was crawling?"

Mike emerged from the doorway. "Come here. You have to see this."

Henry's instincts rarely failed him, and at the moment alarms were screaming in his head. He angled past Seth and stepped forward. "Show me."

◇

CHAPTER 34

Evan cracked open a bottle of water and slugged it down. "There's more. Help yourself."

Seedy said, "This ain't right."

"Yeah, nothing here makes sense. Mays is lying, probably about everything. For the time being, we have shelter, water and—" Evan held up a small metal tool. "A way to open these cans."

"What of the others? What if they get into trouble?" Seedy took a swig from his bottle. "I feel bad we ain't helping them."

"We didn't ask them to help us. We owe them nothing." Evan suspected that fate would eventually drag them into the fray, but that would come later. For now, he needed rest, better yet, sleep. "We'll talk tomorrow. They'll probably be back soon and take off to who knows where, happy to be rid of us. There's nothing but trouble waiting for us in that hotel."

Sleep came quickly.

◇

When Evan woke, the morning light peered through the front window. But this light moved like the headlights of a vehicle.

He whispered. "Seedy. Seedy, get up. We have visitors."

Seedy grunted something incomprehensible, but caught on quickly. Their corner afforded some cover by way of several display stacks.

The door swung inward.

Seedy mumbled. "Maybe it's our people."

An unmistakable Batran hiss filled the small store's dark void. "Did you hear that?"

The other answered. "Relax. See what you can find worth keeping."

"We've been in dozens of these shops … always metal containers with something putrid inside them."

"Here's something interesting."

Evan craned his head. Both Batrans bent over the table with the stacked cans.

"Signs of a live one, don't you think?"

One of the Batrans swung a weapon into view.

A thunderclap knocked Evan back. Acrid smoke engulfed the spot where the two reptilians had been standing. When the haze cleared, one of the Batrans rose from the floor and fired his weapon, leaving a scorch line on the far wall. Another thunder blast filled the air. The Batran flew backwards and disappeared into the shadows.

Evan tried to shake off the ringing in his ears, worried that he might not be able to react to new surprises. He felt Seedy's hand on his shoulder, grasped it, and the two staggered forward.

Mays stepped out of the gloom with a face covered in gleaming rivulets of sweat. Her shotgun fell from her hands.

"N-never shot one of these."

Evan said, "You said it was unloaded."

Her shoulders slumped and she leaned into him. Evan wrapped his arms around her shuddering body.

"They killed my mom."

He lowered her to a sitting position on the floor. "Seedy, check the street. See if there are any other lizards out there."

While Seedy moved to the front of the store, Evan checked the bodies. Both had gaping holes in their chests—impressive accuracy for someone who never used a shotgun. He grabbed up their weapons.

Seedy returned from the window. "Nobody out there. Maybe they be the two we saw, you know, going to the hotel."

"We can't stay here."

Mays said, "I ain't leaving."

Seedy said, "You crazy, girl? They catch you, they'll eat you alive."

Mays's eyes widened. "You lying."

Seedy bent lower to look her in the face. "I know. I was on the damn menu. Evan here, he saved me."

Evan said, "Do what you want. We're leaving right now."

"How you going? On foot? They track you down no time."

Evan pointed to the street. "With a bit of luck, our ride is out there. Coming, Seedy?"

Once outside, the two kept low and in shadows. When they reached the van, Evan glanced back. "Hold it, Seedy. She's coming."

◇

CHAPTER 35

Mike held Henry by the arm while removing his blaster. "Don't blame me for this."

Henry wrested his arm away and stepped into the room. "You shouldn't have gone to all this trouble for me."

The room was sparsely furnished with only an armchair in the center occupied by a female Batran. She spoke in perfect English. "What makes you think this concerns you?"

"Where are the two humans, Sequoyah and Chooli?"

"Safely kept."

There was something in the way she spoke that gave Henry pause—a twist to her mouth, or maybe a pause to show off her pointed teeth.

"Where's your boss?"

The Batran rose. "I am the boss. I am Marth, the Councilor of the colonies."

Henry chuckled, hoping the move would throw her off. "No, I mean the bastards who cleaned up this planet for you, the ones that did all the dirty work, the ones who you're working for now."

"The Soofysh are our business partners. We are simply repaying a favor."

"Favor? Killing a few billion humans is quite a favor. Of course, they left some for you to enslave, and maybe a few to serve to up for dinner."

Marth sauntered closer to Henry and pressed a gangly finger to his chest. "Not much meat here." She hissed, a sound that Henry recognized as Batran laughter. Her sarcasm held a glimmer of hope.

"What do you want with me?"

She walked back to her chair and turned. "You were dead, an exhibit of how things once were. Now, you are alive. You have chosen to attack my people and threatened our ore production."

"If you mean freeing your slaves, it's what I do."

"The only reason we have not killed you is that the Soofysh may have an interest."

"There you go … trying to appease the Soofysh. You don't get it. They only demand, never give. Humans are not the only slaves here."

Marth lingered a moment, perhaps contemplating Henry's words. Maybe he was getting through to her, but then her eyes focused on the doorway behind him."

A Batran voice rasped, "Hello, Seth."

The reptilian at the door bent down to pat the robot on the shoulder.

Henry said, "How do you know his name?"

"I know you, too, Henry."

The deep lines beneath the reptilian's eyes spoke to age along with the dark tone of his neck scales, and the bent over posture. It came to Henry in a flash.

"Genz. Is that you?"

The Batran extended his thin arms and embraced Henry. "All these years, you were dead."

"I may have been to you, but for me just a few days have passed."

Henry held onto the second Batran he ever met, the one who along with Anth had helped him battle against the Soofysh several lifetimes ago. Knowing what he knew now, that victory was hollow and relegated to an ancient, nearly forgotten past.

Marth said, "How sweet."

Genz said, "You have to forgive my daughter. The colony is all she cares about."

"Your daughter?"

"Second child. The first, the one we named after you, died some time ago."

Marth spat. "At the hands of humans."

Genz said, "An accident."

Henry wondered if Genz knew of Anth, and that she was still alive. For that matter, did Marth know?

Genz said, "It was long ago, when Marth took her first steps."

"Your wife, Anth—."

Genz raised an arm and said, "Speak not of her." Henry swore the reptilian winked, as if cutting off the conversation for a reason he was reluctant to share. He might know about Anth, perhaps where she was hiding. Secrets were being kept.

Marth said, "Enough, father. Your opinion is twisted by the passage of time. Come back to the present. This cyborg creature poses a threat to us today."

Genz said, "Have you considered that perhaps you and Henry have something in common?"

"More nonsense?"

Genz brought an arm around Henry's shoulders. "You both hate the Soofysh."

Marth slumped into her chair. "Dependence is not hatred."

Genz said, "And Henry lost his world, his wife and all reason to go on living. Which of you suffers more?"

"There is nothing I can do for him, but I can meet the Soofysh demands. It is my job to assure the welfare of our colony. And this Henry of yours … he threatens us."

Marth nodded her head and Mike approached from the rear.

"Secure this cyborg and get rid of his robot."

Henry's arms were pulled back and his feet left the floor as Mike hauled him to the door.

Genz nodded at Seth. "No need to destroy this mechanical wonder. It is Soofysh technology after all, and can be reprogrammed to serve our needs."

Marth said, "As you wish."

Henry whispered in Seth's direction. "Go with Genz."

"But, sir. You should know—"

"It's all right, Seth. I know."

He and Mike entered the hallway. When the door closed behind them, Mike said, "It's good to see you again, Henry."

"I can't say the same."

An acrid electric stench filled the air. Henry, released from Mike's grip, turned to face the robot.

Mike's body blurred. Miniature lightning bolts shot out from arms and legs. He changed shape, condensing into a dark humanoid mass.

"Miss me, Henry?"

◇

CHAPTER 36

Seedy caught up to Evan. "Ain't seen nothin' like it. Can you make it go?"

"I only know about gas-driven cars from pictures in books, and that was a while ago."

"Damn, Evan."

Mays tossed her shotgun and an armful of cans into the rear of the truck. "Get moving. Likely them lizards be here any time now."

Evan held onto the steering wheel and depressed a pedal. He recalled needing a key, a way to start the thing, but only saw a hole in the dash where it might have been at one time. "Nothing's working. There has to be another way." He loped to the front of the truck. "Here it is." Holding up a curved metal rod, he said, "I'm going to crank the engine. Seedy, step on the pedal on the right."

Evan gave the rod a twist, the engine sputtered.

"Again!"

This time the engine roared to life, spinning the crank out of his hand and wrenching a couple of fingers.

"You can take your foot off the pedal now."

He jumped into the truck and tossed the crank in the back.

Seedy said, "So where are we going?"

Mays raised her shotgun and said, "Where I say."

Evan said, "Put that thing down."

Mays waved it at Seedy. "Don't you get any ideas. Just do what I say."

Evan considered rushing the girl, but in the scheme of things, he had no idea where to go.

"All right, Mays, you're in charge. Where to?"

"Follow the tracks. I'll tell you where to turn."

He glanced up at the hotel and hoped no one had heard the shots or the sound of the truck. Maybe everybody was up on the top floor, and what about that Henry fellow?

Then there was Mays. A liar, a killer, a child—and a kidnapper.

It took Evan a few lurching mistakes to get a handle on shifting gears, but soon they were moving. After a few minutes, Mays said, "Turn here." Her eyes grew larger. She angled to Evan's side, one hand gripping the shotgun, the other, the dashboard. The truck's headlights might yet work, but the risk of being spotted threw that option out. Evan continued on, careening around the remains of vehicles dimly outlined by the faint glimmer of an occasional working streetlamp.

Mays shouted. "Stop here. Right here."

Evan said, "What makes this spot special?"

Mays sent a shiver through him. She grinned and said nothing. A group of shadows moved across the street ahead. The shapes became humanoid and approached the truck.

Seedy said, "It's the Batrans. We're done in, Evan!"

In moments it became clear the shapes were human. Mays opened the door, and said, "My friends."

Evan counted five—two females and three males, teenagers, like her. And all were armed with rifles and handguns. "Who exactly are these friends of yours?"

"We escaped from camps. Been hangin' out here and there, waitin' for the right time. We're gonna send the lizards back to the hell they came from."

"A small group to take on the whole Batran colony."

Mays pointed out the windshield with her shotgun. "Get back to the rail tracks and follow them east."

The corners of Mays' mouth curled up.

◇

CHAPTER 37

"Didn't we kill you?"

"We are many, and we are one."

"I understand why you're here, but what the hell do you want with me?"

"You are our creation, Henry. Does not a mother wish to see her son? Does she not want to share in his growth and learning?"

Henry swore he detected a note of sarcasm. "You're no mother of mine. Nothing's changed. You're the same bastards that killed off the humans on this planet. My planet."

"A necessary step. Colonization is rarely kind to the indigenous. Your own history speaks of wars which killed millions."

Henry hesitated a moment and then said, "Murder is murder."

"Death is inevitable."

The discussion was getting nowhere. He looked back to the closed door. "What happened to your other son … you know, Mike?"

"He is a work in progress."

"And the Batrans … do they know you're here?"

"They know our ship has arrived to pick up their tribute."

"You mean extortion."

"An agreed-to payment for services rendered."

"I'm betting you'll be back for more."

"It is of no concern to you."

"And if they fail to meet your agreed-to payment?"

"Then a different price will be exacted."

"You guys are really a piece of work."

"We are interested in you, Henry. You exhibited some profound abilities that we wish to explore further."

"Yeah. You killed my wife with those explorations."

"For good reason. Shall we say it was for science?"

"Count me out. Take your science and shove it." Henry turned to move away. A kind of electric tingle ran up his spine. A tap on his shoulder turned his blood to ice.

"Liz."

"Henry, why are you being difficult?"

"You're not real." He shook his head and blinked. The apparition remained. "The damn Soofysh are playing with me again."

"That may be, but why not enjoy the moment? I miss you, Henry."

"Don't say that." Henry felt his heart pound. A machine encased in a titanium body doesn't pound.

Liz drew nearer, bringing her lips close to his. Henry shut his eyes and pushed her away. "Get away from me." He gave the empty hallway a frantic look. "Stop it. Stop it."

She was gone, leaving behind an after image seared into his mind. Had she really stood next to him?

A voice intruded in that memory. "See what we can do for you, Henry? You could be with your Liz for the rest of your life. Simply cooperate with us and she will be yours."

"It's a damn illusion. Get out of my head."

"Are we not all caught up in an illusion?"

The tingling faded away. Henry concentrated on calming down, forcing his respiration to slow, his muscles to relax.

"As a token of good faith—"

The Soofysh voice trailed off, coming from farther along the corridor. Two figures emerged from several doors away.

Henry gasped. "Sequoyah ... Chooli."

Chooli said, "What happened? How did I ... we get here?"

At that moment the door to Marth's quarters opened. Genz stepped out with Seth in hand. "Be quick. Marth does not know of this."

Henry said, "But the Soofysh—."

"The Soofysh arranged it. They are much more concerned about their ore shipment than our petty squabbles, and thankfully, seem to consider you rather special."

Henry said, "They're expecting me to ... join them ... that's the best way to put it."

Genz gave Henry a wide-eyed stare.

"Do you know about Anth?"

"You mean that she is alive and hiding in the desert?"

"Damn. What don't you know?"

"I know you must leave now."

Henry extended his hand and Genz grasped it with both of his. "The Soofysh cannot have their way."

Genz said, "I will not be able to help you."

Henry embraced his old friend. Images of their century-old adventure washed over him. Together with Anth's help, they had saved Liz. They were just kids then.

Genz nodded, giving Henry a wink, and entered Marth's chambers. A figure lurched into view at the fire door.

"Mike! You are Mike, aren't you?"

"Who else would I be?"

"The Soofysh come to mind."

"Don't know what you're talking about. I was walking down this corridor and then I kind of blinked. Now I'm standing here."

Henry said, "A lot has happened."

"How did you all get loose?"

"I think the Soofysh arranged for our release."

"In turn for what?"

"No telling what they want, but whatever it is, they usually get it."

Seth said, "Sir, the Soofysh want you."

"That's not happening."

"Sir, one other thing."

"What is it, Seth?"

"Have you noticed that you never see more than one Soofysh?"

◇

CHAPTER 38

Mays nudged Evan with her shotgun. "Stop. Stop here."

As Evan pulled the van over to the side of the road, the engine sputtered and died. It had been difficult to see much without a moon. The glow in the east might have been the presage to a sunrise, but it was too soon for that.

"What's here?"

"Not here." Mays pointed toward the glimmering. "We go on foot."

Seedy said, "What's going on? What're we doing?"

"Not sure. I guess Mays knows."

"I ain't going nowhere."

Mays waited until all her friends were out, and then said, "You, too. Both of you."

Evan said, "Don't know what you're going to do, but Seedy and me aren't interested. If you don't mind, we'll be on our way."

"Ain't happening. You come with us." Mays waved her shotgun at the rest of the group outside. "Come and see."

Evan shrugged and nodded to Seedy. "Fine. We'll tag along, for now."

They joined the group with Mays behind them and followed the rails. It took less than a half-hour to discover what caused the glow. Several lights propped up on scaffolds illuminated a wide flat expanse with parallel tracks running through the center.

Seedy said, "Damn, Evan. Look at all them rail cars."

"Each one full of ore, Seedy." Evan recognized one—the Yellow Death he had seen at the railway station. "That one there's from our digs. But it ain't only our rocks here." Evan pointed at a car topped with something glimmering. "I swear those rocks have gold streaks." He never saw much gold, but knew of the precious metal. His mom had a ring made of it, and she had explained how it was rare and people valued it, people would kill for it. His fingers curled about the ring strung about his neck as his mind slid back to a simpler time.

Mays nudged him. "That way."

The group had formed a line and headed out to one side of the illuminated area, careful to stay in the shadows. Lines of hopper cars covered the entire expanse, each filled to the brim with piles of rock.

Evan gasped. "Seedy, up there. What do you see?"

"Nothing. Just the night sky. Don't see no stars."

"Look again."

A huge black disk hovered over them. The size of the craft, if it was such, blocked out the stars in every direction..

Evan said, "It must be Soofysh. They're here to collect."

"Like the Batrans kept telling us."

Evan turned to Mays. "You know what this is?"

"It's Batran's business. And we going to put a stop to it."

Evan said, "Do you see any Batrans?"

"They be here. We find them and kill them."

"Maybe you don't get it. That giant saucer up there is not Batran. That's Soofysh, and they don't play around. They're here to pick up their payment. If you step between them and their bounty, you and your friends die."

"You talk too much." Mays waved to the others in her group, pointing at the nearest rail car.

Evan grabbed Seedy by the arm.

Mays swung her shotgun about. "Get ready to use those Batran weapons."

Evan said, "Forget it. It's your party. Go get yourselves killed. Leave us out of it." He stood up and crossed his arms, hoping the defiant stance would change her mind.

Mays was about to say something when a flash erupted from the underside of the craft overhead. A blast of hot air smacked Evan in the face and turned all three away from the heat.

Seedy said, "What the hell was that?"

Evan rubbed his eyes to clear them. "Mays, your friends."

A faint red glow on the concrete surface running alongside the nearest train car was all that was left of the young warriors.

Evan said, "We have to get out of here. And now."

Mays dropped her shotgun and fell to her knees. "No, no, no. What happened?"

Evan snatched Mays' tunic and pulled her to her feet. "Answers come later."

They ran to the van while Evan stole glances back at the hopper. Seedy gasped. "I don't think anybody's coming."

"You're probably right. I don't think anybody's here ... at least no Ba-trans."

Evan looked up at the underbelly of the hovering behemoth. "See that thing hanging down. Is that a hose?"

A long transparent tube squirmed as rocks bounced up along its length.

"Damn big hose, Evan. It looks like they's sucking up the ore."

Mays broke away. "Let me go. I got business to take care of."

Evan reached for her, but too late. She picked up her shotgun and disappeared into the gaps between the cars.

Seedy said, "What do we do now?"

◇

CHAPTER 39

Mike climbed into the aircar. "Where to, boss?"

"Damn if I know."

Chooli pulled Sequoyah to her side and said, "Go back. Back to our village. There is nothing here for us … only death."

Henry said, "Where are the two we picked up?"

Mike said, "The hell I know. Whatever happened to them is their problem, not ours."

Henry fought back the urge to agree. After all, those two were strangers. "We don't know why they left. Maybe they were taken."

"By who? The Batrans? Wouldn't we have seen them?"

"Maybe."

Seth said, "Sir, there is a vehicle approaching."

Chooli said, "That sound."

Henry said, "It's an engine … from a car or truck. Same as what we heard … at the hotel."

Although the first level of the parking garage offered some cover, everyone instinctively ducked inside the aircar.

"Where's Seth?"

Mike pointed to the street. "Out there."

Seth skirted behind a derelict and peered over its fender. The object making the sound loomed into view.

Henry said, "That's the van that was in front of the hotel … the one with the two Batrans."

Mike said, "Delivering meat."

The van trundled closer and stopped in front of the train station directly across from them. For a moment, the faded logo on its side looked like a dragon's head. A blink later, it was the face of Jody the Plumber with two hands holding a wrench and a pipe.

"Did you see that?"

Mike said, "Yeah, a van. Was there something I missed?"

"Must have been the light, playing games."

Henry shook off the déjà vu—on a poster in Atlanta, and now on the side of a van. He turned his mind to the taut string of his bow and a deer in the woods. Simpler times.

A pair of Batrans clambered out and went inside a store near the station. Seconds later, two explosions rang out.

Mike said, "Damn. Those aren't Batran weapons."

Henry said, "Too loud."

Seth loped back from the street. "Shotgun reports, sir."

Henry said, "Who the hell has a shotgun?"

Two men and a girl emerged from the storefront. Henry recognized the men. The dark-skinned girl was new. The trio ran to the van. One of the men hunched over its front and cranked the engine to life. With all three inside, the van roared away.

Mike said, "Should we follow them?"

Henry said, "No. Not until we know what happened inside that store."

The van turned and followed the rail tracks eastward. Henry watched until the night swallowed it along with its engine noise. "Mike, come with me. Chooli, you and Sequoyah stay here. We'll be right back."

By the time they reached the storefront, Henry realized he had neglected to tell Seth what to do. Not surprisingly, the little mechanical beat him to the door and eased it open.

"Seth, see anything?"

"Bodies, sir." Seth lit up the scene with a beam of undulating yellow light.

Mike said, "Two Batrans."

Seth said, "They have been shot in their chests, sir."

Henry looked over Seth's head. "No weapons."

Mike said, "Probably taken by our friends."

Henry looked out the window at the hotel. "Funny that no one up there noticed."

Mike said, "Yet."

Seth emerged from a room hidden by the shadows. "Sir, someone was living here for a time."

"Probably the girl." Henry walked back to the front of the store. "I don't like this."

Mike said, "The killing?"

"The whole situation. The Soofysh know we're here. Chances are they are watching right now. And the Batrans … can they be that ignorant?"

Seth said, "Perhaps they are not ignorant, sir. Perhaps they have no choice."

"Then what the hell is going on? What kind of game is this?"

"Seth joined Henry at the door. "The Soofysh run the game, sir. That may tell you exactly what is going on."

When they joined the other two in the aircar, Henry said, "Mike can you catch up to them without being seen?"

"Seen by whom? The Soofysh, the Batrans or the van?"

"Let's concentrate on the van for now."

◇

The flash in the night sky ahead was hard to ignore.

"Ease up, Mike."

"No problem, Henry. What do you think that was? Lightning?"

"Something worse than lightning."

Seth said, "Sir, look up there."

The starless sky took on the shape of a huge circular object darker than the night.

Mike said, "Geez, it's gigantic."

Hopper cars occupied the tracks below the object, taking up a few city blocks, but compared to the Soofysh monster floating above, they looked like a child's play set.

Mike settled onto a street a few blocks away. While Chooli and Sequoyah vanished into an alleyway, Henry followed Mike and Seth to a corner building.

The van sat in the middle of the street between two automobiles. Three figures ran from the tracks toward the van.

Henry said, "Hear that?"

Mike said, "Yeah, the girl … she's crying."

"Not that. It's a kind of grinding sound coming from up there."

Seth said, "It is from the apparatus hanging below it, sir."

Mike said, "Yeah. I see it … looks like a giant tube."

Henry focused on the hoppers and their loads. "And I'm sure that's the ore the Soofysh have come for."

"Meaning?"

"Meaning this is all Soofysh."

Movement caught Henry's attention. The girl ran from the van toward the tracks. The two men moved to follow her.

Henry yelled. "Evan, Seedy. Hold on."

Seqoyah sprinted after the girl, while Mike and Chooli joined Henry at the van.

Evan said, "Where did you come from?"

Henry said, "Shotgun blasts in the middle of the night are hard to ignore."

"Yeah. That wasn't us."

"The girl? What's her story?"

"She doesn't say much, but from what I can figure, the Batrans had a hand in killing off her family … and now, her friends."

"The flash we saw?"

"From up there."

"This time it wasn't the Batrans."

Mike said, "She must be nuts. The Soofysh don't give a damn who they kill."

Evan said, "I think maybe she wants to die."

Henry said, "I know the feeling. What's her name?"

Evan said, "Mays. Her name is Mays."

Sequoyah returned and raised his arms. The girl had gotten away.

Henry said, "Mays has one chance."

Mike said, "Don't say it."

"Take these people to the aircar. Take them back to Anth's encampment. Nobody knows about it. They'll be safe there."

Mike said, "What the hell are you up to, Henry?"

"Seth and I are going for a visit."

"You can't be serious. That ship must be filled with Soofysh."

"Or maybe no one's home."

"Either way, it'll be suicide."

"Please do what I ask. Get these folks to safety."

Mike took a step closer to Henry. "You do know you're acting like a psycho. Everyone knows you want to die. Why don't you be less selfish and think about us, about the rest of the humans you could help."

Henry patted Mike on the shoulder. "Believe me, I am thinking about you and all the rest. I promise you this is not my way out. Get these people back to Anth."

"Fine. But I'm coming back as soon as I can."

"I'm counting on it."

Henry turned away and motioned to Seth. "You coming?"

"I would not have it any other way, sir."

◇

CHAPTER 40

"What is the plan, sir?"

"We need to find that girl. She's going to get herself killed."

The two crouched behind the first hopper in a series which led to the dangling hose at the far end. Cars loaded to the brim with ore occupied six parallel lines of track.

"It's likely that Mays is hiding between those cars up ahead. Maybe you could scoot under them to take a look?"

"Scooting is what I do best, sir."

While Seth vanished beneath the hopper, Henry trained his eyes on the hovering juggernaut. From a distance it was featureless—a Soofysh tendency for simplicity. As his eyes adjusted to the dim lighting cast from the street, the opening through which the so-called hose emerged became evident. A less obvious detail next to it captured his attention.

A few minutes later Seth returned the same way he had left.

"Did you find her?"

"Sorry, sir. No sign, although I did not check the contents of each hopper."

"She wouldn't be that crazy ... or would she?" Henry's voice faded away to a whisper. "I think I see her."

"Is she nearby, sir?"

"Not exactly. Not unless you consider that hose. I think I saw her getting sucked up along with the ore."

"That sounds grim, sir."

"Let's go." Henry ran to the far end of the line, keeping his head down while Seth skittered behind him.

The rumble of moving rock grew louder, making the hopper's walls tremble. Henry pointed at the hose and motioned for Seth to follow. He leaped up onto the rim of the car. The hose swayed like a huge snake—some two feet across with a mouth lost to a spewing miasma of thick dust.

It scraped along the bottom of the car, hungry to lap up the remaining ore. In moments it would likely move on to the next car. Henry leaped onto its corrugated exterior, using the folds in the plastic-like skin for purchase and climbed. The entire operation shifted to the next car, oblivious to Henry's presence or Seth, who dangled from Henry's leg. The hose's girth was too large for the robot's arms to encircle.

"Sir, may I ask what our objective is?"

"Save the girl, Seth. It's what we do."

Henry concentrated on his next handhold while bracing each step with his feet. Less than a minute later they reached the opening through which the hose dangled.

"Too small to fit through."

Henry tried reaching the adjacent panel that had caught his interest earlier.

"Damn. Too far, and besides, I have no idea how to open it anyway."

Seth scrambled up his back and then onto his shoulder. "Sir, I can get through."

The ship shifted, apparently getting in position over the next car. Seth sprang from Henry's back and jammed himself into the tight space between hose and aperture. In a blink he slipped through.

The Soofysh had to have spotted both of them, and probably the girl as well. Why they hadn't been vaporized was a mystery.

The panel adjacent to the hose slid aside and Seth's head bobbed into view. "Sir, take my hand."

Henry pushed himself off the giant tube and lunged for Seth's extended hand. In that ephemeral sliver of time, he thanked the heavens for the treasure his little friend had become. Seth saved his life countless times throughout their adventures together. The death of his wife had led to an urge to end it all. Seth tried to stop him. His unwavering loyalty and positive outlook could not be ignored. The modest robot had become his closest friend, a rare commodity in the world these days.

"I have you, sir."

"You sure do, Seth."

Henry swung himself up and through the open panel. They squatted in a tubular shaft about the height of a human. The latest batch of rocks glided along a curved upward path. The stones made no sound; however, the dancing hose beneath them spoke to another matter.

"We better move. Looks like a fresh load of ore is on the way up."

Henry took but one step before being urged on by a mass of foul-smelling ore from his rear. The gentle barrage carried them both along the shaft until the floor disappeared. He and Seth floated amid stony shards, and moments later, they landed atop a growing mound.

"Unbelievable. There's hardly any gravity here." Henry reached out and slapped at a fist-sized rock. It spun away and bounced down the uneven slope in slow motion.

Seth said, "The gravity here is approximately one-sixth of that outside."

A white patch at the bottom of the stone pile caught Henry's attention. "Is that her?"

They bounded down the pile, careful not to dislodge too many stones, although their current weight would hardly represent a danger to anyone. A few loose pebbles followed, landing in whispers.

The girl came free with a single tug on her arm.

Seth said, "I detect life signs, sir."

"Yeah, maybe she was knocked out on the way up." Henry ran a hand over a wall. "Amazing. Everything here glows."

"It is a form of electromagnetic radiation emanating from the material itself, sir."

"Yeah, it seems everything Soofysh has that quality."

Mays moved her arms and legs, and groaned. She sprang up, swinging her head about. "Who the hell are you?"

Henry said, "We're not the Soofysh or Batrans, if that's what you're worried about."

"You're blue."

"Yeah ... that's a different story. I'm as human as you ... more or less."

"What's that thing?"

"His name is Seth. He's a friend."

"He's a damn robot."

"Yeah, that too."

Seth said, "Pleased to meet you, Mays."

Mays backed up against a wall. "Where you come from? And where is this?"

Her eyes kept darting to and fro.

"We saw what happened. We saw you get sucked up."

Mays leaned an arm against the wall and sobbed. "My friends."

"We know."

"What do you know?" She pushed aside some stones from the pile.

Henry said, "Looking for your shotgun?"

Mays sidled along the curved wall. "What's going on? Everything feels wrong. I feel light."

Henry said, "Soofysh tech. We need to find a way out of here."

Seth pointed up to an oval outline in the ceiling. "A hatch, sir."

"Are you sure?"

"I can see a handle."

"A handle is good."

The hatch was at least 10 yards above them.

"I have an idea, Seth." Henry brought his hands together. Seth caught on, and placed his foot into the cradle.

Henry heaved the robot upwards against the low gravity of the chamber. Seth came up short and floated back down to Henry.

"Okay, then. Plan B." Henry turned to Mays.

"What you want?"

"Let Seth stand on your shoulders."

"You going to send the both of us up?"

"Don't let go of his legs."

Henry launched the duo and this time Seth grabbed hold of what everyone hoped was actually a handle.

"Got it, sir."

Seth twisted his body and the handle turned. The hatch swung down, leaving the pair swaying back and forth.

"Can you hold on, Seth?"

"All set, sir."

Henry climbed to the peak of the ore pile and jumped up, grasping Mays' ankles.

She said, "I'm slipping."

"A few seconds more, Mays." Henry climbed over her body and gripped Seth's arm. In one motion he swiveled over Seth and pulled Mays up. Seth was quick to follow.

Henry said, "Where are we?"

Seth said, "I am not familiar with this vessel, sir."

"I was being rhetorical."

They found themselves in a hallway of sorts. An over-sized oval tube about Henry's height extended in a curved path in either direction.

Seth said, "Perhaps this conduit is an access to other storage chambers."

"If true, then I'm guessing we need to find a way up to where the folks running this ship might be."

Mays said, "Yeah, and then kill them."

She didn't know the sheer power of what they were to face. For that matter, neither did he.

Henry said, "Easy, easy. We don't know what's waiting for us."

"I'm going to kill them all."

Seth said, "It is slightly brighter in this direction, sir."

"Suggesting?"

"Perhaps a junction or exit, sir?"

"Come on, Mays. One way is as good as another."

The three marched along the corridor while Mays kept mumbling and sobbing.

"Sir, have you noticed the air?"

"I'm breathing it, so, yeah."

"It's Earth air, sir."

"Maybe it came up through that hose back there."

"The volume of this corridor would not support your premise, sir."

"You're probably right. Besides, the chamber panel was closed. I'm hoping this is some kind of access corridor and not where the ore goes next."

"You're being optimistic, sir."

◇

CHAPTER 41

If Mike could blush, his face would have turned a dark, smoldering crimson. Anth paced the stone floor fast enough to generate a breeze.

She said, "Why did you leave them?"

Mike said, "Like I told you, Henry ordered me to return. I told him I would be right back."

"And that was an hour ago. He could be captured or dead by now. The Soofysh are nothing to toy with. You know that."

Mike fought back an urge to keep the argument going. Anth was livid, and his own emotions began to surge beyond control, a feeling that surprised him because he was one hundred percent artificial.

"You say you saw Genz?"

"Didn't see him, but I got the idea he was quite helpful."

Chooli, who had been standing at the door, said, "We saw him. He returned the Seth robot to us. And he said the Soofysh arranged the escape."

Anth pirouetted around her desk, and laid both hands on its uneven surface. Her head hung low. After a minute she straightened up and said, "You and Chooli. Go back immediately and get that damn suicidal hero back here. If the Soofysh are behind all this, then Henry is walking into a trap."

Mike paused at the door, thankful that the inquisition was over. "What of Evan and Seedy?"

"Where are they?"

Mike swiveled his head. "What the hell?" The pair had once again managed to disappear.

Anth said, "Chooli, you and Sequoyah, find them." She sat atop the desk. "Mike, get back to that Soofysh depot, or whatever it is. Bring Henry back. Now."

Mike bolted out of the room and flew down the rough-hewn stone stairway, his mind filled with disturbing visions. Foremost among them was Henry in pieces, taken apart by a vengeful Soofysh specter. He ran to the aircar, all the while grunting Henry's name. "How could I be so stupid?"

In seconds he was aloft and heading east.

◇

"I'm telling you, I saw her."

Evan shook his head. "You're dreaming, Seedy. Bee's gone. We need to get going."

"She was outside … when we came in. I didn't think it was possible, but now I'm sure it was her."

Evan dropped his bag. "Damn it, Seedy. We're losing time. They're going to come for us any minute. He glanced at the aircar.

"Hell, Evan. I can't go." Seedy ran back into the cave complex. "She's here. I know it."

Evan lowered his head and spoke to the ground. "Good luck, old friend."

◇

Mike heard a scuffling sound from the rear of the aircar.

"What … who's there?"

"It's me. I sit with you?"

"Mowgli!"

"Ain't just Mowgli."

"Evan. What are you doing here?"

"Mowgli and I have something in common. We're both eager to visit some old friends … back in Atlanta."

Mike turned his head to catch the glint of a Batran weapon. "No need for that, Evan. We're on the same side."

"Are we tin man?"

"I need to get back to Henry. He needs me."

"We need you, too. Don't we, Mowgli?"

The boy said, "My mama … she there, in the under the ground place."

"Yeah, but—."

"And I'm thinking that's where they took my wife."

Mike grunted. Lately, he found himself doing that quite often. "Put that pea-shooter away. I'll get you to Atlanta, but don't expect me to hang around."

"That'll be fine. We just need the ride."

Mike wasn't going to argue the point. It was important to help Henry, and soon.

"How long until we get there?"

"I'm pushing this heap to its limits. I'm guessing about an hour."

Mowgli sat up front next to Mike. Evan slid into the seat behind them and said, "What is it between you and Henry?"

"Everything. Everything is between us."

◇

CHAPTER 42

Mays ran ahead, fading into the hazy wall glare.

"Don't get too far ahead, Mays."

A minute later she yelled. "A tunnel. I found another tunnel."

Henry quickened his pace. "Wait for us."

They nearly caught up with her when she vanished.

"Did you see that, Seth?"

"Indeed I did, sir."

They came to a round vertical shaft, large enough to accommodate the proportions of a typical human being.

"Was she was sucked up this tube?"

"Perhaps, not sucked up, sir." Seth took a step closer to the shaft, placing himself beneath the opening and disappeared.

"Damn." Henry leaned in to take a closer look. "Oh, what the hell." He closed his eyes and took a step.

He had no sensation of movement. A blink later, nothing seemed to have changed. The same vertical shaft towered above him. A glance to the side revealed several shafts headed out at right angles, and one that led down that was new.

"Transport tunnels, that's what these are."

His voice echoed along the metallic walls. He was tempted to shout out 'hello' to see if someone might answer back, when he heard the word echoing down from the vertical shaft above.

"Who is that?"

"It is me, sir."

He yelled back, "Where are you?" A dumb question with no possible useful answer. Nonetheless, it was answered.

"In your cabin, sir."

Intrigued, Henry stepped forward. In an instant his nostrils were filled with the scent of pine trees.

"Good to see you, sir."

Seth stood in front of a familiar log cabin. A balmy breeze licked at Henry's ponytail. He was back on the west coast, standing in his front yard. The twisted gray wood of the porch, the torn screen door, the path leading away into the woods—everything exactly as he remembered. The path that led to a cliff was the one he took a century ago and only a week ago.

"How in the world?"

Seth said, "There is more, sir."

A large black dog trotted out from behind the cabin. It was not a dog.

"Wolfie!"

The wolf was Liz's good friend. Wolfie ran up, stretched up on its hind legs and licked Henry's face. Henry eased him to the ground and said, "Seth, we both know this can't be real. It has to be Soofysh trickery of some sort.

Maybe the damn Soofysh are in my head again."

"Unlikely, sir. The cabin, the wolf, everything here registers as real."

"But what if you are part of the illusion?"

"That is possible, sir."

"He's real too, Henry."

Henry took a step back. "Who said that?"

Seth raised an arm and pointed at Wolfie, who sucked in its oversized tongue and spoke in perfect English. "How do you like it?"

Despite coming through the gaping jaws of a wolf, the ego-rich intonation was unmistakable.

"You are Soofysh?"

"Who else would we be?"

"What's your damn game? What's the point of all this?"

"We want you to feel comfortable, Henry."

"It's not working. All this makes me cringe. I know it's you and your bag of tricks."

"Now, now. You haven't heard our offer."

"You have nothing I want."

"It's your singular ability, Henry."

"You're talking about me and Liz … the way we talked to each other …

thanks to you she's dead, and all that telepathy crap is history now."

A figure emerged from the front door of the cabin. Henry fixed his gaze on the red hair. A sleek female in a tee shirt and jeans bounced down the three steps of the porch. She couldn't be older than twenty. After slowly taking a few steps closer, she threw Henry a very familiar smile. "Henry. It is Henry, is that correct?"

Her voice tore his heart in two.

"Liz?"

◇

CHAPTER 43

The late afternoon shadows were quick to engulf Evan and Mowgli as they stepped out into an Atlanta side street.

Mike said, "Take care Mowgli. You, too, Evan."

Mowgli glanced back at Mike before the two disappeared around a corner.

Mike raised the aircar a few feet and then settled back down. "Damn. Damn Evan. Damn Mowgli. Damn everything."

He turned off the machine. Seconds later he reached the corner and spotted the pair trotting along the sidewalk, heading toward the subway station where he and Henry first encountered Mowgli. It was like he was caught in a film loop, repeating the same scene. Days ago, it was Henry; now it was Evan and Mowgli. There was something unsettling going on down in that subway, and it was drawing them all in.

Abandoned cars adorned every street. Full-grown trees erupted from cracks in the streets and sidewalks. Vines sprawled across building facades.

Mike had loved life in Atlanta, one of the bigger cities in the South. He passed several towering hotels with most of their sky bridges still intact and recalled conventioneers dressed in outrageous costumes carousing in the streets. Some of those cosplays reminded him of the reptilians. He used to love fantasy and science fiction until he became a living cosplay himself, and there were times when he wondered how alive he really was. Was he a mere robot and a defective one at that? But how? He felt alive, although admittedly an emotional wreck with anger bubbling up with every step.

The station was blocks away when the sound of a siren reverberated along the street.

"Damn those two."

Mike skirted from one storefront to another. The wailing grew louder. When it stopped, it left behind a faint trace of a dying echo.

The sidewalk began to vibrate. Something large jerked into view a few blocks distant, in the general direction of Mowgli's subway station. The mechanical beastie used metallic treads similar to the ones he had seen during his last visit, but this monstrosity was at least three times larger, and equipped with spider-like arms—four of them spanning the width of the street. Claws at the end of each grasped a vehicle, squeezed it into a spitball, and threw it into a bin on its backside. It continued in this way, crushing and devouring cars. Several Batrans loped alongside the monster, picking up debris too small for its giant claws. They were moving toward him.

Mike backed away and used his thrusters to glide along a parallel street in the opposite direction. Ten blocks later, he spotted a subway station south of his target—dark, quiet, with no Batrans. Its entrance was partially blocked by a truck. Mike squeezed through the wreckage and made his way down a dead escalator into a soul-consuming darkness.

He stepped lightly, fearful that the crumbling escalator treads beneath his feet might give way. At the bottom, the north tunnel outlined a ticket booth and several turnstiles.

"Perfect."

He leaped over the turnstiles and seconds later negotiated a landing on the rail bed. Only then did he consider the possibility that the tracks might be electrified, especially given that a few lights along the tunnel were working.

"Idiot."

Closer inspection revealed flooding along the floor of the tunnel, only a few fingers deep, but covering the rails. He engaged his boot thrusters to lift him up a couple of feet and followed the tunnel until he reached an aban-doned passenger car. A quick check through its mold-enshrouded windows revealed that it was empty save for a few skeletal remains strewn on floor and seats. He turned off his boots, and because the track bed was dry here, stayed between the rails. The sound of voices coming from somewhere be-yond a curve ahead had him bent low.

"Batran hissing. Sure does carry far down here."

As the way ahead became brighter, he hugged the tunnel wall to avoid detection. A new chorus of voices joined the reptilian hiss—children, human children.

A brightly lit subway station came into view along with two lines of pas-senger cars. A couple of Batrans escorted children along the raised platform alongside. The kids looked no older than six or seven. The Batrans hissed at them. From his limited understanding of the tongue, Mike was taken aback by a surprising revelation.

"They're teaching them their language."

Some children were herded in and out of the cars. Others, older, were segregated into separate groups. The whole scene had Mike mesmerized. He had entertained the queasy possibility that Batrans were raising humans for other reasons. What he saw spoke to a very different objective, although he couldn't completely rid himself of the images he had seen in the museum.

He drew nearer using the second line of cars for cover. When he heard a human voice, a familiar voice, he chanced a peek between a pair of cars.

Evan spoke face-to-face with three Batrans and motioned with his hand as if making a point. "If you want the kid back, you'll give me what I want."

Mowgli was nowhere in sight. The Batran turned to talk to the other two and then said, "How do we know you have the child?"

Was Evan planning to trade Mowgli? And for what? The answer arrived as if he had asked the question out loud.

"I want to see Claire. Now. And only then I'll bring you the child."

The reptilians whispered among themselves again. After a beat, the lead Batran said, "Stay here. We will bring her to you."

Mike refused to accept what was happening. Could Evan be so heartless? Was Claire his wife?

Two of the Batrans left, apparently to fetch Claire. Mike's mechanical heart froze when Evan paused while facing him. It would take the eyes of an owl to spot him in the dark. Evan nodded in Mike's direction. Not knowing what else to do, Mike nodded back, wondering what he had tacitly agreed to, but thankful that Evan did not expose him.

Evan turned away and held his hands akimbo with a finger pointing at his lower back.

"A Batran weapon. What is he trying to tell me?"

The reptilians returned with a human female held between them. Dressed in a tattered tunic and faded jeans, her shoeless feet partly dragged along the cement platform, her head bobbed up and down. When the Batrans stopped in front of Evan, she looked up.

Evan tried to go to her, but was held back by the lead.

"Claire. It's me."

Her eyes widened and mouth opened. She whispered something, and then slumped to her knees while the Batrans hoisted her back up by the shoulders.

The lead said, "You can have her. Where is the boy?"

"What have you done? She's barely alive."

The Batran appeared agitated and moved his hand closer to a holstered weapon. "It is enough that she is alive. We will allow you both to leave. We are growing weary of this talk. Where is the boy?"

Evan formed a fist with his right hand and waved it, trying to threaten the towering Batran he faced.

"Is he crazy?"

In that moment, a shadow flew through the air—Mowgli. The boy must have been hiding atop a railcar. He landed on the Batran's head and wrapped his arms around it.

The other two reptilians dropped Claire and reached for their weapons. Evan fired his, felling one. The second drew his blaster, but twisted to the ground when Mike fired. The lead Batran tossed Mowgli to the side and in one motion disarmed Evan and held him out by the neck with both hands.

"Fool. You were never going to leave alive. Tell whoever is hiding on the tracks to drop his weapon or I'll break your neck."

Mike froze. If he gave himself up, they were all doomed. The flashlight design of the Batran weapon limited its accuracy.

Evan yelled. "Take off. Save yourself."

Mike stepped out. He had a clear line of sight between cars.

Evan yelled again. "Don't. He'll kill all of us."

The Batran said, "Not all. We like the boy."

Mike took another step. "No reason to kill anyone." And without hesitation, fired off his weapon.

Evan's body shook for a few seconds, and then hung lifelessly between the Batran's scaly fingers.

"Fool robot." The Batran released Evan and unholstered his own weapon. His fingers were still wrapped around the blaster when his body shook and he collapsed to the floor of the platform.

Mowgli crawled into view. "You kill Evan. You kill Evan."

Mike leaped onto the platform. "Take it easy kid."

Claire stirred and raised herself onto her elbows. "Evan."

Mike said, "He'll be out for a while, but don't worry, he'll be fine. At least I think I used the right setting."

Claire said, "Who … what are you?"

"I'm a friend of Evan's and this little tiger, he's Mowgli."

Mowgli ran to her. "Mommy, mommy."

Claire's eyes fluttered.

"Now, ain't that something." Mike looked along the length of the walk-way. A few figures farther along the platform approached with speed.

"We need to get out of here and fast." Mike picked up Evan with one arm, and Claire with the other. "Mowgli, you'll have to climb up my back and hang onto my neck."

Seconds later they were gliding over the flooded rails, headed into a darkness that held the promise of both dread and freedom.

◇

CHAPTER 44

She flipped her long red hair to the side as she approached Henry. "That is correct. I am your Liz."

Henry glared at Wolfie. "Son of a bitch. What have you done?"

Wolfie morphed into the shadowy humanoid the Soofysh seemed to prefer. "She is in all respects a perfect copy of your deceased wife. What do you think? Not bad, right?"

Henry lunged at the shadow. His hands tingled as he passed through it.

"Now, now, Henry. Think. You're home, and Liz is back with you."

"All this is an illusion, a specialty of yours. Living in a world of make-believe must give you great satisfaction."

"It does, Henry and you'll find it satisfying too. By the way, this Liz is no illusion. She is a human being like her predecessor, identical to the original."

Clearly the Soofysh were resistant to sarcasm. Henry looked back at the woman who would be Liz. "Do you know what you are?"

"I am a copy of the woman you loved, Henry."

Henry made a show of facing up to the Soofysh. "You went through a lot of trouble to clone her, but a human being is more than the product of genes. We develop a personality that comes from a lifetime of learning experiences. This clone can never be the woman I loved."

"Henry, you underestimate us. We have taught the new Liz much, not only of the world she lived in, but about you too."

Liz cleared her throat. "I may not be the original, but I think you'll find me acceptable … and I can learn."

Her voice, it was Liz's voice, drew him nearer. Her features were perfect—a younger Liz, a version prior to her sickness, from the time before the invasion when they were college students.

She took a step closer, coming within an arm's length. "You have been in my mind for as long as I can remember." She reached out and embraced him with both arms.

Henry resisted the urge to return the embrace. She was not Liz. She could not be. He struggled to ignore her scent, the feel of her body next to him, her languid eyes piercing his.

She whispered. "I love you Henry. In time you'll love me too."

His arms came up, encircling her bodice. And his lips met hers.

The moment halted time. He was back in California sitting on the cabin steps whittling away at a dried pine twig. The smell of roasting venison wafted over him. He looked up to see Liz at the fire pit, slowly turning a spit. She caught his gaze and smiled.

<I'm afraid.>

The voice echoed in his mind. He knew the sound of it. Liz was talking, but not with her mouth.

He focused. <Is that you? Liz?>

At first, only silence. After all, he was never all that good with mind tricks.

<It is me.>

Henry broke the embrace and stared at her. Was it her speaking, or was it the original Liz? Or was it the Soofysh playing at some deeper game?

The shadow spoke. "Nice to see you two are getting along. Willing to stay a while, get acquainted with your new Liz, and work with us?"

Henry had trouble turning away from her, and when he did, the Soofysh had edged closer. Its acrid odor felt repulsive, as did the sight of the entity or entities—an abomination to all that was decent. He stilled his disgust, and said, "I'll grant you that she is similar to my wife."

"Sir, what are you saying?"

Seth rarely interjected himself without being asked.

"Seth, what should I do?"

After a momentary pause, the diminutive mechanical soul spoke in a soft voice. "You should not accept any offer made by the Soofysh, sir."

"I thought you'd say that."

Seth added, "It is only logical. She is not your wife. Everything is an illusion, an enticing prison created by the Soofysh to study you and this human clone. We do not know the real reason why they wish to do so."

The Soofysh said, "The reason is simple. Although we know much about the physical world, what you call the universe, we are only beginning to explore the quantum realm. We believe thought waves may be utilizing novel channels in spacetime. Henry and, it is hoped, his wife may add to our meager understanding."

Seth raised his voice. "To what end? Is it not enough you imprisoned a human mind in a machine? Is it not enough you wasted the life force of his original wife? What will become of these two once you are finished with your experiments?"

Taken aback by Seth's aggressive tone, something that was a rare departure for him, Henry said, "Now, now. It's clear the Soofysh are scientists and—"

Seth said, "And murderers?"

A dead quiet descended upon the group. Henry looked to the new Liz, but her face remained unremarkable, waxen. What scared her so?

The Soofysh said, "At the conclusion of our experiments we will return these two to their original home on this planet. You have our word."

Henry glanced at the new Liz and turned to Seth. "I have to admit that this is quite a surprise. I may have to reconsider."

"What are you saying, sir?"

"We talked about this. Do what I tell you to do, Seth."

The little robot lowered his head.

<Whatever I say, try to look happy.>

<I understand.>

Henry embraced the clone and kissed her. "You will be my wife."

"But, sir."

Henry turned to the Soofysh. "This is not an easy decision for me. But I cannot live alone. I need someone. I will agree to work with you and this version of Liz if you promise to bring us back to my home, my cabin. And allow Seth to leave your ship. He is of no further use to me. There was a girl that came aboard with us. She goes too."

<No.>

<Trust me.>

The Soofysh said, "An excellent decision. You and Liz will be returned. We have no use for the robot or the girl. The ore will be loaded by sunrise, at which point we will leave this planet. We suggest you use the time to get reacquainted with your wife, Henry. Once we are underway, we will have time to discuss details of your participation in this most exciting research."

The Soofysh escorted Seth to one of several tubes.

"We will come back, Seth."

The little robot's head twisted to take a final look or maybe say something more, but he faded away without another word or so much as a wave.

◇

CHAPTER 45

"Hang on." Mike hovered over the escalator, tightened his grip on his passengers, and shot up to street level. He pictured the Batrans running along the tracks—a slow chase over flooded rails. They probably communicated with topside, and that meant a slew of those lizards would be coming into view any moment, maybe in an aircar or two. They'd be coming from Mowgli's station, some dozen blocks to the north.

Evan said, "Where to now?"

"The aircar." Mike nodded back to Mowgli's station. "It's back there."

"That's great."

"We need to circle around. I hope they don't know we came in one." Mike glided across the street and headed west. "A few blocks up and we turn."

At a corner Mike veered downward and the group tumbled into the sidewalk, scattering across the broken concrete. Evan pushed himself up and crawled to Claire's spread-eagled body. "What the hell happened?"

Mowgli nudged Evan's side. "Mommy. Is mommy all right?"

Mike said, "Damn, my boots ran out of juice. That happens sometimes when I run them too long."

Evan said, "Nothing's changed. Claire's still unconscious."

"Is she really the kid's mother?"

"Maybe. At least Mowgli thinks so."

"What the hell were those Batrans up to back there?"

Evan cradled Claire's head, passing his fingers through her matted hair. "They're making babies, human babies."

"Damn."

"They get women pregnant, with or without a human male, and raise the children—teach them to serve … to serve the Batrans."

"They don't—"

"Eat them?" Evan forced out a laugh. "Bullshit. It's something to scare us. They need slave labor, and this is how they get it."

"How do you know?"

"I was captured when I was twelve—the last time I saw my parents. Those bastards raised me, gave me an education. I'm one of their graduates."

Mike wanted to keep the questions going, but more important matters were afoot. "We can't stay here. I'll carry Claire. You carry Mowgli."

They kept up a slow jog, stopping at each intersection to check on possible pursuit. At the fourth intersection, Mike held up his hand and whispered. "Just saw an aircar go by, headed south."

Evan said, "They'll find out we're not there."

Mike said, "And expand the search area. Can you run?"

"I've carried worse loads. Let's go."

The setting sun turned ivy-covered buildings a deep shade of red, as if the devil himself adjusted the lighting. Mike led them through the shadows between, seeking out storefront alcoves for cover.

"Evan, you all right?"

"Yeah, yeah. Catching my breath is all."

A grinding sound, metal on metal, echoed from farther along the street. Mike leaned against a lamp post and checked on Claire. Her half-open eyes glinted in the waning light.

Evan asked, "She's coming to. What's that sound?"

"The Batrans put together some kind of a monster tractor as wide as the street. "They're using it to clean up."

Claire groaned and when her eyes locked in on Mike, she stiffened, struggling to get out.

Mike said, "I get this a lot. Claire, my name's Mike. I'm Evan's friend."

Evan came closer. "It's all right, honey. Mike is helping us escape."

Claire's eyes fluttered and she passed out.

Mike said, "We'll keep going this way … a few more blocks."

At the next intersection, Evan jerked to a stop.

"What's up? You need to rest?"

Evan pointed to the west. "Is that it? Your machine?"

"Sure is."

The gangly contraption spanned the breadth of the street, munching away at the hulks of ruined automobiles. A number of Batrans jogged to either side, and they were making their way closer.

Evan said, "There's no way we can get across this intersection without being seen."

Mike laid Claire on the sidewalk, careful to prop her head against a storefront door sill.

Evan said, "What are you doing?"

"The aircar is a block away … up that street and in an alley to your right."

"I don't know how to work it."

"Wait for me. With some luck I'll join you in a couple of minutes. What we need is a distraction."

Mike stepped out into the street in full view of the oncoming Batrans. The huge tank with its four dangling arms halted and some half-dozen reptilians gaped at Mike as he rounded a corner and headed south. Mike heard their hissing followed by mechanical rumbling. The chase was on.

As he dodged around a few cars, a quick glance back confirmed he had company. Their machine lost some momentum while ramming a few vehicles out of the way, but the Batrans on foot were closing in fast.

Mike turned another corner and pushed through the glass doors of a small hotel. He loped up a central staircase and when he reached the third floor, he heard the sound of shattering glass from the lobby below.

He found the door leading to the roof and closed it quietly behind him, hoping the Batrans would lose some time searching. The giant tractor machine lumbered along the street at the far end of the block. Mike leaped from roof to roof, settling behind a parapet which overlooked the street. A single reptilian sat cradled in a seat at the center of the machine. No others were about.

Mike jumped.

◇

CHAPTER 46

Fine desert sand cloyed to Seth's metal skin, while he strained to get on his feet. The fall from the ship appeared to damage a knee hinge. He flexed it several times and a clicking sound confirmed the problem. The matter did not annoy him. It was one more data point added to his ever-expanding experiential adventure. He would handle it as he did everything—using cold logic, with a sprinkling of human emotion.

"Ouch!"

He looked about, seeking the girl. According to the Soofysh, she was to leave with him. After a few moments hobbling in a circle, he came across a body lying along one of the tracks. A visual examination revealed multiple broken bones and an abdominal swelling consistent with an internal and fatal hemorrhage. The Soofysh were true to their word. Both he and the girl were allowed to leave; however, nothing had been promised regarding their condition.

Years ago, the Soofysh had created him along with a number of others— expendable robots designed to take care of details, conduct maintenance and retrieve things. He was assigned the task of protecting the human cyborg. Henry, another creation of the Soofysh, was special. He had something that intrigued the Soofysh. They wanted him to survive the killing virus in order to study him, and now, his communication with the Elizabeth clone.

Crammed with data about humans, their civilization and history, Seth was programmed to befriend the cyborg. He did his job. Henry survived and was reunited with his wife. They managed to live together for a few decades before health issues took her away. In the decades that transpired something had changed. Henry was no longer a simple project. Henry became a friend. How that happened was a mystery to Seth for he was not programmed for friendship, or for that matter, loyalty. Now, a century later, they were back together again, and he was faced with the most difficult decision of his existence.

He limped away from the girl's body and stared up at the Soofysh ship. Henry's last words kept circling in his mind. The image of his friend leaping off a cliff, heart-broken and distraught at the loss of his wife would never leave him. That moment remained an indelible scar to Seth's otherwise optimistic demeanor. He had chosen to follow Henry over the cliff. It was a decision that surprised him—to never abandon his friend, and he would not do so now.

"You look perplexed."

Seth's internal analysis had muted his otherwise sharp awareness of surroundings. He sought the owner of the voice. A shadow moved into view.

"Genz?"

"Sorry to surprise you, Seth." Genz ran his hand over a device strapped to his chest.

Seth said, "The invisibility module."

"Yes. It still works after all these years. I've found it most useful."

"Why have you come here?"

"I followed you and Henry. I've been watching ever since you two went up into the ship. I started worrying you might never come out. Where is he?"

"He decided to stay, to go with the Soofysh."

"That doesn't sound right. Was it really his choice?"

"The Soofysh presented him with a clone of Elizabeth. They plan to study those two and their ability to commune, that is, without speaking. And, yes, I am sure his decision was freely made."

"Ahh. Seeing his wife, even her clone, must have been overwhelming. But surely there was more to it. Henry is no fool."

"That is true, sir."

"You're being secretive. Why?"

"I need to leave."

"You're not staying here … to try and free him?"

"I am following his orders." Seth paused mid-stride and added, "I believe you may be of some assistance."

"What can I do?"

"First you must inform Marth to leave this city. Tell her to withdraw all her people and any humans in her charge. It must be done immediately. Tell her they must go east, as far away as possible from the ore loading site."

"But why?"

"Sometime tonight there will be nothing left standing within a radius of roughly five miles of this position."

Genz gasped, at a loss of words, and after a moment's pause took a step away and lifted a corner of his robe. He raised his voice a few times while speaking into a gadget at his shoulder. When he returned to Seth, he said, "She is stubborn, but will follow your advice, but only for this evening."

"That will be sufficient. By morning it will all be over. Either the Soofysh will have left, or …"

"Or what?"

"We will see." Seth pointed to the van. "Now you can help me start up that vehicle."

◇

CHAPTER 47

One of Mike's feet slammed into the back of the reptilian driver, sending him tumbling down alongside the machine. He extricated his leg from between two levers and settled into the seat. The driver remained motionless below, clear of machine's gargantuan tracks which kept rolling forward. The others that had been running along the street had joined the pursuit of Evan.

Mike fiddled with the levers and foot pedals, and soon had the mechanical juggernaut accelerating, crushing abandoned vehicles beneath its treads. The noise would be impossible to ignore. He rumbled through an intersection and headed south. The four clawed arms whirled in a circle and smashed into walls and windows.

While under the shadow of a tall building, Mike leaped off and scurried into a ground-level shop. The motorized behemoth continued to wreak havoc, gouging building facades, knocking over lamp posts and obliterating century-old wrecks scattered along the way.

Several Batrans ran in from a side street and loped alongside it, trying to leap over its menacing treads in an attempt to get to the controls. With the distraction under way, Mike slipped out the rear of the shop and headed north.

◇

CHAPTER 48

When the Soofysh left, Henry trudged to the cabin porch and sat with his head bowed and arms draped over his knees. He flexed his fingers and watched, fascinated by them, making symmetric designs in the air. He had never felt lower, not even when he had decided to take the leap.

Liz sat alongside. "I do not understand why you decided to stay."

Henry hardly heard the words. "What? … oh, yeah. I am staying. It's the biggest decision I have ever had to make. By the way, you're not put off by my blue skin?" <Can you hear me?>

Liz's eyes blinked in surprise. "I was prepared for it." <What is going on?>

<Don't be afraid. For some reason our minds can hear each other.>

Liz shook her head. <I've never experienced this.>

<Relax. It's something I used to do with the original Elizabeth, but it was never this easy.>

<Whatever you say, Henry, but it will take some time for me to get used to it.> "You're not feeling well?"

"I lost a good friend, my best friend. Seth and I … we've been through a lot."

Liz put her arm around Henry's shoulders. "I understand. But you are back in your home. Look around. This is our home now."

"Sure looks like it." <An illusion to keep me happy.>

"Give it time." <I still don't understand.>

"I guess so. How about a walk?"

The pair strolled arm-in-arm to the back of the cabin to a small clearing surrounded by pines. Henry glanced at the forest edge and spotted the stone markers.

"No detail overlooked."

As they approached, Henry pointed out the writing on the markers. "That's where I buried my Liz … I mean the original one." He stammered. "And that one … that one is Wolfie's."

Liz said, "Wolfie. Was that your pet?"

"Wolfie was no one's pet."

The presence of the headstones confirmed that the Soofysh must have returned at some point after Liz's death to gather a precise image of Henry's home. The condition of the wood, the size of the trees, all pointed to a time close to his suicide. That meant the Soofysh must have been so impressed with his so-called mental ability, that they took the trouble to prepare for this very day—a staggering level of forethought.

"I want to check on something else."

Liz followed him along a trail which led to a cliff.

"Amazing. It's exactly like that day when I … I can feel the breeze, the smell of the ocean, the pines. Damn … can you hear the sea gulls?"

Liz pointed and said, "What is that?"

Henry gazed into the setting sun. "That tower is what's left of a bridge.

They called it the Golden Gate. It used to connect us to the mainland."

<You miss this place.>

<Damn right.>

"The sun. It's setting like the one outside. I'm going to try something." Henry picked up a stone and hurled it at the sun.

Liz said, "It disappeared."

"Yeah, no clink. We should've heard a sound if that sun was a light fixture. I wonder what would happen if I jumped."

"You wouldn't do that."

"I did once, and look where it got me." The joke had no effect. "Let's go back to the cabin."

<I got the joke.>

<Now you're reading minds?>

"I'm sorry. You are the first human I have ever been with, and everything you say and do is new to me. I was trained to—"

"Love me?"

"I can't help how I was raised."

"I know. The Soofysh are masters at controlling others."

"I was raised by humans."

"You don't say." Henry turned away from the ocean and ambled back to the cabin. "There are humans aboard this ship?"

"I'm not sure if they were real."

"It is hard to figure out what is and what's not."

<I'm real.>

When they arrived at the meadow in front of the cabin, Henry slid his arm over Liz's shoulder. "What do you remember about your upbringing? What kind of childhood did you have?" <Do you know of any way out of this ship?>

Liz's eyes widened for a moment. "I attended a school. There were human teachers … no other children. To me, everything was normal. It was my life." <I do not know of any way off this ship. Until today I did not know I was on a ship.>

"And how did you come to learn of me?"

"I was shown moving pictures of you and Liz … living here, in this cabin. You were happy. We were happy. And there were special sessions—"

Henry felt Liz's shoulder tighten. A tear formed at the corner of her eye and her voice broke. "I don't know what happened then, but I grew fond of you."

"Damn. The Soofysh certainly know their business."

Liz shook her head and straightened up. "I was created for you."

"Don't say that. No one is created for anyone else. You're free to choose your own path. You probably can't see that, but in time you will." <We need to get out of this ship before it takes off.>

"Perhaps you're right."

"Do you know how to make coffee?"

◇

CHAPTER 49

Evening shadows cloaked the alley with no sign of Evan or the other two having arrived at the aircar. Mike sidled along a wall, drawing near to get a clear view of the vehicle's oval outline.

"Mike?" Evan appeared from behind a trash bin with a Batran weapon in hand.

"Damn. You scared the hell out of me."

Evan slid the blaster into his waistband and laughed. It was a short laugh, but a welcomed sound to Mike, who had little to be cheery about.

Mowgli leaned out of the aircar's door. "Mike. Come, we go."

"You bet."

Mike clambered into the pilot's seat with Evan and Claire close behind. "How is she?"

"She's fine." The voice came from the back—pure female and surprisingly strong.

Evan said, "She needs water."

Mike said, "First, we need to get out of here without getting vaporized, then we'll talk about water."

The aircar hummed to life and inched upward between the narrow alley walls. As they passed a dusty window, Mowgli screamed.

Mike said, "What's up? Are you okay?"

Evan pulled out his blaster and said, "We both saw something. Not sure what, but something moved behind that window."

Mike backed up the car a few feet and hovered. "Don't see anything now."

Mowgli said, "There. There," and pointed.

A blurry figure bobbed up behind the opaque glass.

Mike said, "Hard to see what that is." In the next instant, the window shattered with a blinding blue pulse. Mike threw his free arm over Mowgli. Evan fired off his blaster, splintering the car's rear window. For an excruciating few seconds, a veil of dust made it impossible to see. A humanoid shape emerged from the haze, grasping its torso—a Batran. With weapon in hand he toppled through the broken window and plummeted to the alley below.

Mike said, "Nice shot. Damn. Must have been waiting for us."

Evan said, "Your arm."

Mike's arm swung loosely at his side. His hand was completely gone. "Well, what do you know? Mowgli, you okay?"

"Yes. I okay."

Evan said, "You saved the kid."

"Is Claire all right?"

Claire said, "I'm fine, but what about you?"

"I'm down one eye and one hand, and my boot thrusters don't work. I've had better days." Mike nudged the aircar to the edge of the roof. "See anything that looks like Batrans?"

"Seems clear."

"Then we're off."

Mike opted for a zigzag route between buildings and through alleys, favoring the cover of shadows. The thin line of a sunset to the west kept him focused on the way ahead.

When they emerged from the city limits, Evan said, "Where are we going?"

"Henry. I have to get to Henry."

◇

CHAPTER 50

The coffee was perfect.

"I'm going to call you Liz, if that's all right with you."

"It's my name."

"Yeah." Henry lifted his coffee cup. "Do you see what I see?"

"A cup."

"What's on the cup?"

"The letter H."

"Interesting. And yours has a letter on it too."

"E … for Elizabeth. Why is this interesting?"

"It should have dawned on me earlier. We both see the same things."

"So?"

"So … it means that not everything here is an illusion … unless of course the Soofysh figured a way to affect both our minds at the same time."

"I do not understand."

Henry extended his hands. "This could be physically real. The Soofysh ship is big. It could hold all this."

"Meaning?"

<If it is real, then there must be an exit … a door … a way in and out.>

Henry downed the remains of the coffee. "That was really good. Why don't we take a walk?"

"We just did."

"I know, but I want to … It's been a while."

Liz followed Henry outside and they toured the front yard which included a chicken coop.

"Amazing. There are live chickens in there." <I'm looking for an abnormality … something that doesn't quite add up.>

<Because?>

<Because that might be the location of a seam, an imperfection.>

<A spot where a door may be hidden?>

<That's it.>

The pair circled the property with Henry in the lead. A deer trail led to a stand of trees set close together. "Very thick vegetation. Can't get through." <Probably a wall.>

They continued their exploration and after running into similar barriers, returned to the cabin. Henry wandered into his den, surrounded by the familiar smell of moldy wood. His prized possession, an old colt revolver, hung on the wall. A longbow leaned against the corner. A threadbare couch sat below the window overlooking the front yard. He plopped down, letting his frustration ooze its way down into the sagging couch.

Liz said, "I'll tidy up the kitchen. You must be tired, why don't you take a nap? You do sleep, right?"

Henry nodded, braced his head with a throw pillow and closed his eyes; however, his mind would not allow rest. Time was running out. He straightened up and ran out to the kitchen.

"Weren't you supposed to be resting?"

"I'll be right back." <I have an idea I need to test.>

Henry circled to the back of the cabin and followed a path that led down to the shore. The waters of the bay gently swooshed through the pebbles surrounding an inverted rowboat propped up on a set of stones. A pair of oars leaned against it, inviting him to go for a ride.

A fog had settled in across the darkening waters, making the opposite shore impossible to see. Taking the boat would likely lead to the same dead end annoyance he experienced above, but this time with the mist no doubt mysteriously turning him around. The Soofysh were no fools.

He removed his outer clothing, tunic and shoes. A toe check confirmed the water was at a typically bitter cold Pacific temperature. He swung his arms as if the motion would somehow warm his body and plunged in.

◇

CHAPTER 51

Evan leaned over the front seat. "Where is Henry?"

"Where I left him … with the Soo … with the —."

"Mike, are you all right?"

"Why, what's going on?"

"You're acting strange."

"You would be, too, if you just lost a hand."

The aircar took a sudden turn and grazed a parapet, sending a few bricks flying.

"Sorry about that."

Evan grabbed Mike's shoulder. "Something is wrong. Don't you feel it?"

"My nerves. Having trouble concentrating."

"You don't have any nerves. I think you should land."

"Don't be silly. I've got this under—"

Claire said, "Look, look, ahead."

Evan turned in time to see a metal tower which became a wall of metal struts wrapping themselves across the windshield. The sounds of metallic screeching drowned out Claire's screams. Bent rods and braces pummeled the car and the entire structure collapsed over them like a spider's web engulfing a hapless fly.

Evan wrapped his arms about Claire and Mowgli. The entangled car spiraled downward, squealing as it caromed off the side of a brick building, and came to a stop upside down in a parking lot.

Evan listened for a moment, overwhelmed by a feeling of elation that he was still alive, and that Mowgli and Claire survived. The pings of freshly twisted metal surrounded them, gradually ebbing to whispers.

"What happened?" Mike hung inverted from the pilot's seat.

Evan said, "You happened. Something's wrong with you."

Mike released himself and joined the others on the ceiling of the car. "It was an accident. Anyone can have an accident."

"You're not anyone. And you were acting weird."

Mike opened his silvery jaw and said nothing. After a beat, he whispered. "It's the damn Soofysh. Sometimes I see things, and when that happens, it's always them screwing around. I bet they're hardly aware that they're doing it."

"Is there anything we can do?"

"First, we need to free this car from all this crap."

It took only a few minutes for Mike to peel off the remains of the tower, releasing the car from its metal cocoon. All the while Evan kept his eyes scanning the dark sky for any sign of a Batran pursuit.

Mike flipped the aircar over and said, "Evan, I'm going to show you how to pilot this thing, and then I am going to turn myself off."

◇

CHAPTER 52

Even a cyborg needs to breathe.

The depth of the water was over his head, forcing Henry to come up every few minutes. He struggled to stay under long enough to discover how thorough the Soofysh designed the place.

It was the fourth dive that brought Henry to a wall. He followed it in one direction, dragging his fingers along its surface. When he came up for air, a mist blanketed the water, hiding the shoreline. He dove back down, keeping track of how far he had gone in an effort to estimate the way back to shore.

His fingers ran across a break in the smooth texture. He followed it down to discover a door without an obvious handle. Perhaps it was a means to empty the bay simulation, like a plug at the bottom of a bathtub.

He surfaced and retraced his way along the wall. When the shoreline loomed into view, he made a mental note of the door's location with respect to the shore. Relieved to be out of the frigid waters, he looked forward to getting his clothing back on to stave off the cold fog, a detail he was sure the Soofysh were proud of.

"Where did you go?"

Liz stood near the upturned boat. "A swim. I wanted to see if the water was real." <I found something interesting.>

"Your blue skin looks even bluer." <What did you find?>

"Hah. It's an optical illusion." <A door beneath the water.> "Let's get back to the cabin. My skin might not get any bluer, but I'm freezing."

"Good idea,"

Henry was grateful that Liz was a quick study. She knew what to say when speaking aloud.

Once back in the cabin, Henry assumed his favorite pose on the couch. Time was getting short, and he hadn't found a way out of the ship, for that matter, getting out of the simulation was proving to be a challenge.

Liz called out from the kitchen. "Are you hungry?"

Henry pondered the attention to detail in everything the Soofysh created, including Liz's mannerisms that apparently included her cooking skills.

"Amazing."

Liz stepped into the den. "Are you talking about me?"

Henry chuckled, something he never thought he could do again. "I'm talking about this place, and, of course, you."

Liz angled in next to him. "I can't help it. This is what I've been waiting for my whole life."

Henry frowned and fought back the urge to correct her once again. "That may be true for you. But—"

Liz put a finger to his lips. "Don't over think it. Let this moment guide you. No one knows what the future holds." She pulled him closer, and their lips met.

His head swam. The clone might as well have been the original. Captured by her eyes, he ran his fingers through her crimson hair. She felt like Liz. It was easy to imagine it was really her. He pulled in closer. Her warm breath glided over his cheek, her eager body pressed against his. She was Liz.

◇

CHAPTER 53

"We have arrived."

Genz said, "That was a long walk. Why have you brought us here?"

"It was only a few miles."

"It was much more. I'm not as young as I used to be."

"None of us are." Seth paused at the entrance to the nameless town, and scanned the length of Main Street. The freshly risen moon, a smiling arc low to the east, shed its faint glow upon the scattering of buildings lining the street.

Genz said, "Can you see in the dark?"

"The moonlight is sufficient for me. And there is the infrared region. Every object retains a level of heat from the day."

"See anything we should worry about?"

"Not at the moment. Our last visit had some guests drop by, Batrans to be exact."

"It's quiet now."

"I think Henry would say 'too quiet'."

"That, he would."

Seth opted to stay to one side of the main thoroughfare while Genz followed closely behind. "Is there much more to this? My feet are in pain."

"I am sorry for your feet, but the object of our quest is only a bit farter west of this town, and it is imperative we get there as soon as possible."

"I still do not understand the secrecy."

"It is a matter of precaution. You will know everything when we arrive."

The pair passed the toppled steeple of a church on the far side of town and followed a narrow trail into the desert.

When they reached an open area, Seth said, "Stop. Do not move."

Genz edged to Seth's side. "What is it? I see nothing but darkness and the faint edge of the horizon."

"I have detected a Batran positioned near our destination."

"Probably one of Marth's people. She is thorough. Is this where she tracked your group to earlier?"

"Indeed."

Genz touched a device strung on his chest and disappeared. "I will investigate."

Seth followed Genz using his heat-sensitive vision, keeping to the rear and skittering between occasional outcroppings of scrub. The clear night sky offered up a wealth of stars and a sliver of a moon that coated everything below with an eerie silver sheen.

"I know you're there, Genz."

The voice was at once recognizable—Marth.

Genz reappeared and said, "How?"

"I followed you and that annoying little robot." She nodded toward the side of the low-slung building to her rear. "In my personal aircar."

"Impressive. Did you move everyone out of the city?"

"That is being done; however, your call intrigued me. I wanted to find out what you were up to."

"Honestly, I myself do not know."

Seth stepped out from behind Genz. "The time has come to explain, but you must follow me first,"

Seth guided the pair to the backside of the one-story structure where a wrecked jeep leaned against a wide metal double door at the base of a ramp. "Can you move that vehicle away from the door?" Marth gave Genz a look that Seth interpreted as exasperation.

Seth said, "Once inside we can talk."

While the two worked on the remains of the jeep, Seth ran up the ramp and set off to the front of the building. "I will endeavor to open those doors from the other side."

Moments later, the entryway was cleared and Seth invited the pair inside.

Marth said, "What is this?"

Seth closed the doors. "Now we can talk. This structure is equipped with electromagnetic shielding."

Genz raised a hand to cover his eyes against the single overhead light. "Shielding against what?"

"Against being overheard by the Soofysh among other things."

Marth said, "So, I ask again … what is this place?"

"It is a control center for the launch of a missile with a nuclear warhead."

Marth stepped back. "And what do you intend to do?"

"I will carry out Henry's request … which will likely be his last."

Genz said, "You don't mean to launch a missile?"

Marth said, "Impossible. How can anything so old still work? And what is the target?"

"The Soofysh ship."

Marth's voice rose in a shrill. "What? You are insane. That would mean the end for all of us."

Genz said, "You cannot be serious."

Seth paused a moment to consider what a shock this tactic would be to the Batrans. "Henry and I theorize that the Soofysh are one, that is, there is only one being, and that being is in the business of murder and extortion."

Marth said, "Our people have an agreement with the Soofysh made ages ago. They supplied a habitable world, we colonized it, and we are indebted to them. Who knows what horrors would descend upon us if we break that agreement or worse, attack them. Your plan endangers all of us, human and Batran. It makes no sense."

Seth said, "Firstly, they lied to you. You know that they killed most humans on this planet and told you that it was all due to a series of natural disasters."

Genz said, "We know."

"And secondly, have you ever seen more than one Soofysh?"

Marth and Genz remained silent.

"Did you want to remain bound to this monster forever? We can put an end to it this evening, and perhaps save billions of lives on other worlds from similar fates."

Marth said, "Soofysh technology is far ahead of our own. Resistance would mean breaking our agreement, and we would be helpless against such a power."

Seth said, "Helpless until now."

Genz said, "You say you can launch a nuclear weapon to strike at the Soofysh ship back in Albuquerque. What gives you the idea that the ship is vulnerable? The Soofysh have defenses that we cannot imagine."

"I am a Soofysh creation. When I was built, I was made aware of Soofysh technology. It is part of what I am. Under normal circumstances the Soofysh can easily repel a crude missile; however, we have three advantages. While loading ore, the ship's shielding is minimal as are its defenses. The Soofysh are primarily concerned with attack from below, from the ground. And we have surprise on our side."

Genz said, "I do not think surprise carries much weight. You said three advantages."

"That I did. We also have Henry."

◇

CHAPTER 54

The kitchen light filtered into the study and cast a crimson sparkle on Liz's hair. "Would you care for coffee?"

Henry said, "More coffee. That would be great." <We don't have much time.>

Liz stopped at the doorway to the kitchen. "Do you want anything with that?" <What do you mean?>

<What do you know of the Soofysh?>

<They raised me and taught me the ways of humans. You were brought up many times, reminding me of your love for the original Elizabeth and hopefully for me.>

<Did you ever see more than one of them?>

<I'm not sure.>

<So how do you feel about them?>

<They were kind to me and provided human mentors. In return I was expected to care for you.>

<What would you say if I told you the Soofysh have killed billions of human beings to prepare the way for colonization by another species?>

<It is hard for me to imagine such a thing.>

<It is a fact. The world you see around you through this simulation … this is where I … we used to live. The Soofysh killed nearly everyone on this planet, including the original Elizabeth.>

Tears welled up in Liz's eyes. She brought a hand to her cheek and said, "You haven't answered my question."

"And what was that?"

Her voice broke. "Will you have something with your coffee, silly."

"No thanks."

<You said we have little time.>

<I've given Seth a directive. If all goes according to plan, a missile will be launched soon—a rocket, a nuclear one.> Henry saw the confusion wrinkle her face. <A powerful technology that will likely destroy this ship and the Soofysh.>

<I do not understand.>

<It is a weapon which will explode with great force.>

<And what of us?>

Henry's heart sank. Here was Liz, come back from the dead, and he had set in motion events that would kill her again. Was this really the right decision?

<We will die, unless—>

Liz grasped the doorjamb and swung down into a kitchen chair. <Unless what?>

<Unless we find a way out of here.>

<How much time do we have?>

<I have no idea. Each moment is precious.>

"Are you sure? I can heat up some sweet buns." <I was in a daze when the Soofysh brought me here. I cannot recall how I entered.>

<You're being brave, Liz. You must see the Soofysh like a daughter sees her father.>

<I know nothing else. But I trust you, Henry. I'll help in any way I can.>

"You know what? Sweet buns are my favorite. I'll have two."

◇

CHAPTER 55

Marth ducked her head and sauntered deeper into the control center. "These instruments look dead. Your plan, Henry's plan, is completely outrageous. Even if you launch a missile, how are you going to control it?"

Genz knocked a finger against one of the many dull gray screens. "Nothing is working."

Seth said, "The missile is located 213 yards to our north, buried in an underground silo." He pointed at two mechanisms set in the wall, about ten feet apart. "All I need from you is to turn these two keys when I say so."

Marth said, "I'm not doing it. You're crazy. The Soofysh are not stupid. They will respond with vengeance, destroying all that we have built this past century. It will mean an end to our colonies. Father, you must see that. Tell this idiot robot. Say something."

Genz said, "It is true that Henry's plan borders on the insane. It is also true that the Soofysh have killed many. They have lied to us. Our agreement is based on falsehoods. They will likely use us to strip all the resources of this planet … and what happens after that?"

"The agreement ends. The Soofysh leave us in peace."

"What is there to stop them from killing all of us and selling this planet to someone else? It would be easier now—we are few. Even after extorting our natural resources, this planet would be much desired—plenty of water, a variety of climates, fertile ground and abundant animal life."

Marth leaned back on a counter and stared at the floor.

Seth reached up and turned the pages of a notebook. "I will program the missile warheads."

Genz said, "Warheads? How many?"

"Three in this version of the Minuteman missile—each capable of seeking out a separate target."

Marth said, "This is madness. We have no chance against the Soofysh."

Genz said, "If this fails, the Soofysh will blame the humans, not us."

"A thin argument. The Soofysh may choose to hunt down anyone else involved."

Seth said, "The data entry keyboard has ceased to function."

Genz said, "No surprise there. This equipment is ancient."

Seth jerked a line of cabling loose and tore off its outer coverings. After splaying out the bare ends of the wires on the counter, he touched a finger to each.

Genz said, "What are you doing?"

The display screen above the keyboard flashed into life, streaming several lines of text. "Seth said, "The missile system is coming on line."

Genz said, "Nice trick."

Marth said, "You should stop it, not encourage it."

"I've known Seth for a long time. He, not it, is someone I would trust with my life."

Seth said, "The targeting is complete, but something is still wrong."

Marth spit out a hiss in Batran. "Of course there is something wrong. There is something wrong with all of this."

Genz said, "Marth, you may have nothing to fret about after all."

Seth said, "Stay here. I will return soon," and swung open the double door entry.

Genz said, "I'm coming with you." He gave Marth a backward glance. "And do not touch anything."

Marth said, "Ha. I may not be here when you come back."

Minutes later, at the underground missile site, Seth pointed out the rusty sheen of chain link fencing that formed a square roughly 60 yards wide. "We go inside there."

"I only see a concrete structure perhaps too small for the two of us to fit within."

Seth tore an opening in the fencing and said, "The building is an access point." He nodded back at the hint of a curved metallic dome covered in sand. "And that is where the missile is located. The hatch should have opened."

The door to the building looked impenetrable—made of stainless steel covered with dark streaks earned by years of exposure. It offered up no handle or hinge.

Genz ran a hand over its pitted surface and knocked on it. "Not sure what I can do. It feels quite thick."

Seth produced a small screwdriver and pressed it into an aperture at the door's rim.

"Is that a key?"

"It will serve as one."

A few turns and one sharp click later had the door ajar. "Now you can help."

Seth wedged his small frame against the massive door. Genz joined in by leaning in with his shoulder. The door screeched in protest, but eventually succumbed.

"Now what?"

Seth cast his laser strobe into the dark interior and highlighted a metal railing. "We go down."

"I hope the ceiling below is higher than the one here."

Seth led the way along a spiral staircase, which rattled against loose bolts with every shaky step. After about a dozen treads, the two emerged into a cement alcove which secreted another door.

Genz said, "No handle, no lock."

Seth said, "This one has an electronic locking mechanism," and reached up to press one of the ten buttons on a keypad mounted on a wall off to the side.

Genz said, "No electricity."

"We have power back in the launching bunker and the missile signaled a problem to me."

"I am sorry to be negative, but don't you need the code necessary to open this door?"

Seth jerked the keypad off the wall, leaving behind an explosion of thin wires. He used the fingers of both hands to contact each bare end, pausing at various combinations. After a minute, a loud clack preceded the door sliding to the side.

Genz said, "A tunnel. I see light in there."

"The illumination works, probably because it was not turned on until the tunnel door opened. This would further suggest our missile is powered."

"Is the rocket equipped with solid propellants?"

"Indeed."

"Are you sure they will function?"

"No. But then, that question will be answered shortly."

The tunnel opened up on the missile itself. A single cable stretched from the body of the rocket to a coupling above their heads.

Seth pointed up and said, "This is what humans called the nose cone. It contains the nuclear warheads."

"I do not know much of such things. You said nuclear. Are we in danger of radiation?"

"I am not, but you may be." Seth craned his head out beyond the tunnel opening. "I see one of the problems. The dome motor may have failed."

Seth shook the cable.

Genz snickered. "Ha, we often do the same when an electrical device malfunctions."

"Can you go back and try to pull up that cover?"

"I can, but what if the missile takes off?"

"The two keys back in the bunker will have to be turned at the same time to do that."

"That makes me feel a little better."

Genz crawled back out the tunnel while Seth took a closer look at the cable. Gashes in its cracked rubber covering suggested the work of rodents. He gave it a tug, and the cable snapped in two, exposing a myriad of multi-colored wires. Several were clearly bitten through. "I found the problem."

A deep grinding filled the silo, ending with a loud crack.

"Can you hear me?"

Seth said, "I hear you."

"I have the cover fully open."

"Excellent. Please return to the launch bunker. You and Marth must turn the keys at the same time to launch this missile. I need to conduct a repair here. Do not wait for me. The launch is of primary importance."

"But if you are still in the tunnel—"

"I will follow soon. When you get back, execute the launch. Keep the keys turned until the missile takes off."

"I do not know if I can do this."

"Henry is depending on you and so am I."

Seth waited a few seconds, but there was no response. He held the two ends of the frayed cable and knew that he would have to maintain a physical hold on several strands to insure a successful launch.

"Henry, my dear friend, if you can hear me … "

◇

CHAPTER 56

<I'm getting tired of this mental talk.>

<Yeah, me too. But I don't want the Soofysh to overhear us.> Henry finished off the last of three sweet rolls. "That was perfect. I could get used to living here."

"I'm glad."

He had no concrete plan for escape or a potential route out. As the bun's sweet taste faded, he pictured Seth clambering down into the missile bunker. He'd need help with the two launch keys, but he'd find a way.

There were many reasons why the missile might not take off, and many reasons why a nuclear warhead might be ineffective against the Soofysh ship. The whole plan began to unravel in Henry's mind. He hoped to destroy the Soofysh, an entity that existed for millennia and had technology that dwarfed anything he could imagine. But, then again, there might be only one Soofysh, and in addition to being a murderer and an extortionist, that entity was probably adept at lying.

<Liz, I have an idea. You will need to play along with me. We are about to get into an argument.>

Liz held her arms akimbo, which set Henry to thinking of the extent of her Soofysh training.

"Of course, you're glad. Why wouldn't you be? It's what the Soofysh programmed you for."

"Don't say that."

"You're not my Liz and never will be. You're nothing but a lousy copy. Everything here is a charade."

"Henry, you must know I love you. The Soofysh have made it possible for us to be with each other."

<Good one.> "Easy for you to say. I made a mistake. It's all a game, isn't it? I don't want any part of it. You can tell your Soofysh masters I want out."

"How can you say that, Henry? You agreed to work with them … with me … I have no way to contact them."

"Maybe this will get their attention." Henry hoisted the settee and hurled it through the window. The sound of shattering glass made him wince. Was this a good idea?

"What are you doing?"

"I'll tell you what I'm doing. I'm putting an end to this stupid experiment. Your friends, the Soofysh, killed my wife. Don't you get it yet? You're nothing but a lab rat in a cage. We both are." Henry yanked his Colt revolver from the wall, aimed it at Liz and pulled the trigger. "See? Nothing. It's fake like all this … like you."

"Henry, stop it, stop it." <I hope you know what you're doing.>

<Me too.>

He heard the crinkling behind him, cellophane being squashed in a fist followed by an acrid ozone stench.

"Henry, Henry. We had an understanding."

The smashed window was intact and the settee was back with a figure lounging in it that looked human, but remained indistinct like an impressionist's portrait with details lost to a swirling pixilation.

"You bastard. You should have never come back." Henry leaped at the reclining form, but landed in the couch grasping a cushion.

"Now, now." The undulating humanoid shape assumed a position at the kitchen door. "Henry you must appreciate the larger picture. We are here because of a business agreement with the Batrans. You should be thankful that we spared you. Look at what we have done for you … your home, your wife."

Henry slumped into the couch and hugged a pillow. "It's all a fantasy. I can't go on like this. I may have been dead for a century, but I lost my wife last week." Pointing at the kitchen, he added, "That thing … that thing that looks and acts human is your creation and will never be my wife." <Stay with me.>

The Soofysh remained silent, perhaps considering Henry's words for a moment. "The clone is a perfect copy of your wife. And she loves you, Henry."

That last comment bore a trace of sarcasm that Henry hadn't believe the Soofysh were capable of.

"What do you know of love? You're some kind of electromechanical freak without empathy or conscience. I don't know what you really are. Damn, I'm beginning to think you don't know what you are."

"Would it help to know I was once human?"

Henry, taken aback, stuttered. "No way … it can't be." <Now we are getting somewhere. Notice the singular?>

<Careful, Henry.>

"We are much more alike than you realize."

"Why are you telling me this?"

"We will be together for some time. There is no sense in remaining enemies."

"Are you willing to show me who you really are?"

Once again, the apparition paused. "I see no reason why not."

<Singular again.>

"Then do it. Show me. Who knows, maybe you can convince me to work with you, though I doubt it."

The rainbow specter at the door faded away.

Liz said, "What now?"

◇

CHAPTER 57

The rectangular outline of the missile bunker came across as a mere suggestion under a cloudless obsidian sky. Genz loped down the ramp. A shadow within the bunker's edge caught his eye. He said, "Glad you decided to stay. We're going to have to do this together."

Marth stepped away from the double doors. "What makes you think I'm going to help?"

"You're still here."

"Maybe I want to be sure you don't do this."

"Be serious. This is our one chance to rid ourselves of the Soofysh. You know what they are."

"Where is the imp?"

"If you mean Seth, he's in the missile silo."

"Shouldn't you wait until it returns?"

"He's not coming back."

Marth tilted her head. "Why in the world would it do that?"

"There was a problem with a cable. He's back there holding it together."

"That would mean—"

"Exactly."

"Oh well … it's just a robot."

"Seth is Henry's friend. He's not just a robot."

"So it's a he or a she, it doesn't matter. But—."

"But what? He and Henry are both willing to give up everything. And you ask, for what? It should be obvious even to you. They're doing this for us."

Marth shrugged. "And you're sure?"

"I am sure the Soofysh will not stop with this planet. They are a ruthless species without compassion and will continue preparing more unsuspecting planets for other naïve clients. Think of what we do here as saving the lives of countless millions, probably billions. The chance to stop them may never come again." Genz walked past Marth and entered the bunker. "Coming, daughter?"

While he waited for Marth to consider his words, he scanned the instruments along the walls. Metal boxes on either end sported an inserted key. He reached up to grasp one and extended his free hand toward the other. The stretching caused a filamentous membrane to drop down from arm to lower back—a wing long since relegated to a fading memory.

"Planning to take flight, father?" Marth walked over to the key box on the other end of the room "All we have to do is turn these keys?"

Genz nodded. "And keep them turned until we hear the missile take off."

Marth ran a clawed finger over the key.

◇

CHAPTER 58

"Do you know what you're doing?"

Evan took his eyes off the dash and glared at Claire. "No. I don't. All I know is what Mike told me." He pointed at the dash screen. "He told me to keep these numbers the same."

"Those are not numbers."

"All right then, these symbols."

"I can't see the horizon."

"The symbols tell me where I'm going. I don't know what they mean, but I'm steering to keep them from changing."

"Is that what Mike said to do?"

"He said it would take a couple of hours, and then look for a tall building. Henry is somewhere near there, near a rail yard."

"Who is Henry?"

Mowgli said, "He is blue man ... friend."

Evan said, "Get back to sleep. You'll need your energy when we find him."

Claire said, "Blue?"

"Don't worry, he is human, but was put in an artificial body by the Soofysh."

"Why would they do that?"

"Not sure, but like Mowgli said, he is our friend and he helped us escape the Batrans. Mike told me he's in trouble … the Soofysh may have him."

Claire said, "Those number symbols … they are changing."

The aircar lurched to one side and dove

Evan squeezed Claire's arm. "I don't know what is happening. I can't steer this thing anymore."

The aircar surged downward. Mowgli screamed and flew into the ceiling.

"I got you." The voice belonged to Mike. An arm swung over Evan's shoulder and jerked back on the steering wheel. The car's nose pointed upward. "Push down on the throttle!"

Evan said, "It's down to the floor."

The drop eased up a bit. The darkness outside revealed only a flat, featureless landscape without landmarks.

Mike said, "Something's wrong with the power. We're going down. Brace yourselves."

Mowgli s leaped into Claire's lap. Evan leaned over to cover them both. Mike jumped into the back seat. They heard and felt the sudden shock of the aircar grinding into the desert floor. Seconds later, the vehicle's superstructure flexed and the air filled with a series of metallic pings.

Mike mumbled. "That's the second time we've crashed. At least this time it wasn't me at the controls."

Evan said, "Actually, you were the one holding the steering bar."

"A detail."

"Are you feeling better?"

"Don't really know. Right now, we need to get out of this heap and figure out where we are."

Once outside, Claire and Mowgli huddled against the side of the aircar, trying to avoid the wind.

Mike ambled out onto the desert gravel.

Evan said, "It's awful cold out here. Do you see anything?"

"There's a line of mountains to the west. That means we're near … maybe 20 or 30 miles from Albuquerque."

"That's what you call near?"

"You guys will have to stay here, at least until daylight. It'll be warmer inside the aircar."

"And you? What are you going to do?"

Mike fired up his shoes and rose off the ground. "These babies are up and running again. Don't know how long they'll last, but I'm not waiting to find out. I'll be back for you as soon as I can." Mike shot off into the night, leaving behind a moonlit trail of swirling dust in his wake.

◇

CHAPTER 59

Henry followed the Soofysh apparition into the kitchen. As soon as he entered, the kitchen became a dark hallway with glowing panels lining the floor.

The Soofysh waved a hand ahead and said, "It is a short walk."

Liz grasped Henry's arm. <I am frightened.>

<That makes two of us.> He pulled his arm free. "Get away from me." <And remember that at this moment I am supposed to be unhappy, and that includes being pissed off at you.>

Alcoves to either side of the hallway displayed glowing orbs, models of planets.

Henry said, "What are these? Trophies?"

"New colonizations."

"And what of the indigenous peoples?"

The Soofysh uttered a sound vaguely reminiscent of a snicker. "What of them?"

Henry counted dozens of displays within view. "Did you sterilize each of these planets like you did here?"

"Sterilize is such a harsh word. We've had this discussion a few times, Henry. The Soofysh are simply the catalyst for change, and change is inevitable."

There was a time when Henry's people suffered a similar change. There was nothing to be done then. Maybe now was different.

A doorway materialized and the Soofysh said, "We are here. Please enter." With that, the speckled figure disappeared, leaving behind a faint but all too familiar acrid scent.

A human voice greeted him from inside the doorway. "Come in and make yourselves comfortable."

A figure sat at a grand piano. Henry's vision blurred while he absorbed the scene. He struggled to close his mouth. Surrounding the ebony grand, bookshelves over-stacked with leather-bound tomes lined all four walls of an expansive library. A divan, satin plush, sat to the side with ivory-white porcelain urns to either side containing what looked like Japanese Bonsai trees. The scent of cherry tobacco led Henry's gaze back to the piano.

"Surprised?"

The voice had a kind of warm congenial quality one would expect from a grandfather or a favorite uncle. The man who had spoken sat at the piano bench. His baldpate and the gray wisps that curled over his ears framed a robust white moustache that bounced over his pipe. His yellow-green eyes gave Henry the chills. He raised a hand to withdraw the pipe and smiled. A wine red silken housecoat fell short of hiding a pair of incongruous striped pajamas.

"Please be seated."

It was like a movie come to life with details stolen from Hollywood's penchant for cliché. Henry shook his head, "You can't be serious." <Is this what the Soofysh looked like?>

<Actually, yes.>

<No wonder you're fond of him. He could charm the skin off a snake.>

<I do not understand.>

Henry wondered if the Soofysh was at it again—playing with his mind. "Is this really you, and is this really how you spend your time?"

"Did you see me as some ogre, a monster, perhaps with tentacles and long sharp teeth, intent on mindless destruction and mayhem?"

<Yes> "Not at all. My impression of you is that of a spoiled, self-centered asshole with the power to obtain anything he wants. You're nothing but a child, and an evil one at that."

"You are mistaken. I simply perform a service."

"I don't get it. How can you be human? I get the impression that you've been killing people for thousands, maybe millions, of years." Liz tightened her grip on his arm.

"My story is complex, but you're essentially correct. I have been in existence for many of your ages. I've adopted the human form for its practicality; essentially, I am human, at least for the present."

Henry held back the impulse to rush the man, to choke his pudgy neck, see his eyeballs bulge and face turn to a crimson bloat. "And you operate the ship and transact your so-called business all from this room?"

The man laughed, took a deep puff from his pipe, and then pointed to his head. "I can access all the ship's controls from here."

Henry turned to look at Liz. <I hope he hasn't been listening in on us.> "You have everything you want. What the hell do you want from us?"

The man raised his eyebrows much like a teacher would while lecturing a child and pointed his pipe at Henry. "As I've stated many times, it's all about your ability to communicate with Liz. I can tell when you communicate, but cannot ascertain the messaging. It's driving me mad. For example, you transmitted a message during our discussion. What was it? A plan to kill me? Or to take over the ship?" The old codger laughed. "The looks on your faces give you away." He took another drag and exhaled a blue cloud.

"Don't worry. I expected as much. One doesn't reach my age without some talent at anticipation."

"At least tell me your name isn't Soofysh. Your parents must have hated you."

The man stood up from the bench. "You're really trying hard, Henry, I'll give you that." He paused a moment, examining the Persian rug at his slippered feet. "No, you're right. It isn't Soofysh. That is a name known widely throughout this galaxy … you may say it is my business title. I haven't used my real name in such a long time. In any event, it's of no consequence."

Henry approached the man who backed up a step. "Then what do we call you?"

"Easy now. You do realize I can end your existence with a thought."

Henry held his hands akimbo. "I'm not intending to attack you." <Not right now, anyway.>

"You can call me Captain. Appropriate, don't you think?"

"Perfect."

"And before you ask, there is only one of me."

◇

CHAPTER 60

The thrusters burped and then sputtered. Mike's boots were failing again. His night vision queued up a flat landscape ahead. He aimed for a thin strip of a highway headed toward a faint glow along the western horizon.

"That must be Albuquerque."

He skidded to a landing on the sand-covered road. Moonlight glinted from the remnants of vehicles scattered about him, most headed away from the city.

"Poor devils. Running from death only to find it out here."

A gust of wind sent tumbleweeds weaving through the derelict maze, blurring the way ahead. For a moment, Mike saw something move between the cars.

"Man, my mind is running up on me." He spoke aloud both to calm himself and to make sure that the something out there heard him.

The undulating drone of skittering sand had his nerves on edge. He had rarely succumbed to fright, and considering he was entirely artificial, was at the same time impressed that Soofysh technology was able to reproduce such a human trait.

"Who's that?" The voice, human and raspy, came from between the cars.

Mike paused a second to regain his equilibrium and shake off the shock. "Me ... uh ... I mean nobody but me."

The silence that followed clawed away at his sanity. Was he hearing things now?

He raised his voice. "Who are you?" Maybe he should have added 'what are you?' "Damn. This place is making me crazy."

"Not too crazy."

This time the voice came from his rear, a gravelly tone, deep and threatening. Whoever it was had managed to get past him. He strained his mechanical lens to see a way ahead. A tangle of mangled vehicles sifted into focus. Mike pictured the ensuing arguments, made a century ago, followed by the realization that everyone was dropping dead. They must have struggled to flee their cars, not knowing where to run.

The image compelled Mike to crank his legs up to a quick jog. Making new acquaintances in the middle of the desert in the middle of the night was not on his immediate to-do list.

As he cleared the last car, he spied a pale face that popped up from the passenger side of a pickup truck. Its sunken eyes stared out, while thin lips mouthed words that would never reach Mike's ears.

"Damn."

At the sound of an engine cranking up, he broke into a sprint, daring not to look back, his frazzled mind unable to process the impossibilities, all the while fully capable of imagining demons and spirits leaping out of their dried-out corpses.

It was a half-hour later when he slowed down. From time to time a mechanical needed to rest its springs and gears. He gave the road behind him a furtive glance, assuring himself no one or no thing had followed. Only a few wrecks came into view between swirling wisps of dust. He brushed himself and set off on a jog west.

Time morphed into an abstraction. The endless road coughed up an occasional car. He counted each one, concentrating on simple numbers to fight of the image of Henry facing the all-powerful Soofysh. What had Henry gotten into? What was Henry up to? Every time his mind wandered, creatures, grotesque and sharp-toothed, passed in and out of view along the roadside.

"Damn Soofysh."

He was certain his waking nightmare came from another kind of monster—the same beings who created him from the human he once was. From that day, he had fought to resist them. They were back and he felt his resolve faltering. The closer he got to the Soofysh, the more those fierce illusions were likely to overwhelm him.

He turned his attention to Albuquerque's far off lights looming on the horizon.

◇

CHAPTER 61

"I cannot do this." Marth slammed the side of the key box with the back of her hand and leaned against a console. She felt herself caught between two forces—keeping her colony safe and ridding her Batrans of the Soofysh terror forever. Her father and Henry had driven a sharp wedge between those choices. She teetered at the edge of a cliff, destined to fall no matter what she decided.

Genz gripped the key at his box. "We have gone over the reasons many times. None of them are stupid. Now, be reasonable, daughter. This is our best hope for freedom. Henry is depending on us."

Marth turned away, but of a sudden she lurched at Genz and grasped his hand, pulling at it. "It's not worth it. We have to pay the Soofysh. It's in our contract."

"What are you doing?"

"You are threatening our existence. The Soofysh will exact vengeance against everyone, human and Batran."

She jerked his arm. The key box separated from the wall sending sparks flying. A surge of paralyzing energy stiffened her body, while wrapping an arm about her father. They landed on the floor with Genz writhing alongside her.

"Papa!"

Smoke snaked along the ceiling of the narrow room, cloaking the fluo-rescents. Other than a twitch of his arms, Genz appeared lifeless.

"Papa, wake up."

She hoisted his body to a sitting position, propping his back against the wall. A wet gurgle emitted by his throat and a flutter of his eyelids brought her closer. She whispered, "Papa, can you hear me?"

Genz nodded and his mouth moved, exhaling a deep, labored breath.

She brought her head down to listen.

"Get … Seth. He … would know—"

"Know what? Speak, papa. Know what?"

Genz slumped to the floor. Marth searched the room for something, for anything that might help her revive her father.

"Seth. Get Seth."

She ran to the doorway and sprinted to the flat building in the distance.

◇

CHAPTER 62

Henry said, "Only one?"

The old man shuffled away from the piano and pulled a book from a nearby shelf. "See this?"

Henry nodded, not knowing what to expect next.

"This book is an original first edition. 'On the Origin of Species,' by a fellow by the name of Charles Darwin. Are you familiar with it?"

"Everyone is. How the hell did you get it?"

"I bring to your attention the message it contains."

Henry knew where this was going. "Mass extinction by an alien isn't covered by Darwin."

"Evolution, Henry. Survival of the fittest species … In your case, humans lose out,"

A surge of anger narrowed Henry's eyes. He staggered for a moment, regarding the entity. It looked human, but was most definitely not. It had no empathy, only greed—a vile, personal greed to control and manipulate. The world, for that matter, the galaxy would be happy to be rid of it.

The Soofysh paged through the book, seemingly searching out a specific passage.

Henry leaped across the room with hands extended.

<Henry, no!>

◇

CHAPTER 63

"Councilor."

Marth turned to the voice. "I ordered you to stay with the aircar."

A Batran with weapon drawn glanced backward at his comrade and bowed. "We were worried. It is our duty to protect you. Forgive our impatience."

The Batran turned to return to the aircar.

"Wait. My father lies inside this bunker. He has been injured. Have your assistant take him back to our secondary quarters for treatment immediately. Tell him not to go back to our command station and do it as fast as possible." Marth held up a communications device for both guards to see. "And stay there until you hear from me."

Her heart sank. She looked on while her unconscious father was carried out. She should not have lunged at him. Now he might die and it was her fault.

She scanned the bleak landscape and focused on the far off small building. Somewhere in there a little robot was trying his best to insure the missile would launch. He might be perched right next to the rocket, likely to perish with the blast—pure loyalty to his master, and to a cause that was burning a hole in her chest.

When the aircar lifted off, she motioned the remaining guard to follow her back into the bunker. "We have something important to attend to."

◇

CHAPTER 64

Henry's hands plunged through the Captain's chest. His fingers closed on something soft, squirming. The Soofysh creature lurched backward, pulling Henry atop its prone body. An instant later, Henry lay face down on the plush library carpet, his hands empty.

A voice came from somewhere impossibly distant. "Such a reckless move for someone of your intelligence."

Henry raised himself to a knee. The Captain was caught off guard—not infallible after all. "You think you're a damn god, superior to us in every way."

He turned to face the Soofysh and gasped. The Captain was gone leaving behind a swirling mist. In seconds that too was gone.

Liz said, "What happened? What did you do?"

"I have no idea." Henry scanned the room. The door they had entered was gone, but on the opposite side, beyond the dying swirls of a multi-colored mist, a narrow passageway took form between two towering bookcases.

"Let's get out of here."

"Where are we going?"

"It doesn't matter." Henry had the creepy notion that the Captain might pop up any instant, maybe this time turning into the tentacle monster he described, hell-bent on destroying everything in its path. And then there was the passageway, showing up the way it did. His optimism waned with the realization he was a sheep and the Soofysh, the herder.

He paused a moment as his hand felt its way across the smooth textured wall. An image of his last remaining friend loomed into view. He pictured Seth in the missile bunker. The robot would need help to turn both keys. A thousand complications rose up in Henry's mind, and every one of them, impossible to overcome. But this was Seth. Seth would insure that the missile launched, somehow. The end of the world was on its way, slated to arrive any minute, for that matter, any second.

"We need to find a way out of here … I mean out of this ship."

Liz said, "You angered the Captain."

"I doubt it has human feelings … probably no feelings at all."

"Like a robot?"

"It's no robot."

The way forward took on the look of a corridor, complete with ceiling and walls, curving at times with odd lighting effects from above and below. A movement ahead, much like curtains drawn aside, halted the pair.

Henry's eyes were the first to readjust. "I see something green … trees."

The two stepped forward and tumbled to the ground. Henry felt the texture of grass beneath his hands. The scent of ocean filled his nostrils. "We're back at the cabin."

Liz ran to the porch. "Yes, yes, we are home."

Henry followed her, all the while scanning the front yard's treed meadow, as well as checking behind him. "So it seems." Of course, it was not home. It was a prison. Henry hopped onto the porch and into the cabin. He emerged seconds later.

<Liz, I need to tell you something.>

She sat down on the porch steps.

<As you know, I've set into motion events that are likely to kill us both.>

<I understand. I also understand that your plan may not work.>

<In any case, there will be an attack on this ship at any moment.>

<And?>

<And I'm not sure if I … I don't want to lose you again.>

<If what you say comes to pass, you'll be dead too.>

Henry struggled with what to say next when a shadow fell across the porch, and along with it, a unique cherry aroma. "Conspiring against me again?"

The Captain appeared a few feet away with the setting sun outlining his rotund frame.

Henry said, "Of course we are. Wouldn't you?"

The Captain chuckled and blew out a puff. "There is nothing you can do that I have not anticipated. You are my guests until I deem otherwise. And if you cooperate, I may fulfill my promise to bring you back to Earth."

"And when might that be?"

The Captain's eyes rolled up. "Oh, I would estimate that happening within 200 of your Earth years."

"Two centuries?"

"Don't be alarmed. While you remain on this ship, your natural aging processes will be inhibited. You will not age."

The Captain's eyes focused on Henry. "Of course, that doesn't matter to you, because we insured your body will last, but to Liz … she will remain young for hundreds of years. You will enjoy each other's company without aging, without disease, without the fear of death. What say you to that, Henry?"

"And what if we don't cooperate?"

◇

CHAPTER 65

As a rule, robots do not engage in worrying. A full fifteen minutes had passed and Seth had detected no electrical signal. Was there a short somewhere along the line? Was there an issue with Genz and Marth?

What was he to do? Too much time had gone by. Something was wrong.

He was about to let go when a series of relays clacked up and down the missile's length. The firing circuit came alive. At any moment he expected the missile's solid propellants to ignite, sending the deadly payload soaring into the night sky, and leaving him a smoldering heap of ashes.

But nothing happened.

Seth extended his head through the tunnel's opening and listened. The relays had ceased caterwauling, leaving one barely detectable chirping in their wake, emanating from the nosecone itself—the nacelle with the nuclear warheads.

With one appendage still clasping the cabling, insuring a good connection, Seth reached out and slapped the nosecone. Having elicited no effect, he kicked at it until suddenly a roar erupted from below.

◇

CHAPTER 66

"That would be a shame."

Henry took a step toward the Captain. "You don't know the meaning of the word."

"Now, now, Henry. Earth is hardly your world anymore. In fact, you never did fit in, did you?"

"How do you—"

"I know much of your culture. Humans are a biased lot, a tribal society. You don't trust anything that doesn't look like you. I don't have to remind you how the white race treated yours, do I?"

<He's good.> "Thanks for your concern, but I don't need your sympathy or pity. There's only one race, the human race. We may have had our problems, but they were our problems, not yours."

The Captain chuckled once again, and each time he did, Henry's mood turned darker. Everything was about to come to a bitter end whether the bombs succeeded or failed, nothing would be the same.

The Captain waved at the idyllic surroundings. "Illusion or not, for the next 200 years this is your home. Everything you treasure is here, including your lovely wife. What else could a man ask for?"

"Freedom."

"Another illusion. No one is free, Henry. And all I ask for is some of your time to study your gift."

"Why don't you dissect my brain and figure it out?"

"I have considered that option. It remains a possibility if our analyses fail."

Henry looked back at Liz. <Trust me.> He reached into his pocket and brought out a large kitchen knife.

"The knife is of no consequence."

"Maybe to you, but what about me?" Henry raised the blade to his neck. "Thanks for making it sharp. It should be easy to cut through my neck and slash through those blue arteries. No blue blood, no living brain. End of experiment."

The Captain lowered his pipe. His voice became deeper, commanding. "Henry, what are you trying to accomplish?"

"This." Henry ran the blade across his neck, or at least he tried. His arm refused to move.

"Henry!" Liz came running.

<Stay away.> He put the full force of his concentration on his arm, willing it to move. His artificial muscles knotted with the effort, while the Captain showed no outward concern. <I'm starting to lose grip.>

<Why? Why are you doing this?>

<Distraction. The Soofysh admitted everything here is controlled by his mind. When our bombs arrive, I want him to be busy with me.>

<But you do not know when that will be.>

Henry gasped at the rising pain. <It better be soon. And I'm sorry it has

to end this way.>

<As am I.>

◇

CHAPTER 67

"Damn. What the hell?"

A shooting star lit up the night sky. Its bright trail caught Mike's interest especially because this one took on a spiral course upwards. It winked out and a small burst of light gave birth to three new curvy lines, flying off in different directions like strands of spaghetti.

"Who's shooting off fireworks?"

Two of the spaghetti lines darkened and winked out. The third left a sputtering trail as it plummeted to the ground.

He recalled the bunker. "That's a damn missile."

Mike squinted and brought up a hand. A growing dread in his gut sent him for cover behind a clump of rocks.

"This ain't good, Henry. What did you do?"

◇

CHAPTER 68

Henry gripped the knife in both hands and fought to bring it closer to his neck. His arms ached with the strain, his fingers slipping.

The Captain took a step closer. "You cannot kill yourself. I will not allow it."

<That's it. His weakness.>

Henry spat in the Captain's direction. "As long as I am alive, I will not … we will not … take part … in your damn … experiments."

"Time has a way of changing attitudes. It may take years, tens of years, but eventually you will cooperate." The Soofysh made a half-turn and waved his arm to dismiss the pair. In that instant, the knife vanished.

With control returned to his arms, Henry reached down, grabbed a clump of earth in both hands, and flung it at the Captain. The clod vanished an arm's length from its intended target.

"So childish, but I should have expected such a reaction from a backward species."

As Henry searched for anything to keep the Soofysh occupied, a loud thunderclap nearly knocked him over. The ground beneath his feet pitched back and forth. The Soofysh collapsed to his knees. His pipe flew out of his mouth and his head blurred.

A dark crack formed overhead. The fracture enlarged, sending blinding white jagged streaks across the artificial sky. Bursts of even more intense light erupted along those cracks, each carrying with it a burst of scorching heat.

Henry looked for the Captain, but the Soofysh was gone.

"We need to get the hell out of here."

He grabbed Liz's hand and led the way around the cabin and down the path to its rear. The dense forest cover provided some relief from the growing inferno above. When several tree tops burst into flame, he lifted Liz into his arms and leaped down the trail, unsure of where it ran because of smoke and ash peppering the way ahead. By the time they reached the shoreline every tree behind them was ablaze. Smoldering branches and embers hissed as they landed in the bay.

Blisters appeared on Liz's shoulders.

"The shoreline … it's receding." Henry wrapped his arms about her. Rising steam blanketed the roiling water. "We're going in."

The two slipped under the surface of the water. Liz broke away but kept up with Henry.

<When you get some air, be quick. It's an oven up there.>

A strong and turbulent current pulled them forward. Henry lost sight of Liz. In moments he was sucked into an underwater vortex that spun his body through a serpentine corkscrew.

<The door I told you about. It's open.>

Henry barely finished the thought when he surged through the dark maw. For a moment he flew, untethered to the world. As the water peeled itself away from his body, he sucked in the precious warm air buffeting his face.

<Henry, I'm falling.>

<We both are.>

Moments later they were under water again.

Henry fought to reach the surface. An enormous waterfall cascaded from the ship, pushing him down, threatening to keep him under. He gave in to the raging flow, feeling himself swept along, hopefully away from the wounded ship and its Captain. The nuclear explosion ran through his mind—the mushroom fireball, radiation, fallout, the destruction—why was he still alive?

His head smashed into something. Air became a distant concern, unimportant. He felt water streaming over his body, sending it tumbling into a warm, welcoming glow. The world became liquid and he, a denizen of the deep.

◇

CHAPTER 69

The fluorescents died and the bunker shook, sending Marth dropping to her knees. Rumbling radiated from the concrete floor. A thousand thunderstorms exploded in quick succession.

Her guard disappeared into a dark recess behind an instrument panel. Marth regained her legs and followed the narrow counter to the entry doors where an intense yellow light streamed in through a crack in the seam. Rocks pelted the doorway, followed by a choking cloud of dust.

Marth pushed open the doors and was greeted by a swirling ball of fire and smoke. The roar of the rocket engine fell away and its blazing exhaust column shrank into the heavens. The missile sputtered and exploded into three distinct lines, each of which took on its own curved trajectory downward.

She was frozen, mesmerized by a sight no reptilian had ever seen. The three lines twisted about each other. One vanished, then another. Her eyes were fixed on the third, until some deep instinct for survival called her back into the bunker. Its trajectory continued downward until it met the horizon.

She raced into the bunker and smashed into the guard who had been gawking at the same spectacular sight.

"Get back inside. Hurry."

Marth pulled on the doors which failed to completely close. That is when night became day.

"Help me."

Even with the guard to help, the doors left a narrow opening between them. A moment later, the metal handles became hot, forcing the two to scramble to the rear of the room.

A thud followed, unleashing hell. The entire bunker heaved upward as if smacked by some giant's hand. Anth gripped the counter. Her feet left the floor only to crash back. She rolled under a pile of collapsing instruments. Bookshelves and equipment rained down from above. The doors had sprung wide open to reveal a glow outside and a crackling—the desert was ablaze.

After several minutes, Marth shook off the debris and took a tentative step outside. A miasma of smoke and embers swirled around her, stinging her eyes. A deep crimson radiance in the east blocked out the stars.

"Albuquerque."

She gagged on the bitter air and thought of her people in the city, hoping that they had obeyed her instructions to get out. What of her father?

"I might have killed everyone."

"Unlikely. The Soofysh ship was about 15 miles outside the city. Your people were beyond the blast radius, although there would be no avoiding some heat and a significant pressure wave."

"Who said that?"

"It is I, Seth."

The robot limped to her—his brass sheen darkened by several irregular black streaks across both head and torso. When he drew closer, a missing arm became evident.

"How did you—"

"Councillor Marth, good to see you. I do not know exactly what happened. I recall the missile's engines igniting, then nothing until I regained awareness farther along the tunnel. That is when I realized my arm—" Seth raised a hand within which he grasped the remains of his other arm, "had become dislodged."

Loose strands of wiring caught Marth's eye. The hand at the end of the severed arm continued to grasp the remnants of a cable. She shook her head. "It is a wonder you were not destroyed,"

"A wonder."

She stepped out, gingerly avoiding several floating embers. The robot leaned to one side.

"Are you all right?"

"I am significantly disoriented. You should leave immediately … the fallout … is radioactive … go now." Seth wavered and then collapsed.

Marth ran to him. He lay on the ground with his loose arm atop his chest. Although her knowledge of radioactivity was superficial, she respected its deadly qualities.

"What happened?" The guard emerged from the now skewed bunker, rubbing his head.

"We need to go."

The guard pointed at Seth's prone body. "What is that thing?"

Marth said, "Not a thing ... a person."

Someone stepped into the nuclear twilight.

"Father! How—?"

A second guard came into view at Genz's side. "He demanded that we return, Councilor."

Marth said, "How did you survive the explosion?"

Genz said, "We were far enough away, although the aircar suffered some damage. In fact, we lost power and were forced to land not far from here."

Marth said, "The city … is it still intact?" Her heart weighed heavy with worry for the hundreds of Batrans in Albuquerque.

Genz said, "From what we saw, the destruction was limited to a few buildings, mainly those closest to the blast." He looked at Seth's body. "What of Seth?"

"Damaged by the missile, but I think he will survive."

"He?"

"That robot is unlike any I have ever encountered."

The rumbling in the distance turned all heads.

Genz said, "More explosions."

Marth turned to her guard and said, "Pick up the robot and his arm, and follow us. Your aircar better work."

◇

CHAPTER 70

A car engine coughed and sputtered. Chug-a-chug. Chug-a-chug.

"You coming to dinner or you gonna lie there the rest of the day?"

Henry knew the voice, but it seemed far away.

"Your brother's gonna eat all the fry bread."

Chug-a-chug. Chug-a-chug.

A cool breeze whipped across Henry's face. It was night. Light from nearby dimmed and brightened in cadence with the sound of the stammering engine. He sat in a patch of grass, surrounded by the heady scent of prairie dropseed. It smelled like movie popcorn—buttered popcorn.

He shook his head. The light drew him back to a swaying electric bulb hanging under the eaves of a trailer. He knew the trailer.

"What are ya waiting for?"

Three figures sat around a table. One huddled beneath a buffalo skin. His mom was always cold.

"Where am I?" He asked the question, but knew the answer.

One of the figures stood and raised his arm. "Get your butt over here now."

His father had no patience.

Henry toddled over to the table, surprised at how tall everything was. He sat down on a bench next to his brother, older by two years. James tilted his head and threw Henry a smirk.

James passed away later that summer. The memory stunned him. "What is going on?"

His father sat back down. "I'll tell you what's going on … you're having supper with your family."

The aroma of wohanpi filled his nose. The bison stew was a rare treat. James lifted a ball of fry bread coated with powdered sugar from an empty bowl and waved it in front of Henry's face. Henry reached out to snatch it, but his brother chomped off a piece and laughed.

It was ages since he had a taste of his mother's cooking. She used her sing-song voice. "That's a good boy."

"Mom, you know this is my favorite."

James handed him the remains of the bread.

His father said, "Where you been? We been calling you for a while now."

Henry stopped mid-swallow. Where had he been? The image of a mis-shapen figure flitted by.

"I was taking a nap, wasn't I, dad?"

His father threw him a wide smile. "If only it were so, son."

Henry ran a hand over his jacket and rubbed his pants. "It's weird, dad. I had this feeling I should be all wet."

"Finish up that stew. Then you gotta go."

His mother's hand came up and grabbed his father's shoulder, like she was trying to stop him from talking anymore.

"He has to know, Elizabeth."

Elizabeth. Liz. Yet another image, this time of a smiling young girl. It came and went. Henry's gut tightened.

His mother said, "What's wrong, Henry?"

His father whispered. "He don't know yet, but it'll all come back."

His brother nudged him. "You ain't here, bro. You ain't here, but stay if you want."

Henry dropped his spoon and gazed at the guttering electric bulb. Was he in some kind of a dream? Nothing felt real.

"It ain't no dream, son. You gotta make a decision. Stay here or go back."

The images piled up and made a story, a sad and miserable story that made him want to stay with his family forever. But it was unfinished. There were people depending on him, pulling at him. How could he abandon them?

He glared at his father and gritted his teeth. "I get it."

"Maybe so, maybe not." His father came around and hugged him. "You know we love you and we want you to stay, but you have something important to take care of, don't you, son?"

"It's still my choice, right?"

His father stepped away and nodded.

Henry's legs weakened and he braced himself up with his hands on the table. He felt his face getting wet. He gasped for air. "What is happening?"

His father said, "You've made your decision. No tears, son. We'll still be here when you visit again."

"But I want to stay. You don't know how hard it's been … so many years."

"We know."

The bulb dimmed. The night swallowed the trailer and the table.

A moment later he raised himself on all fours from a torrent of scalding water.

◇

CHAPTER 71

A glowing orange ball rose above the horizon. Mike felt its heat and ducked behind a thrust of rocks. Seconds later, a crack of thunder shook the ground. Gravel erupted from the sand and beat against his stony barrier as they skittered past him. The ground itself seemed to heave.

A minute later it was all over.

The fireball faded, leaving behind a shimmering miasma of lightning bolts and smoke in the distance. Soon, the wind settled and the cool night air returned.

He continued to stare at the whirling specter, ebbing to an angry dark crimson now, until it diffused, leaving behind tinsel-like tendrils of smoke reaching into the sky. It took a few minutes more for those medusa-like tresses to fade away. Mike gripped his handless arm. What he witnessed had him frozen. A newsreel clip flitted through his mind—soldiers at a test site, all wearing sun glasses. They were warned that staring directly at an atomic bomb explosion was likely to blind them.

"What an idiot."

He blinked a few times and looked about. The clear night sky offered up brilliant starlight that highlighted tufts of scrub all around him. Perhaps for the first time since being converted to a mechanical, he thanked the Soofysh for their advanced technology, specifically for the resilient design of his optics.

"I was staring at a nuclear explosion with my one eye. Lucky I didn't blind myself."

Although his emotions were modulated by electronics, he did notice a kind of lighter feeling to his mood. Something had changed.

"The Soofysh, the damn Soofysh. They're not in my head anymore. Maybe they're gone."

He guessed the blast had erupted on or near the Soofysh loading site, some half dozen or more miles away. He tried revving up his boots and, to his surprise, they engaged at full power, sending him cart-wheeling to the desert floor.

"What an idiot. Yeah, I said it again." Speaking out loud had a calming effect, and calming was what he needed most right now. He clambered to his feet and engaged his boots once again, this time with care.

"I'm coming, Henry, and you better be in one piece."

◇

CHAPTER 72

Henry spat out a mouthful of water. His head throbbed and his vision doubled. The image of his family waiting for him would not go away. He yearned to go back, back to whenever it was, whatever it was. Delusion or not, a return to a life before the invasion, to a life with meaning, remained locked in his mind.

No tears, son.

He was sure those words would haunt him for the rest of his life.

The foot-deep water churned in dizzying eddies making it hard to get up without falling back in. Hot air carried smoldering ash that surrounded him and sizzled as it fell into the water. Nothing of the railcars or of any buildings remained standing.

He shouted into the maestrom. "Liz, where are you?"

<Liz, can you hear me?>

Maybe she was unconscious. Maybe worse.

"Maybe this is hell."

He wiped his head with his hand. It came back covered in a slimy goo—blood, bright blue. The sight made him run for no obvious reason. The direction did not matter.

"Liz!" <Liz, can you hear me?>

After falling a few times and calling out her name at every turn, he gave in to the grim realization that she was nowhere nearby. Hope was all he had left, hope that she had survived. His entire being screamed to continue searching for her, but he had more pressing matters to attend to—making sure the Soofysh abomination was gone.

At least he was still alive.

A dark shape, spanning much of the horizon and glowing at the edges, blotted out the stars. An edge of the Soofysh ship touched the ground. Still in one piece, but now with a significant tilt.

"Damn, it's still here."

He waded toward the behemoth a mile or so away, all the while both terrified and impressed that it remained intact. But intact it was not. A number of fractures came into view through the rising steam, some of which were wide enough for a truck to drive through.

Water gushed out from one of the larger breaks in the ship's hull. As he approached, the air grew hotter.

"What's left of the San Francisco Bay, no doubt."

Henry pictured the river of water carrying him and Liz, wending away into the darkness, into oblivion. Being immersed in that water probably saved his life.

<Liz, where are you?>

The pinging of metal snapped his attention back to the ship. He had no time for sorrow. No time for tears. If the creature inside the ship was still alive, it would be severely pissed off.

Henry pushed through the surge of streaming water, and used the edge of the opening to swing himself inside. A smear of light, perhaps what was once the sky, sputtered from up high. The bay had largely emptied, leaving behind steep metallic walls without a hint remaining of the forest cabin and cliff.

Henry stepped through the knee-deep quagmire to get closer to the walls and looked for a way into the rest of the ship. A jagged series of cracks led to an opening some a dozen yards up, dark and irregular, and about the height and girth of a man. Using smaller fissures as hand-holds, Henry clambered into a corridor. He felt his way along its walls, noting the empty alcoves that once held models of planets—planets whose innocent inhabitants, billions of lives, were all gone, reduced to mere Soofysh trophies.

A prickly feeling tickled the back of Henry's neck. Was the Soofysh still alive, and worse still, was it watching? The feeling worsened as he entered what was left of the Captain's library.

A pulsing glow from the ceiling reflected off a mist crawling along the floor. For a moment, Henry expected ghosts to rise from that mist. Books were scattered amid collapsed shelves. The piano stood on end in a corner. Remarkably, its stool remained exactly where it had been earlier.

Henry scanned the perimeter of the room. Fractures laced the walls and ceiling. A large tome caught his eye and its title caught his breath—The Bible. Transfixed for a moment, he wondering why the Soofysh would ever be interested in such a book. Then he thought of the history of the Earth, its many religions, its countless wars—the torturous journey of humankind over thousands of years—generations hopeful to create a better society snuffed out in an instant by a monster with barely a concern other than for itself.

He sighed. "There are still some of us left, you piece of shit."

The piano bench nagged at him.

"Having fun, yet, Henry?"

A tall figure entered the library. Its silvery sheen was all too familiar.

"Mike?"

"None other."

"How—?"

"I saw you climb up."

"How do you feel … I mean—"

"Fine. No delusions, illusions, or whatever. And you?"

"A headache."

"That bump on your head looks serious."

A series of loud cracks interrupted the reunion.

"It's amazing you survived … for that matter, this ship. What are you doing here, Henry?"

"Unfinished business."

"Where's Liz?"

"I wish I knew."

"Damn, hope she made it."

"Me, too."

"The Soofysh is probably dead. Why don't we get out of here?"

"Not yet. If I survived, that bastard might have as well. Besides we don't really know what the hell it is."

"You expect to find it here, in this … library?"

Henry stared at the piano bench. "That bench bother you at all, Mike?" Henry grasped its edge. "It's stuck to the floor."

Mike leaned in and gripped the other side. They looked at each other and heaved. The top of the bench snapped off.

Mike said, "Well, what do you know?"

Henry said, "Buttons. Lots of buttons." He reached in.

"Wait. Those damn buttons could do anything."

"What's the worst thing that could happen?"

Mike scanned the room and shrugged. "Maybe this is it. Go ahead."

Henry punched each button in turn. Nothing. "These probably operate on something like electricity. The power in this ship may be gone."

"Give me a shot." Mike depressed various combinations of buttons to no effect. "Damn. Damn the Soofysh. Damn the ship. Damn all this shit." He struck the console with the back of his hand and a portion of a wall squeaked open.

"You're a genius, Mike."

"That I am."

The two sidled through a narrow opening into another room. The floor was uneven and Henry stumbled.

"You okay, champ?"

Henry shook his head. "My head. Everything is spinning."

"Let me take a look." Mike ran a hand over Henry's head. "Your fake hair has a new part, and there's a nice deep hole … You might have a tear in that titanium skull of yours."

Henry dropped to his knees—his human brain could be injured, or maybe dying. He brought his hands to the floor to steady himself. The room continued in a slow carousel movement.

"Mike, is it me, but is the wall moving?"

Mike took a step nearer one of the walls that extended down from the opaque heights of the ceiling. "The cracks … they're shrinking. It's like the wall is trying to repair itself."

Henry leaned against the opposite wall. "I think so. Some kind of memory metal. You have to admire Soofysh technology."

"What's wrong?"

"This might be happening all over the ship … which means it is repairing itself. We have to find the Soofysh fast."

"I wonder what this room is for?"

"Only one way to find out." Henry staggered forward into the gloom.

"Let me help you. My one eye has a wider range of vision than normal humans."

Henry gave Mike the lead.

As they ambled forward, bright patches along the walls came to life. The sounds of pinging metal rose from a murmur to staccato.

Henry said, "Still dark. What do you see?"

"Not much … wait, there's something ahead … looks like a chair."

The radiance spread across the far wall. A box-like shape on the floor materialized.

Henry reached down to pick up a hunk of metal the size and shape of a baseball bat.

Mike said, "It is a chair, and it's facing … what is that … a screen?" He sauntered over to the chair and sat. "This could be the control room."

Henry swung the metal bat with all his strength, smacking the side of Mike's head. The robot leaned to one side, his body still.

Henry drew nearer, keeping his makeshift weapon at the ready.

Mike straightened and turned his head. "Why did you do that, Henry?"

The calm tone of the voice gave Henry chills. He swung again, smashing the heavy metal into Mike's face. He reeled backwards, teetered out of the chair, and crumpled to the floor with arms and legs twitching.

"Because you're not Mike."

◇

CHAPTER 73

The shock wave hit them broadside and spun the aircar, Marth screamed. "Set it down!"

"No power! The controls do not function, Councilor!"

Genz said, "The nuclear blast … electronics … fail." He recalled a time when Henry had disabled the Soofysh with an electromagnetic pulse and he knew that nuclear explosions unleash electronic havoc.

The aircar tumbled into a downward spin. Genz pushed aside the pilot.

Marth whimpered. "What is happening?"

Genz began succumbing to the dizzying gyration. "There is a restart." Marth and a guard crashed forward into the windshield.

His hands felt disembodied as they fumbled beneath the console. A switch. He slapped at it. The aircar's magneto-powered engines sputtered and hummed. The sound was joy.

Genz pulled up in time to settle the aircar on the ground, turning a potential crash into nothing more than an ordinary landing. He cut the power, and slumped back into the seat. "Marth, are you all right?"

His daughter rolled back into her seat, while her guard angled in next to her. "I was sure we were going to die."

"So was I." Genz took a closer look at Marth. "You are sobbing."

"What did we do? We ended the world. The Soofysh will destroy us all."

The same consideration had bounced around in Genz's mind; however, the Batran relationship with a monster had to end at any price. "We could not go on like this."

"Why not? We had the humans to do the work. The Soofysh were happy with us." Marth pointed at the glow in the sky. "Now look. Do you think they're still happy?"

Genz shook his head. "Soofysh happiness is none of my concern. We need to go there and make sure the Soofysh are destroyed."

"And if they aren't?"

Genz had no answer.

Marth spat. "Do what you want. You have killed us all."

The two sat without speaking for a few minutes.

"That was close, sir." Seth grasped Genz's shoulder and added, "Where are we heading?"

"Glad to see you have regained consciousness."

"I am glad too, sir."

"Looks like your missile landed."

"By the size of the blast, I would say one of the three warheads reached its target."

"Nonetheless, it was quite an explosion. I'm not familiar with the technology, but isn't radioactivity a concern?"

"There will be a high level, enough to kill both humans and Batrans."

Marth said, "Then we cannot go there. Genz, turn around. We'll go home."

Genz said, "Home? Where exactly is that? Albuquerque? Atlanta?" For a fleeting moment he pictured Henry's cabin on the west coast. Simpler times.

"Anywhere, but here."

Seth said, "The radiation that is dangerous to life has not fallen yet, but will soon."

Genz said, "Then we go and find out if Henry is still alive. It is the least we can do."

Marth said, "Henry, Henry, Henry … he's all you think about. What has he done for us? Only bring the wrath of the Soofysh—."

"Enough, Marth. He is my friend, and that is all that matters."

Genz turned to Seth. "Is he still alive?"

"Hard to say, sir. But he is my friend too."

"Then we go."

The aircar rose and flew off toward the ebbing glow on the horizon.

◇

CHAPTER 74

The floor swallowed Mike's body, leaving behind nothing but a smooth surface. The wall cracks continued to coalesce.

"Damn. What the hell do I do now?"

As if in answer, the wall screen glowed brighter. An image flickered on—a line drawing. An animated cartoon character in full color bounced into view. A rabbit with drooping ears and a carrot in its hand hopped along a forest trail. After taking a bite of the carrot, it turned to look at Henry and said, "What's up?"

Henry tried in vain to fight off the utter incomprehensibility of the scene. Here he was, trying to destroy the Soofysh, a mass-murdering fiend and now he faced a cartoon character. What the hell was the Soofysh playing at?

"What is this? What are you?"

"Henry, you should be saying, 'You wascaly wabbit, wait 'til I get my hands on you'."

The rabbit took another bite and a step forward with its face taking up most of the screen. Over-sized eyes bulged out while its pupils rolled around like little black marbles.

A distraction. The Soofysh was buying time. It wasn't ready to deal with him while the ship burned energy, repairing itself.

Henry nodded. "I get it. I know what you're up to."

The explosion may not have killed the Soofysh, but it was clearly weakened, maybe more vulnerable. There was no other explanation for the cartoon. It needed to keep Henry occupied—an act of desperation. Ironically, it was the same tactic Henry used. He had to find it before it managed a full repair.

"Do you, Henry?" The rabbit danced in a circle, singing some mindless tune.

The ship and the Soofysh—maybe they were one and the same. Henry recalled his last encounter about a century ago. It was a small saucer then, and when it encountered an exploding tank shell, everything disappeared— the Soofysh and its ship. Whatever technology was afoot, it had to do with the manipulation of matter. A self-repairing ship might fit the definition of a living entity more than a mechanical marvel. The thought sent a shudder through him.

A second rabbit showed up and stole the first rabbit's carrot. They chased each other in a wider circle. Meanwhile, Henry heard the walls chattering, squealing.

He tore his attention away from the screen. The Soofysh may be weak at the moment, likely worried that Henry might come across its Achilles' heel. But where was that heel?

The shimmering light from the wall screen outlined a few details of the room. One of the wall panels opposite had a different texture and part of it assumed the shape of a door.

Henry pushed against it to no avail. Several other rabbits joined the circle and the group broke into a marching parade, singing "Henry! Henry! Henry!"

He ran a hand across its corrugated surface and stopped at a protrusion. The singing behind him became chaotic, the wailing alley cats.

A single press on the bump triggered the panel to slide aside, releasing a plume of steam through the opening which remained narrow. The panel may have hung up or was reluctant to fully open. That last thought gave Henry pause—if the ship was Soofysh, then it, too, would be his enemy, seeking out any means possible to stop him, or possibly destroy him in a fit of unrestrained revenge. Survival had to be its all-consuming goal, a trait common to all life forms.

Henry readied himself for a leap through the opening.

"Need a hand?"

The silvery sheen outlined an all-too-familiar figure.

"Not you again."

"Hey, good to see you, too."

Henry raised the metal bat.

"Now, hold on. It's me, Mike." He raised both arms in a defensive move.

"Your hand. Did I do that?"

"Lost it in an accident. I should've been here sooner. Anth'll be pissed off."

Henry lowered his weapon. "You sound like the real Mike."

"The real Mike? What have I been up to, Henry?"

"It's what the Soofysh have been up to."

"That gash on your head … that must be it. You seeing things?"

"There's nothing wrong with my head. Tell me, what do you know about Liz?"

"Seriously? She was your wife. She died long ago. Are you feeling okay?"

"Nothing else?"

"This is stupid."

"I need you to answer."

"You loved her. And after she died … you took your life."

"Anything about a new Liz?"

"What are you talking about?"

Henry lowered his head and sagged against the edge of the opening. "You're Mike all right. There was another Mike who knew of the clone, a Liz copy created by the Soofysh. You wouldn't know that."

"Now you're sounding crazy again."

"I'll catch you up later. First I have to finish what I started. We may be running out of time. The Soofysh is repairing this ship and probably itself in the bargain. I've got to find it before that happens."

"You've just unloaded a lot of crap on me and … I have to say you sound a little nuts."

"I don't expect you to come with me. In fact, it might be better if you got the hell off this ship. Don't get me wrong. I appreciate that you came, but this fight is mine, all mine."

Mike rested his intact hand on the edge of the opening. "Listen, Henry. The Soofysh have been screwing around with me for as long as I can remember. If you think being in this body is some kind of delight … I have to tell you, I miss being human. That's something they took away from me. This here's the last dance, and Henry, I'm with you."

A creaking sound made Mike's hand jump. "What the hell? Did the panel move just now?"

Henry said, "Like I said, it's fixing itself." He paused a second and said, "Mike, about your eye—I'm sorry."

"Forget it. That's in the past. 'Sides I would have done the same. Right now there's bigger fish—."

"Yeah, yeah. I'm glad to have you by my side."

As the two slipped through the opening, Henry heard it snap shut behind them.

"Are we falling?"

Mike said, "Not that I can tell … I feel like I'm floating."

Immersed in complete darkness, Henry had no sense of the size of the room, or any sense of up and down. "I can't tell if I'm moving."

"This sucks."

The odor of the air had become heavy, oily.

"Smells fishy."

"Do you feel that?"

Mike sounded farther away, like he was drifting off. "Feel what?"

"A breeze. I feel a breeze."

"Maybe that's a way out."

"Trouble is … how do we get to it?"

"Hey, I bumped into something." Mike's voice drifted farther off. "It's round … the size of a big beach ball … soft, too. I got my arms around it … and—"

"Mike!"

"Mike!"

◇

CHAPTER 75

The breeze ticked up into a gale and slammed Henry into a wall, sliding him along its rubbery face. He tried to gain purchase, to stop his movement, but there was nothing to grab. Bouncing along its oddly warm surface, he resigned himself to a fate his imagination suggested would likely be grim.

A feeling of utter loss welled up in Henry's mind, but it wasn't his. His thoughts had latched onto something outside himself, something desperate, something struggling to survive. An image of the ship sprang up, and along with it, the ghostly shape of a fetus.

"Henry!"

Mike's voice sounded nearer.

"I'm here!"

"So am I. But where is here?"

As if in answer, a sliver of brightness appeared.

"Go for that light, Mike."

They snaked along the wall with the wind nudging them onward. The narrow opening grew into a jagged tear, large enough to slip through.

Mike said, "Is this a way out?"

The two tumbled into an opaque white world. Seconds later, Henry soft-landed on a solid surface, thankful that some semblance of gravity had returned. Regardless of which way he turned his head, everything looked the same—featureless and very white.

Mike lifted himself up. "I guess that wasn't the exit."

At least Mike provided a visual point of reference—he was the only non-white object within view, although his metallic sheen made him a challenge to see.

"We're still stuck inside the ship." Henry pointed up at a tiny black scar in the sky. "That must be where we came from."

"Weird."

Henry teetered and collapsed onto the billowy flooring.

"You okay?"

"Dizzy. It's this place. Did you notice how warm the floor is?"

"It's a wonder it didn't go up in the blast." Mike pointed out a few drops of blue on the floor. "You're bleeding, Henry."

"It must be the hole in my head." Henry rose. "I can handle it."

Mike came alongside and wrapped an arm around Henry's torso. "We can handle it."

"Everything feels alive."

"More like creepy." Mike paused a moment to look around. "Then … you know, it does sort of look like—."

"A cell?"

"I was going to say an egg."

"That's a cell, too. The Soofysh were collecting ore—all the stuff the

Batrans brought here. I wonder."

"Sounds like extortion."

"The Batrans considered it payment for services rendered, but I'm starting to think it was for something else, something critical to the Soofysh."

Mike slapped the side of his head. "Food?"

"Food. Fuel. Raw materials. Whatever this ship needs to keep going."

"I hope it gets indigestion."

"Yeah … I'm hoping for something more deadly."

Mike pulled a slow 360. "I'm not seeing any way out of here."

"It doesn't matter. I don't plan on leaving. That hole up there … we need to go back."

"Back?"

"The beach ball you hugged … I don't think that's what it was. Are your magic boots working?"

Mike powered his feet and hovered over the flooring. Henry climbed up on his back and in seconds they floated outside the frayed opening.

Henry said, "The wind died down."

Mike said, "Maybe it was a leak … coming out of this hole."

"I think we're running out of time, and I don't have a clue what to do."

"Let's start with my beach ball."

The light from the opening fell on the sphere inside, casting it as a blur, a vague suggestion in the deep dark. The lack of gravity allowed them to push off the wall and head toward the enigmatic orb. The problem was immediate—there was no obvious way to steer, or to tell how far away the sphere was.

"Hold on. I can get us near it." Mike kicked in his boots and almost immediately, they crashed into the sphere, rippling its soft surface.

Henry said, "This is way bigger than a beach ball."

"I swear it was smaller when I ran into it."

"Is that humming I hear?" Henry touched his head against its soft, plastic-like surface and sure enough, the sphere sang in low tones, like a basso warming up. The undulating riddle looked to be about six or seven yards wide.

Henry ran a hand over its surface. "It does feel alive."

"What the hell are we going to do with it?"

"Are you seeing this?"

The membranous orb brightened. Something inside stirred and glowed.

Henry heard a metallic click and Mike screamed. "There's something on my back!"

◇

CHAPTER 76

"So good to see you again, sir."

A shiny bronze head bobbed up behind Mike.

"Seth! Damn, you surprised us."

Mike said, "You scared the crap out of me."

Henry laughed and said, "How did you get in here?"

"I climbed up to a room that appeared to be a library. The controls on a piano bench led me here."

Henry said, "You make it sound easy. Great job with the missile launch."

"I am glad you survived, sir. Marth and Genz managed the actual launch, but only one of the three warheads reached the target."

"Are those scorch marks?"

"I was a bit too close to the launch, sir."

"Your arm?"

"It is with Marth and Genz. They are outside in an aircar. I see that you are injured, sir."

"Yeah. It's just a hole in my head."

Seth said, "And Mike, your hand—."

"One is all I need."

Seth said, "We cannot stay here, sir. There is the question of radiation. The fallout has begun."

"Even inside here? Are we in danger?"

"Mike and I are less likely to be affected, although the ionizing radiation may affect our electronics. It is your organic brain that is of concern, sir."

Mike said, "Yeah, with that hole in your head, I could say something here."

The sphere's surface swelled and shook off the trio, leaving them floating a few feet away. Part of its surface protruded out and took on a humanoid shape that coalesced into an old man with a pipe in his mouth.

"Isn't this special? Henry and his two pets."

The Captain was back; however, some details were amiss—an absent nose and mottled face were among those most obvious. Was the Soofysh struggling?

Henry said, "So, it's true. You and this ship … you're one and the same."

"Very smart, Henry, but what you did was not, although your bomb created no more than a minor setback. We will be whole in no time at all, whereupon severe measures will be taken."

The humanoid spectacle shrunk and became one with the heaving sphere.

Henry said, "The Soofysh is right. We can only watch the ship, and it, pull themselves together."

"Sir, a suggestion?"

Henry said, "Go ahead, Seth."

Mike said, "This should be good."

"I brought something with me that may help."

Henry said, "What? I don't see anything."

"It is outside, sir, and too heavy for me to carry up here."

Mike said, "We don't know which way that is."

"No problem. I left the doorway ajar. I suggest Mike gather us up. I will point out the way."

Moments later, the three drifted away from the throbbing mass and into a deeper darkness.

Henry said, "Can't see a thing."

When they bumped into a wall, Seth guided them to a narrow gap.

Mike said, "How?"

Henry pointed to an object in the gap. "This is how." Half a book protruded through the opening—a bible showing the way.

When they were back in the library, Henry said, "It looks different in here."

Mike said, "Yeah, those shelves weren't on the wall when I came through."

Seth said, "Mike, please go outside. The object we need is near the opening."

Mike said, "And what does it look like?"

Seth said, "A missile nose cone, somewhat damaged."

◇

CHAPTER 77

The groaning of metal reshaping itself was getting on Henry's nerves. Several bookcases crawled up along the walls and set themselves in place, complete with books.

"What's taking him so long?"

Sharp footfalls interrupted the cacophony. Mike stepped out of a shadow lugging a three foot long object roughly cone-shaped. "This son-of-a-bitch is damn heavy. And you do know I have only one hand?"

Seth said, "It is mostly made of tempered steel and uranium, and an explosive device which is the detonator."

Henry said, "Why didn't it explode?"

Seth said, "Corrosion, sir. In layman terms, it's stuck; however, I am sure I can encourage the device to detonate."

Henry said, "What do you mean, 'encourage'?'

Seth said, "Once primed, I'll take it back into the nucleus of this ship and set off the charge. It may or may not result in a successful nuclear fission, but I surmise it represents the only chance we have of ending the Soofysh. I will wait for you two to get out. Use the aircar to get to a safe distance, at least five miles away."

Henry was taken aback by Seth—his most trusted companion. In a desolate world with few humans remaining, he offered to sacrifice himself. Greater love hath no man.

Henry said, "No."

"But, sir—."

"This isn't your fight, Seth. We've come a long way together, but—"

"Sir, if I may. You are human. I am but a robot, in other words, expendable. I will feel nothing."

Mike said, "He's got a point, Henry."

"Sorry, guys. You're not getting it. Everything I've ever loved is gone. The Soofysh took my wife. The Soofysh made me like this. The Soofysh have murdered countless souls not only here but in God knows how many other planets. It was my fight a century ago, and it's my chance to finish it now.

"And Seth, you're not a robot to me." Henry nudged Mike away and pried open the nosecone's compartment. "What exactly needs to be 'encouraged' in here?"

After Seth explained, Henry lifted the bulky mechanism. "You're right, it's heavy."

The hole leading to the Soofysh inner chamber began to shrink. "Hurry, help me get this thing through."

At the opening, Henry said, "You two have been with me practically forever. I consider you my friends. And, Seth—"

"I know, sir. I feel the same way."

Henry turned toward the sphere. "Give me a push."

The pitch dark enveloped him and his bearings went astray. The glowing nucleus spun, as if orbiting around him. It blinked, and all he could do was to keep a tight grip on the nosecone. He had trouble organizing his thoughts, but was sure he had to connect something to something. What was it? The question had hardly ended before a dead black world swallowed the ragged remnants of his consciousness.

◇

CHAPTER 78

Henry squeezed his eyes shut and opened them wide. He was moving. Rather, he sat in a chair in something that was moving.

"Is this a trick?"

He recalled the many times the Soofysh had set up shop in his head.

"Sir, you passed out. We are in an aircar."

"What about—?"

"When you lost consciousness, Mike stepped up."

Henry looked out the window of the aircar. Early morning sunlight reflected off the Soofysh ship in the distance. It looked whole and had straightened itself out. In fact, it looked ready to take off.

"It's untouched."

"Did you really think your crude weapon would destroy me?"

The voice came from the rear. The two Batran guards that had been sitting there turned into a sickly pink haze. The Captain leaned forward and made a show of waving a blaster weapon. "I am going to enjoy this."

Marth said, "I told you. Look at what you've done. We are doomed."

Genz said, "Calm down. If he wanted us dead, we would already be."

"How quaint—father and daughter. Not to worry, you two will be dead … all of you Batrans … everyone on this planet will be dead. Failure to comply carries a hefty penalty. What a waste. I'll have to start all over again. This time I'll be careful to choose reliable partners."

Henry said, "Don't you mean slaves?"

"Business. It is all business."

"Your business is about to close down permanently. And with it, you."

"An empty threat. You cannot comprehend my power. Over the millennia I have accumulated the technology of hundreds of civilizations. It is my desire to be helpful, to share in that bounty, to be of benefit to others."

"What a crock. We've been over this. You're nothing but a murderer and extortionist. It's time to put you out with the garbage."

The Captain shook his head in a disturbingly human manner. "Henry, it's a shame you did not take my offer … you and Liz would have spent a pleasant life together, and at the same time made significant contributions to science."

"Yeah, your specimens, and that was your one weakness, the one thing you couldn't resist. You had to find out how we communicated. You were consumed by that desire and you let your guard down. After all, what could the tattered remains of human technology do to someone so powerful, so clever … so damned conceited?"

"I admit you did surprise me, but surprises are over. My ship and I will be fully restored shortly. And when we are, we will clean this place up. I have a waiting list of eager colonizers who would love to settle here.

"A few fly-overs will be sufficient to deliver the agent required. This time I will insure complete sterilization of all bipeds, Batran and human."

Marth said, "But can you not give us another chance? The attack on you was not our idea. This Henry thing … it was him. I tried to stop him."

She paused to whimper in a convincing if somewhat overdone manner. "We promise that the humans will not interfere. We will be happy to provide you with anything you need."

The Captain aimed his blaster at Henry. "You know, I think I do not want to wait. I have to admit, there is something of an enjoyment in removing the irritation you have become."

Seth inserted himself between Henry and the Captain, "You will need to destroy me first."

"A fine toy, Henry … one that I may have overdesigned."

Henry wrapped his arms around Seth and closed his eyes. "A friend is … something you'll never have."

Seconds went by. The Soofysh was behaving in an entirely uncharacteristic manner. With its staggering resources, it could have ended Henry in a number of imaginative and likely painful ways. Instead it opted to use a Batran weapon.

Henry said, "What are you waiting for?"

"Something in my ship. I feel it."

That was the moment. Henry grabbed the extended blaster. The Soofysh and he rolled from side to side in the rear seat, pulling at the weapon with one hand and pummeling with the other.

The aircar landed with a jarring bounce and spun to a stop with passenger doors splayed open. Henry grabbed the Captain's arm and shook it, half-expecting it to turn into some ethereal mush. But the arm remained solid, as did the Captain. The blaster flashed and a hole appeared in the aircar's roof.

Seth launched himself into the melee. A beat later, he and the weapon flew out of the aircar. Disarmed, the Captain grappled with Henry and the two rolled out onto the desert floor.

Henry let loose a blow to the Captain's head. "Having a problem with your disappearing act?"

The Captain grumbled and ran head-first into Henry, sending the two sprawling. "I have some business to attend to. You'll be doing the disappearing."

The Soofysh staggered to his feet and began to fade, but failed to dematerialize. He looked about as if confused.

Henry pointed at the horizon. "Maybe that's your problem."

The mushroom cloud was unmistakable. A churning incandescent ball rose over the horizon, and gave birth to a fiery orb rising from its center.

"What have you done?"

"Say good bye to your ship."

The Captain fell to his knees. "This cannot be."

Henry drew closer. "Everything has an end, even you."

The Captain's white hair turned dark. His clothing squirmed and in moments, he became a dark outline with only a hint of a humanoid shape. That shape elongated and stretched out, snake-like, without an obvious head or tail.

"Is that what you really are? A damn snake?"

The snake continued to elongate and widen until it became several yards long. A dragon's skull formed at the nearest end. Yellow-green eyes filled in its sunken sockets while a toothy mouth erupted below them.

Henry felt the air heat up, but it was not due to the dragon.

Seth tugged at Henry. "Sir, we need to get in the aircar. The shock wave will reach us any second.”

Henry tore his attention away from the Soofysh monstrosity. “You’re right.” He motioned to Genz and Marth as he and Seth ran back to the aircar.

They leaped in and slid the doors shut in time to see the windows crack as a fierce storm roiled outside. The heat in the car mounted. Marth and Genz hunkered down beneath the console, while Henry joined Seth behind a seat. Rocks and desert scrub pounded the car, sending it rolling.

When the dust settled, the car lay on its side. Henry pried the door open and chanced a look around. Dust devils littered the landscape scooping up pebbles and debris.

Henry heaved himself out and landed on a thin strip of spongy flesh. More remnants of the Soofysh dotted the landscape. The sound of a thump nearby turned his head. A dragon’s head stared at him with its sightless eyes and mouth frozen in a wide grin. Its body, oozing oily fluids, leaned on the roof of the aircar.

“Damn. You’re still alive?”

Its mouth barely moved—the voice, a whisper. “I thought of you as a father thinks of a son. I created you.”

“A father? You don’t know the meaning of the word.”

Dark spittle ran down its jagged chin. “And this is how you repay me?”

“You’re mad. I owe you nothing. I only wish you could suffer as much as the millions of souls you murdered.”

“I am dying. I have fear.” The dragon worm slid off the aircar and col-lapsed into a viscous elongated mass. Its body trembled as its head reared up. “And I will take you with me.”

A deformed wing emerged from the writhing mass and shot straight out at Henry. Seconds later it exploded in a blue haze. A second explosion vaporized what was left of its head, leaving the rest to liquefy and percolate into the dry desert soil.

Seth stood at the aircar doorway and waved a blaster at Henry. "I thought it would be prudent to end its suffering, sir."

"More than prudent, Seth."

The two stared at the stain on the ground that had been one of the most feared entities in the galaxy. After a minute, Genz stepped out and said, "Henry, help us get this thing upright."

Henry joined the others and in short order the aircar was set to go. As he clambered in, he gave the Soofysh remains one last look.

Seth said, "You have succeeded, sir. You have destroyed the Soofysh."

Henry patted Seth on the head. "You know better."

When they reached altitude, Henry said, "Can you see it? The ship, is it still there?" All that Henry saw were dark, roiling clouds.

Seth said, "Nothing remains, sir. It is all gone."

Henry thought of Mike. "So is a friend."

Seth said, "He wished you to know that he was happy to help, to put a stop to the madness, sir."

"His own as well as ours."

"Why so, sir?"

"He fought to be himself every step of the way. That artificial brain—"

"He worried he would lose his humanity, sir?"

Henry nodded. They sat in the car in silence as it glided over the desert, listening to the sound of the wind across its broken windows and gaping hole in its roof. Minutes seemed like hours. When they landed to size up their situation and decide on a path forward, the winds had died down. The sun peered out from beneath the dark atomic mist in the distance like it was waking, wondering what all the fuss was about.

A tapping on a window drew everyone's attention.

A giant rusty robot bent down to look inside the aircar and said, "Can I be of assistance?"

◇

CHAPTER 79

A woman on a horse awaited them at the trail leading to Chaco Canyon. Henry was the first one out. "Chooli, it's great to see you."

The woman leaped to the ground and embraced him. "We did not know what happened to you. Anth was sure you had perished. Your head … are you all right?"

"More or less. But enough about me."

Chooli stepped back, startled by a pair of Batrans joining them.

Genz said,"Good to see you again, Chooli."

Chooli said, "Anth mentioned you. You are her … close friend?"

"Very close."

The second Batran, a bit shorter, approached.

Chooli said. "And who is this?"

"My name is Marth. I am—"

"Genz! Marth!" Anth stepped out of a tunnel entrance along the steep canyon wall and loped over to the group.

"Mother, you're alive?"

The three Batrans wrapped their arms around each other and fell silent.

"It is quite moving, sir."

"That it is, Seth. Those three had been separated for quite a while."

More figures clambered out of the aircar.

Henry waited a moment to get Anth's attention. "This is Evan. We picked him up on the way here."

"We have met."

"And his family, Claire and little Mowgli."

Mowgli hugged Anth's leg.

"I remember this one, too."

Claire said, "It is hard for me … Batrans were never—"

"Kind?"

Evan said, "This is what I told you about, Claire. Look around. There are people like us here. We will be safe."

Claire kept a grip on Evan and said, "But these are Batrans." She whimpered, not with glee, but with fear.

"Hey, Evan!" A hefty figure came running out of the tunnel entrance pulling a woman along behind him.

Evan said, "Seedy!"

"Look who I found!"

"Claire, look!"

"Bee!" Claire loosened her grip on Evan and ran. The two women embraced and cried, while the men did much the same thing. Henry was sure that this time the tears flowed from joy.

Chooli said, "Are you hiding others in that car?"

Henry laughed. "I'm afraid that's it for now. But there will be more."

◇

Tall tales filled the afternoon along with food and drink. By the time evening had arrived, so had exhaustion. Henry bid the Batrans a good night and retired to a room he shared with Seth who flexed his freshly repaired arm.

"How does it feel?"

"Like new, sir. And your head?"

"Anth did a good job. The headaches are gone. It was good to see her and Genz together again. And their daughter … the leader of the colony back in Atlanta. It may take some doing to have her see things differently."

"Did you convince her about humans? To free them?"

"She's headstrong, but logical. With the Soofysh gone, they won't need to keep mining to the extent they have, and it means no need for slavery."

"I hope so, sir."

"Why do humans concern you so much, Seth?"

"I should have told you this long ago, sir."

"Okay, what are you keeping from me?"

"As you know, the Soofysh created me."

"I know that. We saw a number of similar models when we first encountered the Soofysh back in Cheyenne Mountain."

"Correct, but they were incomplete."

"In which way?"

"In a rather important way, sir."

Henry brought his arm around the robot. "What is it that you're trying to tell me, Seth?"

"I am not quite the robot you think I am. Like you, I too have a human brain … a part of one, actually."

Henry shook his head. "How?"

"It was Mike who told me this … before—"

"Before he set off the bomb."

"It was when he revived us back in Atlanta. It would appear I was the first successful transplant, but the Soofysh only retained a portion of my human cerebrum probably to see if their technology would work. My previous life is a blank, but I do remember being placed near your cabin to look after you, to ensure no harm came to you."

"Because the Soofysh was studying the telepathy between me and Liz?"

"I believe so."

"Huh, that's an eye-opener. Wait a minute … I've never seen you eating. Wouldn't you need to eat?"

"My electronics were designed to provide sufficient energy for my organic tissue. This discovery opened my eyes too, sir."

Henry chuckled. "That's a cliché, Seth, but this sheds a whole new light on our relationship."

"Another cliché, sir."

"You're something else, Seth. I can't expect you to keep serving me. You're human and deserve your freedom."

◇

CHAPTER 80

Sequoyah poked his head into Henry's room. "Awake. Awake. Come."

The words were few, but the agitation was clear.

Henry and Seth were followed Sequoyah through the maze of tunnels leading to the outside. The morning sun snaked shadow lines on the red sandstone making it difficult to see what Sequoyah pointed at.

Seth said, "There, sir."

A silvery glint bobbed up over the horizon. It grew and others joined it. Something marched toward the settlement, something metal.

Dozens of natives spread themselves over the tops of the stony outcroppings surrounding the canyon, armed with bows, some with Batran blasters. The air grew still as if the tension itself brought the wind to a halt.

As the advancing figures took shape, several tall ones came into focus—giant robots Henry was thoroughly familiar with—the same ones in charge of mining operations.

Seth said, "Wagons, sir."

About two dozen wagons ran alongside the robots blurred by patches of flying dust. People filled each one. They waved and hollered. Their voices rang with delight.

Henry said, "Son of a gun. That bucket of rust came through."

Sequoyah ran out onto the canyon floor and waved to the surrounding cliffs, calling off the armed reception.

As Anth approached, Henry said, "What do you think?"

"It is gratifying. I feel this is a new beginning. And we owe all of it to you."

Henry patted Seth on the head. "There were many others who were willing to give up everything to see the Soofysh come to an end."

What would Mike have said now? Aw shucks, I ain't no hero.

Anth said, "You were the key, Henry. No matter what anyone says or thinks, without you none of this would have happened. I have my daughter back, and Genz. There is a path forward for all of us now." She looked at Marth who stepped out at that moment. "With her help we will work out a way to share the Earth as equals."

For a fleeting moment Henry pictured his family living in a trailer on a reservation. They had sacrificed everything to send him to school, to educate him, to make sure he would be a success. And there was that special night at the dinner table, a dream or a vision, he would never know. No tears, son.

He brought a finger to his eye.

"Is everything all right, sir?"

"It will be, Seth. It will be."

◇

CHAPTER 81

Genz said, "Quite a mess."

Henry said, "It's home. Where's the rover? He pointed at a narrow gap between newly grown trees in his front yard. "It was right there."

Genz steered the aircar to the meadow. Several pines sprouted from high grass which waved green and yellow under patches of morning sunlight. The surrounding foliage could have been tossed up by an impressionist's soft brush strokes.

"We picked it up when we retrieved your bodies."

Seth said, "I can see the cabin, sir."

"How many times have I told you not to call me sir?"

"A habit, sir."

Henry shook his head and focused on the one-story log structure. The wood-tiled roof was largely intact along with windows—surprising for something over a century old; however, even before they touched down, some discouraging details emerged.

Henry said, "It's going to need some work."

Genz said, "I do not recall a tree growing out of your front porch."

"Yeah, there's that."

The three porch steps had been swallowed by a greedy mass of shrubs.

Seth skittered up to the screen door and opened it. "The hinges still work, sir." When the door fell to the side, he added, "Perhaps not one hundred percent, sir."

Henry held back a chuckle. He wandered around the cabin to the forest edge in the rear. New growth had sprung up, bringing the woodland closer. He ambled between a few trees and stopped at a mound of dried out pine needles and leaves.

"I'm still here, Liz." Henry bent down and cleared the stone and a smaller one next to it. "Hey, Wolfie, you keeping her company?"

Henry recalled how inseparable the giant wolf and Liz had been—playful and protective of each other. And there was the time Wolfie undid her knitting on purpose. He dropped to his knees while grasping the top of Liz's stone. "Damn, I miss you, honey. You wouldn't believe what I've been through. Without you, everything's so meaningless."

"I miss her too, sir, but your life has been anything but meaningless."

Henry rose, finding Seth and Genz standing nearby.

"Genz said, "Forgive the intrusion, Henry. We all miss her."

"I appreciate that … I just can't … I need to stay here for a while."

Henry turned back to the stone markers while the other two made their way to the cabin,

◇

It was early next morning when Henry entered the kitchen. Seth and Genz had done some housecleaning overnight. Dishes were sorted, counter tops and table were cleaned up. The smell of fresh coffee surprised him.

"There's no way you made coffee."

Seth said, "I found some dried out beans, sir. I used water from the hand pump and some tricks in the brewing."

Henry wasn't about to ask what those tricks may have been, and he was sure he didn't want to know.

"Good to know the pump's still working."

Genz said, "It took some effort."

Henry sipped and sat at the kitchen table. "Woah, not everything is the way I remember it."

Genz said, "I warned him, but he insisted."

"That's okay." Henry rose from his seat and poured the coffee into the sink. "It's the thought."

He walked past the entryway and into the den. A pat on the sunken couch, released a cloud of dust. Some wall hangings yet remained. One was of particular interest.

"My Colt. It's still here."

Genz said, "You'll find your bow in the corner."

Henry removed the 1873 Colt revolver from the wall display and plopped into the sagging couch. After a second plume of dust settled he gave the weapon a closer look, bringing it up to smell it. He twirled the cylinder and said, "This has been cleaned, and recently."

Genz said, "That was my idea. I found some oil in the drawer, but I'm not sure about the bullets."

"Given that they've been sitting here for some time, I wouldn't be sure either."

Henry caught sight of his bow and said, "They probably have the same chance of working as that bow."

Genz said, "We found no string."

"That's fine." Henry replaced his revolver on the wall. "It's one more detail I need to attend to. There's plenty of time." He turned to gaze out the front window.

Seth said, "Do you hear it?"

Henry scanned what little of the sky peeked in through the trees. A dot emerged from behind a branch. "Are we expecting visitors?"

Seth said, Yes, sir."

The vehicle landed next to Genz's aircar in a narrow clearing. Anth and Marth emerged and met Henry at the base of the porch.

"What brings you two out here?"

Anth said, "We came to wish you the best of luck. I don't understand why you chose to live out here, alone." Her gaze wandered to the rear of the cabin. "Well, perhaps I do."

Henry nodded.

Marth said, "And we wanted you to know that our Atlanta colony has agreed to free the humans. The word is out, and all our colonies will follow suit. Humans will be welcomed in the city as equals, although I expect many will decide to leave."

Henry said, "Can't blame them."

Anth said, "They will be free to settle wherever they feel comfortable."

"How many are we talking about?"

"Several hundred in Atlanta, but there are others in smaller settlements throughout the south."

Henry mulled over the low number and wondered if it was enough to carry on the human race. There was a good chance these were the last days of humanity. The Soofysh may have been right—change was inevitable. Nature would take its course, and perhaps the Soofysh was part of that process.

"That's certainly good news. I appreciate you two coming all the way out here to give me the official word." Henry waved at the cabin. "I'm sorry, but we're a bit limited with food supplies at the moment. There is some coffee, but I would advise against it."

Marth ran back to the aircar and came out holding a deer carcass by its antlers. She dragged it to the group and smiled. "Do you think this would be enough?"

◇

Henry balanced his heels on the porch banister. His chair creaked much like the wooden railing. A mild morning breeze carrying the sweet lavender perfume of pine allowed Henry a brief glimpse of the lone aircar crouching between swaying grasses. He ran his hand along the rough bark of the skinny pine tree erupting through the porch floor.

Seth ambled alongside. "Do you want me to cut this tree down, sir?"

Henry considered the sapling, how it struggled to live. "I don't know. Maybe we'll fix up the porch and let this fellow keep going. What do you say?"

"Fascinating idea, sir."

Henry had given up chiding Seth for using such a formal address.

"What are you thinking about, sir?"

"Not much, Seth."

"Are you content, sir?"

Henry thought back to when he had attempted to kill himself. Losing Liz had defeated him. Now, he felt differently. Humans were no longer hunted down They were finding their way through the remnants of their ancestors' world. The picture gave him some hope. Maybe he had made a difference, though the irony did not escape him—at one time Native Americans were given much the same freedom. The Batran colonies would be expected to remain a challenge. Old habits were hard to break. In the end, the Earth was changing. For the better or the worse, he was a part of it.

"Yeah, you could say that. The trouble is that being content is a temporary condition." Henry stood and said, "Look at this place. It's been a week, and we've hardly made a dent."

"I have been trying, sir. Your den is nearly back to the way it used to be. I've planted herbs in the garden and rebuilt the chicken coop, although I still have to find some chickens."

"Commendable. And I have been slumming."

Henry walked out to the front yard and grabbed a rust-streaked scythe. "Time to mow the lawn."

As Seth returned to the cabin, probably intending to prepare breakfast using the supplies the Batrans had left them, Henry gazed out at the back meadow. Satisfied with all the work it took to chop down the trees that had blocked his view of the two gravestones, he nodded and turned back to the chore at hand. He was mid-swing when he heard a whisper.

<Henry.>

{{{END}}}

ABOUT THE AUTHOR

As a scientist, **Dr. Arthur M. Doweyko** has authored 140+ scientific publications and patents, invented novel 3D drug design software, and shares the 2008 Thomas Alva Edison Patent Award for the discovery of Sprycel, a new anti-cancer drug. He has had a life-long interest in art as well as science, notably writing and painting.

His favorite writing genres are science fiction and fantasy with a particular fascination for Serling's *Twilight Zone* episodes, as reflected in his short stories. He is the author of several award-winning works: Novels *Algorithm* and *As Wings Unfurl* and numerous short stories, many of which appear in his anthologies *My Shorts* and *Captain Arnold*. *Captain Arnold* garnered the 2021 Royal Palm Literary Best Published Book Award (2nd Runner up). Besides fiction, Arthur also writes non-fiction, and his essay, *Five Reasons to Wonder*, took 2nd Place in the 2019 Writers Digest Competition. The first novel in this *Wind-In-Trees* trilogy won the Kallisto Gaia Press Novel Prize.

Recently, Arthur was honored by winning the 2022 L. Ron Hubbard Illustrators of the Future Contest, a highly competitive international contest culminating in a Hollywood extravaganza attended by some of the best illustrators in the country.

Wind In Trees

Ghost

By Arthur M. Doweyko

Forward

More than a century ago, the reptilian Batrans colonized Earth which followed its sterilization of nearly all human life thanks to a sinister entity known as the Soofysh. In return, the Soofysh demanded payment in the way of the planet's resources, however, in recent years they were vanquished by the reptilians with the help of one of the surviving humans, blue-skinned Henry Wind In Trees, a Lakota Sioux who was forcibly converted by the Soofysh to a human-looking cyborg as one of their experiments. Over the years, Batrans and humans found a way to work together, inhabiting separate parts of the Americas suited best to their biologies. Cold-blooded Batrans preferred the warmer, equatorial climes, while humans favored more temperate zones.

Batrans settled on the North American and European continents, however, the lack of communication with the European colonies prompted a group of North American Batrans to search for answers.

Chapter 1

Early one cloudless summer day, two dozen reptilian souls along with a handful of humans boarded a small, refurbished cargo ship in the port of a city once known as Miami. They headed east across the Atlantic toward a fate no one would have expected.

Seven days into their voyage, Urth, the Batran commander of the vessel met with his second, Dayth, for dinner. The chatter of crew and passengers filled the cramped space. The heavy aroma of freshly killed hog had Urth looking forward to the meal. He unbuttoned his woolen jacket to let the steamy warmth of the Mess hall seep into his torso.

Dayth said, "Cold up on the bridge, sir?"

"Something's wrong with the heating system. Our captain is beginning to look like an icicle."

"Sir, according to the navigator we are about two days out from the UK island."

"I'm not sure how much longer I can take this trip."

Batrans, being cold-blooded did not fare well without the heat of the sun. However, the mission to discover what had happened to their colonies in the east held great importance, sufficient to push the boundaries of comfort beyond normal limits.

Urth glanced at the humans sitting at a separate table and whispered to himself, "How can they consume burnt flesh? It's unholy." He bit into a hog leg and ripped out a mouthful of the heady meat with his needle-like teeth.

Dayth said, "Strange tastes for a strange species, sir."

"Still nothing on the airwaves?"

"Nothing, sir."

The ship lolled from side to side forcing Urth to hold on to the end of the table. "I hate this weather."

Dayth said, "I'm afraid that scanning suggests high winds for the rest of the trip, sir."

Urth had hoped that the weather itself may have been the problem with communications. They had tried all the Batran comm channels, as well as a number of Earth-based radio wavelengths. The absence of any signals at all left Urth with a dark foreboding. Something was seriously amiss.

A low-pitched chirping filled the Mess hall calling for the end of dinner and return to duty stations. Batrans and humans shuffled out, while a fresh group took their places.

Urth waved at his table companions while remaining in his seat. "I'm staying for a bit. Not feeling too well."

Dayth said, "Try the pills the humans use, sir."

"They don't work on me."

"See you on the bridge, sir?"

"I'll be there shortly."

The Batrans had prepared for cold and wet conditions, but sea-sickness left them exposed, affecting some more than others. The roaring wind gave birth to enormous waves that tossed their vessel in a nauseating, endless dance.

Urth held his head with both hands and planted his elbows firmly on the table. He tried thinking of a warm and bright day atop a grassy hill with a gentle breeze licking at his face. He raised his arms to unfold membranous wings beneath, and leapt up to glide over the meadows in the valley below, intent on following the meandering path of a glittering stream.

A thud from above almost knocked Urth from his seat. The metal on metal grinding which followed threw his eyes wide open. Batrans toppled from their seats and dishes flew off the tables as the ship listed. The main lighting winked out, leaving only a few emergency lights on.

Urth staggered to his feet and leaned on a nearby wall as the ship teetered. A moment later, the ship appeared to have righted itself. The calm felt like an illusion, like something really bad was about to happen.

Urth spoke into a wall-mounted comm. "What happened? Did we hit something?"

The speaker emitted nothing but static.

Urth yelled back to the mess hall. "Stay where you are. I'm going up to the bridge."

He felt his way up the stairs and out onto the narrow deck With little to see in the waning twilight, he braced himself against the torrential sheets of rain and ascended a ladder. When he arrived at the wheelhouse, his jaw dropped. It was gone.

"Impossible."

Urth flicked on a hand-held flashlight and clambered over the twisted end of the ladder, all the while clutching at his jacket in an effort to deflect the icy downpour. The ship's funnel, slightly askew, coughed out wisps of dark smoke which flew off with the unrelenting wind. The bridge had been sheared off at its base. Without a command and control center the ship had no way to steer itself, no navigation and no communication. In short, they were doomed.

Dayth came up behind Urth and yelled to be heard.

"What happened up here, sir?"

"It's gone." Urth was at a loss.

"Sir, is the backup steering and navigation system functional?"

Urth said, "Weren't you on the Bridge?"

"I was checking on the menu in the kitchen when—."

"When this happened. What did you say?"

"The backup, sir."

"That's right. I had forgotten, and in fact, was not completely sure it existed. Yes, yes. It should be in the steering gear room down below astern. Get some help from the crew in the mess hall and let me know what you find."

Dayth scurried down the ladder and disappeared into the ship.

Urth directed his flashlight beam over the wreckage. The brackets had the appearance of being physically torn away, as if something took hold of the bridge and wrenched it off.

It could not have been the wind.

A second thud shook the ship and dropped Urth to his knees. The flashlight flew off as he grasped the twisted ends of the ladder to avoid being swept away. The ship listed once again, but this time remained askew.

External lights painted the bleak metal hull with a macabre undulating yellow glow. Sea water gushed into the mess hall and the stern descended into the swirling gloom. Urth held on to a rung with the rising waters crashing over him. The paralyzing cold penetrated his scales, loosened his grip and sent him falling into the roiling sea. He closed his eyes and saw his wife smiling, her arms reaching out. Her name crossed his lips with his last breath.

Wind-In-Trees Upheaval